Tyler Echohawk ghosted down Center Street and stopped under the jail's overhanging porch. He knew that within the hour sunlight would come, driving back the shadows of night. From the folds of his rain slicker, he lifted out his six-gun and eased up to the closed door, his heavy rap hitting just below the barred window.

"Hey, it's me, Tyler!" He pulled his hand away, thumbing back the hammer, teeth bared in killing anticipation.

Inside the jail, Lon Echohawk had dreaded the arrival of this moment. He hadn't yet determined if he had the willpower to kill his own flesh and blood. He stood behind the desk, one hand wrapped around his Colt, and he called out.

"That you, Tyler? The door's unlocked."

He saw the door opening slowly, a vague shadow outlined in the doorway. He saw it was Tyler . . . and then he saw the flame leaping from Tyler Echohawk's gun. . . .

ROBERT KAMMEN
FIVE CROSSINGS

ZEBRA BOOKS
KENSINGTON PUBLISHING CORP.

ZEBRA BOOKS are published by

Kensington Publishing Corp.
475 Park Avenue South
New York, NY 10016

First Printing: September, 1993

Printed in the United States of America

One

The Carbon County Coroner's report read that the Mex sheepherder froze to death with a bullet in his head.

It wasn't until a month later that Sheriff Lon Echohawk took in the scene of the crime: just a stretch of prairie dusted by last night's snowfall. Jutting into the steely sky were a few mountain peaks, while northerly Casper Mountain was a long hump of rock heavily covered with pines. Beyond the shallow grave sat Echohawk's two deputies on their horses and sheepherder Felix Montaya huddled on his mule. Under Lon Echohawk, the grey lifted a hoof to stomp down on the frozen ground, a metallic-like sound swept away by a cold March wind.

"You were saying . . ."

Montaya gestured at a nearby fenceline and replied, "I found Juan there . . . in the barbed wire. I think he didn't die right away, but that day it was so cold—"

"Cold steel done him in," said Echohawk.

"How many does this make?"

"Even one's too many." Gazing around, Sheriff Lon Echohawk thought that grim testimony to the killing was the sheep wagon burned down to its axles, the woolly humps of dead sheep either littering the ground or wedged in the barbed-wire fence. Any way you cut it, this was a lonely place to die.

There were a lot of other lonely and barren stretches of Carbon County, which until a couple of years ago had extended from Colorado clear up to Montana. At that time, the northern part that traversed the Big Horns had broken away to form Johnson County. But it still left Lon Echohawk with hundreds of square miles in which to enforce his brand of law. A scarcity of money, along with what he called rank stupidity, held him to five deputies, when even five more wouldn't be enough. There were the sheepmen and cattlemen who were always gunning for one another. The lawless breed either committed crimes here or availed themselves of the Outlaw Trail that curled along the mountain ranges. He could paper an outhouse wall with the readers spindled in his office.

Echohawk took note of the morning sun's vague presence behind the clearing clouds, then of the pained look on Raleigh Carr's face as he swung out of the saddle. Carr had been a lawman in other places, too, and was as dependable as they came, in Echohawk's opinion. The middle-aged deputy sheriff had big ears that stuck out from the sides of his head, along with stringy brown hair and a beard that could use some trimming. Carr wore leather chaps, mostly to ward off the

6

chill, with his spurs chinking as he walked his horse over to the fenceline. Partly hidden by the bronc, he turned his back and let go a stream.

Hack LaVoy, the other deputy, was a reedy five ten. His attributes were a dry sense of humor and his keen tracking ability. Whereas the other deputy sheriffs enjoyed the night lights of a cowtown, LaVoy would just as soon be at a place like this. His sheepskin lay open to reveal the badge pinned to his vest, along with the single-action Colt .45 in the worn holster. He had a wry grimace as he regarded the wind picking up. Under the low brim of his worn hat, he looked over at Raleigh Carr, about to swing back into the saddle, and called out, "Was me, I'd wipe the sheepshit from my boots first."

This provoked a hesitant smile from the sheepherder.

Shifting his weight in the saddle, Lon Echohawk said quietly, *"Podria usted decirme,* Senor Montaya, how many there were . . . or if you'd seen them before."

"No se lo puedo decir." He gestured at a nearby elevation. "I was beyond that. I heard just the *pistolas."*

"Well, I'm obliged to you," said Echohawk. At this, the sheepherder reined his mule around, whipping it into a slow canter. Echohawk knew there was more the Mexican could tell him, that Montaya had probably seen the killers. And left behind by Felix Montaya was a lingering fear: the dead sheep owned by the Durbin brothers. The problem was that both cattlemen and woolgrowers claimed public grazing land. Out of it had come bloody gun battles and a lot more shallow graves.

The slant of Lon Echohawk's gaze went to the mound of loamy earth. In him was this sense of regret, for in time the grave would settle lower to merge with the earth, be lost to memory. "It still galls me, that coroner's report."

At times like these, the deputies knew it was best to refrain from voicing their opinions around the sheriff of Carbon County. What they now viewed from astride their horses was a hollow-cheeked man in workaday clothing. He was a shade taller than both of them and had a sparse but solid frame. The coal-black hair was a legacy passed on to him by his Pawnee grandmother, who'd died shortly before he was born. His grandfather, now dead and a Scotsman, had endured being called a squawman. To honor the woman he'd loved even after her death, David Graham took his wife's last name. Later on, David Echohawk left eastern Oklahoma to become a part of that great migration striking westward through territorial Wyoming on their way to Oregon. But the man who eventually became sheriff of Carbon County left the wagon train, deciding to remain in Wyoming instead.

Leaving behind a silent prayer for the dead sheepherder, Lon Echohawk spurred his grey into motion. More keenly than the others, he sensed the presence of a maverick spirit ruling over this rawboned frontier of plain and mountain. In many places in Carbon County he'd stumbled across unmarked graves of whites and redskins alike, and the bones marking the graveyards of ancient beasts. For hundreds of years, nomadic tribes had hunted these lands, leaving their dead and ancient customs behind, along with their gods. Most recently it had been the Shoshone and the Sioux waging war against one another, other Indian tribes, and the white man. And so it was that the killings went on, to appease these restless spirits, mused Echohawk.

The report about the Mex sheepherder had been stagecoached down to the county seat at Rawlins, along with word of some outlaws hiding out near where the North Platte River gorged through the Fiery Narrows. By his reckoning, they should come upon the narrows around noon. The other way, which had been under discussion, was to head more to the west by Goose Egg Ranch, then take the easier route around the mountain into Casper.

But Lon Echohawk cleared this all up. "Once we've scouted out the narrows, we'll take the back door onto Casper Mountain."

Nodding, Raleigh Carr said, "Now they've found silver up there, too."

"Up there, too" was the mining camp of Eadsville, another one of the reasons Lon Echohawk had the rest of his deputies working out of Casper. The camp was laid out around a large spring of glacier-cold water, and had a stamp mill and a smattering of cabins. At last report someone had opened a roadhouse, although the miners still made that steep trek down the face of the mountain to avail themselves of the saloons and notorious Sandbar District of Casper.

"Casper . . . things'll get worse over there once they finish laying track."

Hack LaVoy squinted away from the sun as it rose above the clouds, shafts of sunlight piercing through gaps in the Shirley Mountains to the southeast. He tugged the brim of his hat down and said to Echohawk, "Bring in more settlers . . . and a lot of scumbags. What about this feud between Casper and that Bessemer town?"

"It's just that both towns want to be named county seat. But it could be that the territorial governor'll veto those ambitions again."

Echohawk went first through the scrub trees that lined the Little Medicine Bow, whose brackish waters fed into the larger North Platte. Once they'd cross, it was just a matter of beelining northerly, as it was mostly prairie clear to Casper Mountain. But for now they holed in amongst the trees, dismounting to shuck coats and check saddle riggings. They passed up the chance to refill their canteens, though their horses moved in closer to slake their thirst.

Over the rump of his horse, Raleigh Carr said, by way of conversation, "You figure Frank James'll pass through these parts?"

Shortly before pulling out of Rawlins, a telegram had arrived citing the presence of the notorious James brothers in Wyoming. It seemed the Jameses and others on the dodge were being forced out of their old haunts by relentless lawmen. This only added to the problems of Lon

Echohawk and his handful of deputies. It would be a feather in his cap if he captured either Frank or Jesse, but unlike a U.S. Marshal, he wasn't seeking glory and its attendant miseries. And still gripping Lon Echohawk was the cruel fact that the Mex sheepherder had been killed in cold blood.

"Yup, even one's too many."

Mid-afternoon found the sky had cleared and most of the snow had melted away. About a mile west lay the North Platte River, which the lawmen had viewed from the crest of a humpbacked hill. They'd kept heading due north, knowing the river would curl back toward them before gorging through the Fiery Narrows. Back in the 1840's, an expedition led by General John C. Fremont, which included noted plainsman Kit Carson, had dared brave what Fremont coined the Grand Canyon of the Platte, only to have their rubber boat wrecked in the treacherous rapids. Echohawk knew these scrub hills, tawny with old grass, were a favorite hiding place for rustlers.

He voiced his concern to Carr and LaVoy. "We'd better keep to that draw yonder."

"Mo Baxter was reported sighted up around here."

"Baxter and one other. Figured, after they escaped from territorial prison, they'd shy away from these parts."

"Only proves some ain't too swift," said Hack LaVoy. "As I recollect, this draw ends just short

11

of the narrows." Now he loped his bronc ahead without being told to do so. It was just natural for LaVoy, as he could pick up and read sign better than his companions.

Carr and Echohawk held their ground about thirty rods back, Echohawk having unsheathed his Winchester to cradle it in one arm as he swept wary glances at pockets of brush on the hillsides. A quick movement off to his left proved to be a mule deer darting out of a brushy draw. Over the crests of hills, the metallic-blue sky threw back a glare painful to a man's eyes if he fixed on it for any length of time. Echohawk's grey whickered when it caught the scent of water. Ahead of them, Hack LaVoy reined up just as an eagle swept skyward, clutching a trout in its talons. The others pulled up alongside LaVoy, gazing out over the edge of sheer red rock cliffs at the river clawing its way through the narrows.

"Seems peaceful enough."

"Always does," affirmed Echohawk as he reached back to take a field glass out of his saddlebag. He scoped in on the river, comprised here of rapids and whirlpools buffeting against rock walls, following it to the east until it curled around a canyon wall. The cliffs were grey granite, dropping down some three hundred feet, with more cliffs beyond the river cutting off their glimpse of the prairie.

As he fingered at something that had gotten lodged in his eye, Raleigh Carr remarked, "Seems to me it would be more profitable robbing those miners than rustling cattle."

"Miners've got to eat."

"Yup, could be Mo Baxter hazed those steers up to Eadsville—not that smart a move."

"Just hope the pair of them are still up there," Lon Echohawk said. "You boys hungry?"

"Is hunger when your belly starts humpin' agin' yer backbone?"

"Missing a few meals has sure slimmed you down, Hack."

"That ain't slim, that's this sawbones down at Rawlins telling me I was a walkin' cadaver. Just cartilage and bone."

Through a flicker of a smile, Echohawk said, "Thin men are harder to hit."

Back where the cliffs guarding the Fiery Narrows began tapering away, the lawmen had taken note of a line shack and a corral showing signs of recent use. Keeping to their saddles, they started angling northeast and away from the river. Guiding them was ground that had been chewed up by a small bunch of cattle and fresh cowpie, as Hack LaVoy coined it. Then at dusk, Lon Echohawk announced a nearby creek bank would be a good place to start a campfire. He'd decided there was no need for haste, as the trail they'd been following headed straight for Casper Mountain.

They shared a ration of beef jerky and beans, while the Arbuckles sated their thirst. Then Echohawk opened a can of peaches he'd packed in his saddlebag, along with a fistful of wanteds that he now removed as well.

"This one has a general description of Mo Baxter. Got this big mole under his left eye, and that nose of his, appears to have been broken in a couple of places."

"Was Baxter, I'd stay out of those places. What about the other one?"

"Yeah, here we have Rafferty . . . Ben Rafferty. Says here he's an Arkansan."

Raleigh Carr ran an appraising eye over the crude drawing of the outlaw. "Pure quill hillbilly. He opens his mouth, we've got him nailed proper. Tall and skinny an' red-haired. How many more readers you pack along, Lon?"

"Just a sampling of men we're after. Some'll kill their own kind, head other places to rob and die. This Casper town, gonna sprout soon's the railroad pushes in. More trouble for us."

"Wild enough now."

"Spookier at night."

Echohawk rose to step over and hunker down by the creek, where he washed out his cup and tin plate and fork. A signal to the deputies that they were moving out. Soon, mounted, they headed more directly toward Casper Mountain, rising to meet a full moon. Nightfall found the wind cutting away, too. They encountered a few barriers, but it was mostly the upward flow of meadows their horses loped over, the cliffs here dark red. After a while, the mountain rose again and the horses slowed to a plodding walk.

More than once Lon Echohawk had taken this

14

vague trail, passing both ways. In the thickening darkness, deer were beginning to emerge from where they'd been hiding, flitting downward to lusher grassland. The mountain wasn't all that high at around nine thousand feet, and it was flat-topped and thick with pine trees. Snow still lay in hidden crevasses deep in the pine forest, farther up along the rimrock, the higher altitude holding a growing chill. As the last meadow fell behind, they found the trail leveling off, curling through pine trees and naked aspens.

"Campfire off thataway," LaVoy said softly.

"Not all that far to Eadsville," said Echohawk. "Miners, probably." Now he got the point.

With the pines hemming in close to the narrow trail, Echohawk was able to see from astride his horse quite a ways under them, as there were very few low branches. The grass beneath the trees was cropped short from lack of sunlight, and he could detect movement coming from around the campfire, could make out at least four men. Loping around a bend in the trail, a log cabin threw out window light, and beyond that was the mining camp of Eadsville.

The camp was spread out over an area of about ten acres, makeshift cabins, tents, and a nearby pile of logs giving off a piney aroma. It looked peaceful enough to Lon Echohawk, as he dragged the scent of pine, along with the aromatic smell of Raleigh Carr's tailor-made, into his lungs. Coming around a large shed, the trail spread out more and Echohawk pulled up to dismount.

Carr said, "It isn't all that far down to Casper.

'Cause if Mo Baxter sold those cattle, that's most likely where he'd head."

Lon Echohawk read into the deputy's words that he was leery of laying out his bedroll on this cold mountaintop. A feeling Echohawk shared. Up here sound carried, the lowing of a steer coming to them even now. "What, they rustled about twenty head? Anyway, they should be at that new place, that road ranch."

Somewhere glass shattered, followed by a shout of protest, some laughter, then silence. Hack La-Voy looked at the man who'd hired him. "At least somebody's havin' a go at a good time."

"Gold dust and hard liquor; a hellish combination."

"How do we play it?"

"I'll avail myself of the front door. The two we're after have no great reps as gunhands, but hard liquor could make them nervy. Okay, let's head where it's a mite warmer."

Echohawk had stowed the readers in his saddlebag, believing his sheriff's badge was all the writ he needed up here. The camp was barely a year old, and he knew its founder, Charles Eads, as a square shooter. Other than that, it was a place catering to outcasts of society as well as to miners. The buildings of the townsite were tightly packed, with higher reaches of the mountain quartering around. The largest building was the stamp mill, which they moved past to encounter a couple of miners coming out of a tent, proceeding ahead of the lawmen toward a ramshackle pine-framed building.

16

Lon Echohawk cut around to the back of the building, where he could make out the black shape of cattle in a new corral and where a saddled horse was tied up. "Just might have to arrest the owner of this roadhouse for receiving stolen property," he said.

"Proper he gets his day in court."

"But first there's Baxter and his cohort." Echohawk tied his reins to a corral post. He left his deputies to move along a side wall of the roadhouse, from here passing along the unpainted pine log facade. The open front door revealed a boxy interior with an elbow-to-elbow crowd—miners, some cowhands, and a bunch of whores posing as barmaids. He took in the broken windowpane as a mule got to braying. An easier sound than a gun barking. For even this was a chore they'd tackled more than once, Echohawk's body bearing scars left by slashing knifes, attesting to his being hit by leaden slugs.

From the hard-packed ground out front, his spurred boots hit new planking covered with sawdust and debris. Scarcely a caring eye went to the newcomer, but one of the barmaids headed toward Echohawk, only to be detained by a drunken miner.

Quickly, Echohawk consigned to memory the placement of the bar and those manning it, three bardogs, the flight of stairs striking up along the east wall, a pair of pug-uglies whom he pegged to be bouncers. There were as many milling about as were seated at the gaming tables, reinforcing his feeling that those rustlers were here. As for

17

Lon Echohawk, his face showed only the anticipated pleasure of having a drink, his ambling
stride taking him to the front end of the bar. He
thumbed out a silver dollar, the sight of it bringing forth a bartender.

"Whiskey?"

"Yup . . . and maybe you can help me . . ."

"Yeah?"

"I've got some cattle to sell."

"So?" The bartender reached behind for a bottle
of whiskey, then turned back to pick up a shot
glass, pausing now to let his eyes roam over the
stranger. Around a frosty smile, he added, "See
Healy over there. An' that'll be another dollar,
mister."

Fishing out another silver dollar, Echohawk
didn't know if prices were that high or if he was
paying for what the bardog had just told him,
though his smile remained in place as he watched
his money disappear once the bardog began to
wait on others. He swung his attention to the tables, having little trouble picking out the owner
of the roadhouse, who was dealing out cards. The
man's hair was wavy, with touches of grey thread-
ing through the black. His suit also black, and in
his cravat was a diamond pin. The aquiline face
adorned with a fawning smile told Echohawk all
he wanted to know . . . mostly that the other
players were being fleeced by this Mr. Healy.

Of more interest to Lon Echohawk was the
player seated across the table. He sipped at the
whiskey, murmuring to himself, "Red-haired and
rail-thin; got to be Ben Rafferty." At that moment,

18

easing in through the back door were his deputies, to whom he threw a signal by reaching up to adjust his trail-worn Stetson.

He took his time working his way around the gaming tables. At one of them, where the game was five card stud, a man with a florid face glanced up to see, among the onlookers, the sheriff of Carbon County. Echohawk returned the hard gaze with an easy smile and said, "Howdy, Spud."

"Yup," came the man's uncertain reply. "Just passin' through . . ."

"On my way to Casper," Echohawk responded. "I'll probably see you again."

"Yeah, probably."

He didn't bother looking back at small-time outlaw Spud Larkin, knowing all the chap had on his mind at the moment was to vacate the premises. Echohawk noticed his deputies were standing so they could watch both the action going on at a roulette wheel and their sheriff, who came up to the table where Healy, the owner of the roadhouse, was just dragging in another pile of chips.

Sather Healy grinned out, "Gents, I'm buyin' drinks around."

"I'll take mine at the bar, as it's quits for me," groused a lanky miner as he heaved up to vacate his chair.

Easing around the table, Echohawk settled into the chair. He found himself seated next to Healy, who said, "A no-limit game, stranger."

"I'm more interested in cattle."

"That a fact?" Crafty eyes played over Echohawk's face, and then he added, "Could be lookin' to buy some more. How many you bring in?"

"Those out back belong to you, Mr. Healy?"

"Yup, and prime stock, too."

Out from under the table came Lon Echohawk's right hand, which was gripping his Colt .45. It held briefly to the owner of the roadhouse, flinching back in surprise, then swept away to cover Ben Rafferty seated across the table. "Rafferty, I've a warrant for your arrest!"

A wild glare, as of a mustang suddenly realizing it had blundered into a trap, came into the outlaw's eyes. He let his hand slap down to his holstered gun, freezing as from behind came the dry crackling of a hammer being thumbed back, with Raleigh Carr punching the business end of his revolver into the outlaw's neck. Across the table Hack LaVoy got behind the owner of the roadhouse, entertaining similar intentions.

Said LaVoy: "I'd dislike mightily ventilating that pretty coat, sir."

Sheriff Lon Echohawk pushed up from the chair. "The pair of you are going down to Casper. By morning, Healy, I expect your lawyers will bail you out." His attention was drawn leftward to a couple of bouncers moving in, flicking beyond that to the bar, where one of the bardogs had just brought up a Greener. "Call off your dogs, Healy, or there'll be some bloodletting, mostly yours."

Paling, Sather Healy blurted out, "I . . . believe me I didn't know those cattle were stolen . . ."

20

"Or that that deck you've been usin' is marked? What's it to be, Healy?"

"Simmer down, boys. Just a little misunderstanding. Go about your business." Now he grimaced when the cold ring of steel handcuffs encircled his wrists. "It'll be a damned cold ride down to Casper. Perhaps we could wait until morning."

"We could but we won't."

A half hour and a few miles downslope from the mining camp, and still on the northern point of Casper Mountain, the lawmen and their prisoners were gazing, as they rode, at lights poking through trees lining the North Platte River. Skylined far to the north were the dark humps of other mountain ranges, below them the switchback road, with Lon Echohawk concerned about what Casper was becoming.

Mostly a town destined to grow, he mused. So far it had been rustlers, bank robbers, gunhands . . . a breed of outlaw he understood. In a month, two at the most, they'd finish laying track for the Fremont, Elkhorn, and Missouri Valley Railroad, a fanciful name sure enough. Even now a lesser brand of outlaw could be found lurking about Casper, con artists and card sharks. Also waiting for the expected inflow of civilization were land speculators, two-bit lawyers, and a lot more women of the night setting up residence in the Sandbar. It would be a tall order, and one he didn't relish, to sustaining law and order there.

He glanced over at Raleigh Carr, asking quietly, "Is it worth it?"

"These long days and longer rides . . . you tell me, Lon."

"Wish I could. It still rankles me . . . that coroner's report about that dead sheepherder . . . froze to death with a bullet in his head."

"County Coroner Hardesty has a callous sense of humor, I reckon."

From here on, both men lapsed into the silent reverie of their own thoughts, for Lon Echohawk this being his concern with what tomorrow would bring. He knew that as sheriff he was outnumbered by the lawless breed. And what about these maverick spirits holding sway over this westerly landscape? He didn't consider himself all that superstitious, nor did he feel that the Indian had put a curse upon this land. Yet it was there, a deeper something that made men go outside the law.

Inwardly, he said, "But, as the Bible reads, let tomorrow's worries wait unto tomorrow. . . ."

Two

In the year he'd been here, Sean Fitzpatrick had earned the rather dubious reputation of being the champion of the downtrodden and the lawless. Over that time, the young Irishman came to realize rawboned Casper had a future, along with a bloody and glorious past, for through here passed the famous old trails used by thousands of migrants—the Oregon, Mormon, and Bozeman Trails, the fabled Texas Trail, and the North Platte River Road. Scarcely mentioned or even remembered was the oldest trail of all, the Holy Road of the Teton Lakota.

This had been one of the favored hunting grounds for both the Sioux and Shoshone. The floodplain of the North Platte was wide and quicksandy, the river taking a southerly sweep around the blunted edges of Casper Mountain, a view Sean Fitzpatrick had from his second-floor office in the Pennock Building, the lower floor housing the Liberty Gunshop and a jewelry store. And as usual, the young barrister had fallen behind in his rent. He was tall and lean, and black-

23

haired, which made his brown eyes seem even darker. He had a clefted chin, which he'd nicked while shaving this morning. Lately he'd gotten to wearing western boots and a Stetson, the arbiter elegantiarum of acceptance out here.

Pensively, he gazed northward along Center Street, through the smoke curling up from his hand-rolled cigarette. The fog was lifting away from the river to drift his way. On the opposite street lay the saloons and gaming houses. Starting on the next street, to the west, were the whorehouses making up the infamous Sandbar District. He had defended some of the whores in the local court of law, along with his share of petty thieves and outlaws. His most recent case involved the cutting edge of Apache justice suffered by dance hall hostess Lou Polk. It was her misfortune to be abducted by her jealous housemate, a renegade named Dagae Lee. That wild ride of about a week saw him chopping her nose off and leaving Lou Polk to die out on the prairie. Somehow she made it back to Casper, and the last Sean Fitzpatrick had heard she'd taken to wearing a wooden nose.

He smiled at this as he turned away from the window to regard the two men who'd ambushed him on his way over here this morning. First there was Casper Town Marshal Phil Watson, sprawled in a rickety chair and staring through sullen eyes at the old grandfather clock ticking away in one corner. His companion and partner in horse stealing, as just confessed to by Watson, sat back by the door. This was Jess Lockwood, a bland, small-framed man. Every other minute Lockwood would bolt up from the chair to take a furtive glance out a window.

It was a simple but sordid tale that Sean Fitzpatrick mulled over as he eased onto the swivel chair behind his desk: The horses had been stolen by these two men, then taken to the Fish Creek Ranch owned by Tex Calton. Fitzpatrick looked at Watson and asked, "Now, you claim that Calton knows these horses were stolen?"

"Sure. We ain't the only ones Calton bought stolen horses from."

"Why this sudden beating of the breast?"

"Came here because you ain't all that partic'lar about your clientele."

"It seems out of sorts, Watson, your telling me all of this."

"It's because them lawmen showed up," shot out Jess Lockwood.

"Lockwood don't know nothin'," Watson said sullenly.

"He must, or you wouldn't be here," countered Sean as he stubbed out his cigarette in a metal ashtray.

"Awright," groused Phil Watson. "Some lawmen from Sundance showed up to arrest us. I don't figure it's legal, them draggin' us off to that one-hoss town. Extradition, Fitzpatrick, I want you to file a writ of extradition, as I ain't goin' over there to Sundance to stand trial."

"Sorry, can't help you," Sean shrugged. "Extradition only applies when a crime is committed in another state or territory."

"I see 'em, Phil! Headin' for your office."

He glanced at Lockwood hovering by a window, then back at Sean Fitzpatrick. "There's got to be somethin' you can do, damnit, lawyer."

"As you confessed, Marshall, you're a horse thief. Out here, that's a hanging offense."

Watson jumped up, snarling, "You uppity Irish—" He speared Sean with a menacing glare, spinning away to tramp out of the room, while Lockwood took the time to close the door behind them.

Once the floorboards out in the hallway stopped creaking, Sean Fitzpatrick eyed the .44 Navy Colt in the top dresser drawer. He wasn't certain if it even had loads in its chamber. Sometimes he'd toy with the notion of going out to do some target practice. He was one of the few men residing here bold enough not to pack a weapon. Or foolish enough, he mused. Back in Ireland, and then later when he finished college in Boston, he had duked it out with larger men in boxing matches at small clubs and saloons, as a way of financing his education. But out here men used different weapons than fists—knives, shards of broken bottles, and guns. Another thing about Casper, he'd found out, was that it never closed, not even for the Sabbath.

"This Colt's too heavy to pack around," he said, the urge for another smoke bringing his eyes to the sack of tobacco. "And smoking . . . been doing too much of it lately."

The hunger pangs told him breakfast was in order. But force of habit made him first glance at his appointment book. One name, that of a businessman from Bessemer, had been penciled in for eleven this morning. Joseph Baldwin's daughter worked here in Casper, as a waitress at the Colonial House. She had made the appointment, in fact. He could tell that Carol Baldwin had been deeply concerned about the welfare of her father, who worked for a land company run by a man named Harold P. Fleming.

"Fleming's a fellow barrister and financier," pondered Sean. Outside of this, he knew little besides the fact that Fleming came from New York and seemed to have his hand in a lot of business ventures. There were some rumors, which Sean had coupled with bar talk, that gave a clearer picture of Fleming.

Sean knew Lawyer Fleming was heavily involved over in Bessemer, a smaller town some twelve miles southwest of here. Both towns were fighting tooth and nail to be named the new county seat, that is, if this proposal to hack another hunk out of Carbon County was approved by territorial decree. The ranchers were dead set against this happening and weren't overly pleased the railroad was coming to Casper. To them this meant not only settlers but also more sheepmen would move in. Into a territory that cattlemen considered their personal fiefdom.

"Trouble is money to a lawyer," mused Sean. "But trouble'll mean more killings. . . ."

Turning away from the window, he stepped over and took his coat off a wall hook, leaving his office without bothering to lock the door. Out on Center Street, Sean kept to the shadowy side of the wide thoroughfare. Even at this early hour, there came the thudding of hammers, the softer sound of saws teething through wood, as carpenters kept putting up buildings. The craft of masonry was also evident in a few brick buildings under construction.

He nodded back at a man slouched in front of the Crystal Saloon, who greeted him with a watery smile and the words, "You got a spare dollar?"

"Might have. Awful early for drinking."

"Not when it's all you've got."

Around an agreeing shrug, Sean fished out some change as he said, "At least you're an honest drunk, Toby. I could spring for breakfast—"

"Stomach's all burned out; but obliged." He wrapped a bony hand around the silver dollar. "Oh, I seen the town marshal leavin' your office. Kind of strange the hurry he was in . . . him and that Lockwood."

"They've got reasons."

"Stolen hosses have anythin' to do with it, Mr. Fitzpatrick?"

"That," grinned Sean, "and some starpackers from Sundance showing up. Take care, Toby." Striding upstreet, he knew it wasn't unusual that out here lawmen worked on both sides of the law. Be it rustling horses or cattle, or doing strong-arm work for men running the casinos and saloons, or other shady work, just so's a man could make a dirty silver dollar.

As he expected, the Demorest Home Restaurant

was drawing its usual morning crowd. The interior was a collection of red and white wallpaper, white tablecloths on round red tables, and booths running along the side walls. Two bits got any customer a trio of eggs, hash browns, and a big wedge of beefsteak served on a platter, with biscuits and gravy on the side. He paused just inside the doorway to flick a glance at a table occupied by the editor of the *Wyoming Derrick* and a couple of city councilmen. Many's the time he'd bent the elbow with editor Milt Sundby at some local saloon. Their friendship went back to the days when Sean had arrived and put out his shingle. They'd established a sort of barter deal, Fitzpatrick handling some legal matters for the *Derrick* in exchange for free advertising in the paper. By rights, he owed Sundby first crack at printing the misdeeds of the town marshal. But the presence of the councilmen, especially Rafe Bascome, brought Sean's eyes deeper into the crowded restaurant. Right away he picked out the beckoning hand of Sheriff Lon Echohawk, who was wedged into a back booth with his deputies, and Sean headed that way.

Still in the forefront of Sean Fitzpatrick's thoughts lay the shadow of resentment he felt toward Councilman Bascome. Bascome was part of an inner circle that ran Casper politics, and he owned several businesses, among them the Silver Bow Saloon. Sean's troubles with Rafe Bascome had started earlier this year. At the time, Bascome had brought charges of thievery against one of his retail clerks. In his role as defense lawyer, Sean soon learned that another clerk was the culprit, this worthy being charged with the crime. But it was Bascome's damning indictment of Sean, that he was nothing more than "damned shanty Irish trash," that wouldn't go away. This had been a signal to Sean to avoid the man whenever possible.

It was as if light had touched a painting relegated to some dark corner. This show of anger by Bascome at the courthouse had revealed to Sean a certain ugliness of character, in that the high-minded businessman did not tolerate losing . . . and something else. "Bascome's eyes . . . those of someone who's killed before . . ." Afterwards, Sean had inquired around town about Rafe Bascome, what little he came up with revealing no clue as to the man's true character. Got plenty of money, he mused, along with connections to Cheyenne and Denver. Now he shaped a smile as Sheriff Lon Echohawk made room in the booth.

"Morning, Sheriff. Reckon your being back means our local justice of the peace will be busy."

"Back again and bone-weary. "I've got a prisoner needing legal advice, so he claims. Interested?"

"Maybe. You heard about Watson?"

Raleigh Carr smiled. "Couple of starpackers just nailed him tryin' to vamoose out of here. Pitiful sight, a lawman being cuffed and thrown into the calaboose."

"One occupational hazard that goes with the territory."

"Like lawyers handling the estates of the aged and infirm," said Echohawk. He had spoken with no malice intended, for he knew the reputation of the man easing down alongside him, who handled cases other lawyers shunned. He was well aware, too, of Sean's nightly sojourns through the back streets of this river town. His eyes had checked out, with some regret, the fact that Fitzpatrick was unarmed, but the sheriff let this lay as he added, "The name Mo Baxter gets mentioned in any saloon, I'd appreciate being told about it."

"Seems to me, Baxter's serving time."

"Was." Echohawk reached for the pepper shaker, as a waitress came up to take Sean's order of steak and eggs and fried spuds. His eyes slid to Hack LaVoy wolfing down a heaping forkful of hash browns, the fork spearing at the plate again for more of the same, which caused the sheriff to merely roll his eyes in mock sympathy. "Hack, you've got the fastest fork in the territory, I swear."

"Your ma ever te'ch you any manners?"

"No, Raleigh, I reckon not. Or maybe Hack's plumb hard of hearin' . . . only heard the dinner bell echoing fifteen minutes after the rest of 'em were chowin' down."

"Yup, skinny as Hack is, got to be it."

"Ain't skinny, but all whangbone and rawhide."

"Don't talk with your mouth all full like that," chided Lon Echohawk as his grinning eyes lifted suddenly to survey the goings-on in the cafe, his stare deepening. Then he knew and the smile spread, lifting the corners of his mouth.

"Grown considerable . . . but sure enough it's my kid brother. Ease aside, barrister." He pushed out of the booth and strode frontward. The object of his gaze wore dusty clothing and had a six-gun strapped down at his left hip. Has his ma's eyes, mused Lon, but he's no longer a gangling younker. Suddenly aware of the badge bearing down on him, Tyler Echohawk glanced that way as he stiffened, and just as quickly a smile appeared.

"You old warthog," he said chidingly.

"Land, you've grown a heap," said Lon as he grasped his brother's outstretched hand.

"Missed you down in Rawlins. But a lawman?"

"Beats shoveling road apples down at the stockyards. The folks are okay?"

"Pa bought a hardware store over at Albany. Ma's just dandy. But they sure do miss you, Lon."

"Feel the same way." He took in the mass of coal-black hair tumbling about as Tyler Echohawk reached up to remove his hat. Then he added, "Come on, I want you to meet some friends of mine."

The grandfather clock wedged in a corner of Sean Fitzpatrick's office ticked away, approaching the hour of eleven-thirty, and Sean was beginning to believe Joseph Baldwin wouldn't be showing up. Other clients had dropped in, and with the arrival of the stagecoach from Cheyenne, Sean noticed the shadows along the side wall being pushed back by the sun coming onto noon.

He remembered the worry expressed by Baldwin's daughter, but Carol Baldwin had told very little to Sean except for the fact that her bookkeeper father worked over at Bessemer. His thoughts drifted to last night, just after he'd dropped into the Frontier Saloon. There, a raven-haired barmaid had had a startling resemblance to Megan. Megan Randsley of the lilting laughter and gold-flecked green eyes. Just before pulling out of Boston, he'd announced his intentions to marry Megan. But his letters back home to her had told of the uncertain life out here. Or perhaps he was just getting cold feet.

"Comely women like Megan won't wait forever," Sean murmured as he pushed up from the swivel chair and strode over to a window. The stagecoach was waiting idly in front of the Wells Fargo office, the snow having melted enough to muddy up the street. To the west, he could make out a section of road that passed over the toll bridge spanning the North Platte. Beyond that and where the river bent to the south lay abandoned Fort Casper. Farther on a freight wagon passed along the mountain road leading to Bessemer, then beyond to the ranches scattered throughout Carbon County.

"Guess Mr. Baldwin won't be showing up," he said quietly. "Though it's not all that far to Bessemer." That town, he mused, is sure beating the drums over this county issue. But he knew the creation of a new county seat would see an end to those long stagecoach rides down to Rawlins. At that moment, Sean remembered his promise to Sheriff Lon Echohawk to go over to the city jail.

Donning his Stetson, he went downstairs and stepped through an open door leading into the Liberty Gunshop. Barely glancing up was Ray Walker, who stood checking the workings on a Henry rifle. Walker had a wide frame and wasn't all that tall at around five nine. He wore a blue apron over a plaid shirt and dark brown trousers. A stub of cigar protruded from one corner of his mouth, and he spoke around it in a Kansas-ricochet drawl. "You come to pay your rent, counsellor?"

"Only a couple of weeks behind," Sean responded as he took in some handguns laid out neatly in a glass-topped case.

"Make that a month and two weeks," corrected the gunsmith. "What you need are better clients."

"A sodbuster I defended is bringing in a couple of sacks of spuds."

"Spuds, uh? That brood of mine can use 'em. No wind today, it seems."

"Wait'll this afternoon."

"Yup, always seems to hit about then. You know what they say"—he came over holding the rifle. "If you're gonna raise younkers around here, make sure you plant 'em deep. That .32 rimfire—"

"Yeah, Ray, what's your asking price?"

"Someone threaten you, Irish?"

"I just . . ." Sean's eyes darted to the front window and the woman hurrying past it, then he spun around to intercept her at the bottom of the staircase, the daughter of the man who'd failed to keep his morning appointment. "Miss Baldwin, easy now, lass."

Through her tears, Carol Baldwin blurted out, "My father . . . they found him out there . . ."

He slid an arm around her quaking shoulders and walked her into the gunshop, where she slumped into a chair. Gently, Sean said, "Go on, Miss Baldwin."

"They found him out there . . . out there by his buggy. They said it was a road agent . . . his wallet had been taken, but . . ."

"Is he . . . dead?"

"Yes, Mr. Fitzpatrick. I . . . my father told me many things. Enough to know that something was wrong . . ."

"You said your father worked for Mr. Fleming . . ."

"Please, I . . . I must get to Bessemer. Tell Mother what happened . . ."

"You can take my buggy," the gunsmith said to Sean. "I'll go harness my horse and bring the buggy around back."

Coming to mind for Sean Fitzpatrick were the stories circulating around Casper in which a cloudy picture had been painted of Harold P. Fleming. A lot of it was pure out-and-out resentment over the fact that lawyer Fleming was heavily involved over in Bessemer. The man might be a high-binding land speculator and somewhat of a politician, but murder? wondered Sean.

"A harsh indictment," came Sean's unspoken opinion.

35

In fragments amid Carol Baldwin's grief, there emerged the story of how her family had left Cairo, Illinois to at first take up residence in Denver. Her father had been hired on as a bookkeeper, but then Joseph Baldwin took a higher-paying job with a land company.

"The one owned by Mr. Fleming?"

"Yes, to come here."

"And your father," prompted Sean Fitzpatrick as their buggy jarred out of a pothole, "felt that something was amiss?"

"He didn't tell me all that much . . . rarely brought his work home. It was something about the company records . . . that they'd been tampered with . . ."

"What about Fleming himself? Did your father voice any opinions?"

"Only . . . only that Mr. Fleming could be a hard taskmaster at times."

With the gravelly road rising along the higher reaches of Casper Mountain, the bay slowed into a labored walk. Tugging at his hat as the wind suddenly picked up, Sean stole a glance at Carol Baldwin. She'd thrown a cape over her long gingham dress, her light brown hair a mass of tight curls spread over her shoulders. Her tears had dried up now that she'd accepted the shock of what had happened. Sean refrained from further talk, letting his thoughts center more on Harold Fleming. In a silent refrain, he murmured, "The man employs a few unsavory characters." And yes, remembered Sean, about a month ago he'd seen Fleming over at Rafe Bascome's Silver Bow Saloon, just the pair of them hunkered around a back table. Perhaps his dislike for Bascome was spilling over onto the illustrious Hap Fleming. But the fact remained Fleming's bookkeeper had just been murdered.

Once the blunted mountain wall fell behind, the road cut close to the home buildings of the Goose Egg Ranch, visible to the east amongst clustered trees. Then it went down a sloping ledge onto the flood plain of the North Platte River. As Sean reined the gelding into a canter, the road curved toward a plank bridge that spanned the swollen river, scrub trees and brush lining the opposite bank.

"Company," he muttered when a horseman eased out into the open and reined onto the bridge. Sean began to wish he'd packed his six-gun, but then he realized it was Sheriff Lon Echohawk he was approaching. He brought the buggy onto the narrow bridge and up to Echohawk, lifting a hand to remove his hat.

"Sorry about what happened, ma'am," the sheriff said quietly. He brushed a finger along his forehead to wipe some sweat away, as his horse swung around a little to get at some loose hay strewn by a buggy wheel. "I was told back in Casper some outlaws were involved in this. Strange they'd beeline toward Bessemer."

"Any idea who they were, Lon?"

"Not at the moment."

"Unless—"

"Something I should know, counsellor?"

37

"Miss Baldwin's father had an appointment. Seems he worked for Hap Fleming."

"My father was a bookkeeper."

"Worked for Fleming over in Bessemer," pondered Echohawk. "Has other office help, too, and a bunch of salesmen."

"Sheriff, my father wouldn't have made an appointment to see Mr. Fitzpatrick unless he knew something was wrong. For the last month, he . . . well, he was terribly upset, but he was always one to keep things to himself."

"Doesn't leave me much to go on," said Lon Echohawk. "So, I reckon you'd better head on in, folks. But in a couple of days, I'd like a word with you, Miss Baldwin. You too, counsellor."

As the buggy lurched forward and came off the bridge, Lon Echohawk held there, the wind throwing hot summery air and stirring up a little road dust. Down where the ambushers had lurked in the bushes west of the river, he'd picked up some shell casings. There had also been some discarded cigarette butts and an empty whiskey bottle. After the body had been taken back to Bessemer, Echohawk had followed a plain trail left by the killers, losing it on the outskirts of Bessemer. Damn bold of them, he mused. His hunch was they either worked for Hap Fleming's land company, or had been hired special just for this job.

He set his horse at a canter to the east, reckoning that he'd pull into Casper around sundown. Another long day in the saddle, and always the chance that when he checked in with his deputies, he'd be told some other crime had been committed. He groused, "The commissioners running this county are gonna authorize me more men or . . ." Echohawk stopped in mid-sentence, turning his thoughts to the recent killing. For certain, this wasn't just another holdup. As for Hap Fleming and his land company, Echohawk had heard about some of the strong-arm methods used by Fleming's so-called land salesmen. Man's greedy, for darn sure. But it's more than that, he felt. Yup, something a lot more than greed got that bookkeeper killed.

Some four miles to the west, Sean Fitzpatrick came around a curving bend, where the road flattened out onto high rolling land that overlooked the North Platte. There was a scattering of buildings ahead, and the lowering sun burned hotly beneath the brim of Sean's hat. "Carol," he said, "this town isn't all that big. So it doesn't seem logical to have the county seat located here."

"Mostly, this is Mr. Fleming's notion."

"Town lies halfway to nowhere. But Fleming's selling town lots and county land through his promotions. And the railroad . . . seems this place is out of the way for that, too. Again, Carol," his tone softened, "I'm sorry for all that's happened."

"We'll bear up under it." A smile widened her lips. "Mr. Fitzpatrick, we don't have much money, but if there's any way you could help us find those who murdered my father . . ."

Wheeling into the shadow cast by a mercantile store, Sean said, "My solemn promise on that. Forget about the money, as I feel obligated."

"But that isn't right."

"What isn't right, Carol, is that some men think they're immune from the law. Injustice, I know it well. Whether it be here or in Ireland. It'll be my task to have the scales tip the other way, the good Lord willing."

Three

"That should cover it."

"There's still a lot of risk involved," responded line superintendent Martin Colhour over the mournful wailing of the train whistle. They were in Colhour's pullman car, hooked to a work train plying northwest. Up until a month ago, he'd never laid eyes on this land speculator from Casper. But even had Martin Colhour known something of Harold Fleming's past, ten thousand dollars was still a goodly sum. Mostly, though, it had been Fleming's persuasive oratory that both of them could be rich men when this was over.

"The only risk, Colhour, is if one of us should speak out of turn, so to speak," chided Hap Fleming.

The deal he'd made with Colhour was twofold in nature. First, the line superintendent agreed to slow down the laying of track. And then, Colhour promised he wouldn't reveal just how far into territorial Wyoming the Fremont, Elkhorn, and Missouri Valley Railroad planned to extend its line.

To a man like Hap Fleming, it was the pure

joy of gaining something by using illegal means. He loved twisting and reshaping the law to achieve his ends. Out here, that meant putting together enough capital to become part of a larger game he envisioned unfolding within the next couple of years. This railroad was part of it, details that he'd smelled out at the territorial capital in Cheyenne and before that in Denver.

Habitually clad in banker's black, he seemed perfectly at ease in this elegant Pullman car. Muttonchops white as a new snowfall enhanced the wide jawline, the thick mane of greying hair flaring over his ears. His eyes were a disarming mellowy blue and centered in a blotchy face reddened by the sun. Many a man, be he rich or poor, had come to regret ever having run into Hap Fleming.

The third man in the Pullman car was hunkered down a short distance away before an open window. A confidant of Fleming's, he had also fled New York one step ahead of the police. The rap sheet on Barney Cleever back in the borough of Manhattan listed most of the crimes he'd committed, along with the years the bunco artist had spent in prison. He had a foxy smile in a swarthy face and reeked of cigar smoke, cheap cologne and mothballs. Cleever was one of three men heading for Casper at Hap Fleming's behest. He had on a bowler and an ill-fitting brown suit, and there were soup stains on his cotton shirtfront. The tips of his fingers were tobacco-stained, and Cleever was bemoaning to himself the sorry fact he'd run out of cigars. What he could glimpse through the window were rolling hills sloping down toward the North Platte River, guarded by trees. Closer, a speck of movement caught his eye, in the form of a large Great Plains toad hopping away from the dust that had been strewn by the passing train.

"Out of place," he lamented, "same's me." For Barney Cleever considered himself to be a misplaced city dweller. And not quite like that toad but rather like an owl, as it was at night he had prowled the streets of Manhattan. He'd found Denver to his liking, but the Mile High City was run by a clan of con men headed by a French-Canadian named Lou Blonger. So once again he threw in his lot with Hap Fleming.

As the train began slowing down, Colhour said, "End of the line."

"Well, Mr. Colhour, you seem troubled by something . . ."

"Not troubled so much as curious. We both know oil money is backing my railroad. Meaning it isn't homesteaders that'll bring in money to these parts, Mr. Fleming."

A smile flickered across Hap Fleming's thick lips, remaining in place as he drummed his fingers on the desktop. He knew that line superintendent Colhour meant to up the ante, had expected this move. His thoughts drifted back to New York and the stories circulating there that oil had been discovered out west. One report had been of half-breed brothers selling oil lubrication someplace out near the Seminole Mountains, to emigrants for axle grease and to cure sores on the feet of livestock. Even before this, mountain men had told of the tar springs near Lander in territorial Wyoming. A few speculators had come in, only to be driven out by the Sioux and Shoshone. Ever the opportunist, Hap Fleming had decided it was divine fate his having to leave New York and head out to Denver. Headquartered there were major oil interests. And for a man like the disbarred barrister, it was only a matter of time until he'd pieced together the next move of a big player, the Crown Oil Company. Casper, a cow-town strung along the North Platte, would be the hub of the new oil industry. Oil deposits that lay just west of there, at such places as Poison Spider Creek, Big Muddy, and Bessemer Bend, were dubbed the Shannon Field by Crown Oil.

Immediately, he stagecoached to Casper, and within a week's span he'd scouted out the terrain, over in Bessemer and where oil had been found, all the while local newspapers proclaiming daily the battle between Casper and the settlement of Bessemer to become the new county seat. Then came the announcement by Governor Moonlight's office that the governor had vetoed this attempt to split Carbon into two counties. This was a move that played into Hap Fleming's greedy hands. He set up a land company in Bessemer with confederate Ole Lundahl, who resembled a Lutheran minister more than a bunco artist, and opened another land company in Casper, even though he realized Bessemer was in an isolated location and in time would be just another ghost town. Using his money and considerable charm, the crafty entrepreneur got behind a move by the citizens of Bessemer to draw up another petition to split Carbon County. Over in Casper, Hap Fleming's agents added their voice to the fray.

From here on, Fleming's brazen advertisements brought in homesteaders and businessmen. As his fortunes improved, Hap Fleming dispatched his agents out to buy up mineral rights to land claimed by homesteaders and ranchers alike, and what land he could claim as well. He knew that in the boom times to come, Casper would be the linchpin city. Oil magnate; there came an inner glow.

Which went away when Hap Fleming regarded, with a smile, the man across the desk, asking, "Shall we clear the air, Mr. Colhour?"

Martin Colhour was a large and thickset man, used to the rough and tumble of building railroads. Cynically, he replied, "I know all about your land companies, Fleming. How you've been cheating folks out of their hard-earned money. Money used by your agents in an attempt to get into the oil business."

"Seems you've done your homework," he said softly, knowing unregretfully that Colhour had just signed his death warrant.

"Let us just say, Fleming, I'm going to be your silent partner."

"Indeed?"

"Or we end this charade now, sir, by the simple expediency of my ordering my men to lay out more track."

"Aren't you at all concerned that I could get

word to your bosses, Mr. Colhour, as to your involvement?"

"You won't." Hap Fleming rose in quiet expectancy. "Because there's too much at stake—millions, I figure. I'm in for a fifty-percent cut of everything. Well, Mr. Fleming?" He nodded at the gesture of supplication. "Okay, I'll hold back on daily operations. Which'll bring us into Casper in late summer. Also, I'll expect an extra ten thousand each and every week." Rising, he turned away to throw over his shoulder, "You know the way out."

It was only when Hap Fleming's carriage had pulled away in a northwesterly direction from the railhead that the venom of his thoughts came spilling out to Barney Cleever, who was pulling the cork from a flask of whiskey.

"Colhour shall regret being so greedy."

"You gonna pay him ten thousand a week?"

"Seems I have no other choice, Barney. He'll most likely keep the money in that safe I saw in his Pullman car. Another two months and I'll be in a stronger position. Then my friend Colhour breathes his last."

The man driving the carriage reined over a long hillock, and then he stopped in the middle of the rutted trail and gazed back at his companions. He was one of a trio of easterners summoned here by Hap Fleming. Sporting a hatchet face, Darby Connor had trained racehorses and been an up-and-coming middleweight boxer. But the lure of making easy money, as explained to him by Hap Fleming, had them team up to fix races at racetracks around New York City. From there on, Connor had gotten involved in other con games . . . including murder. He became known as a reliable hitman, using his fists or a shive or a gun to kill.

"I brought some grub along, Hap, in this hamper. Didn't want to tell you back there about one of your bookkeepers."

His eyes on Barney Cleever, who was lifting a sandwich out of the hamper, Fleming said, "You wouldn't mean Baldwin?"

"Like you said, it didn't seem right that bookkeeper always wantin' to work on after everyone else was done for the day. We caught up to Baldwin hightailin' it toward Casper." He doubled up a scarred fist. "A few shots to the belly and he was spillin' what he knew. He was fixin' to see some lawyer over in Casper. Some Irishman . . ."

"Hmm, could it have been Sean Fitzpatrick?"

"Yeah, Fitzpatrick."

Fleming tossed the sandwich he'd been chewing on back in the hamper and lifted out a bottle of whiskey, before settling back against the padded seat cushion. Worry flickered in his eyes. Here he was, involved in the biggest con game in his life, and obstacles were cropping up. The question he sought to answer was whether or not Joseph Baldwin had ever gone to see that lawyer before. Fleming murmured, "I believe it would soothe my thoughts if you broke into that lawyer's office, Darby. Perchance you'll find something; then again, maybe not. And it wouldn't hurt any to keep an eye on Fitzpatrick."

47

"Trammel can take care of that."

"The hard case from Oklahoma? Yes, I like his style. One other thing. Soon's we hit Casper, go tell Watson I want to see him."

"Watson's no longer town marshal. He got arrested for stealing horses. They dragged him off to Sundance to stand trial."

"Damn, he was proving useful to us."

"Right now Ed Rinker's holding down the job. Man ain't all that swift."

"No, not Rinker. I'll have to get together with Rafe Bascome."

Not only had Hap Fleming purchased quite a bit of real estate in Casper, but the money he'd funneled to Rafe Bascome was paid out in bribes to other city councilmen, ward heelers, and to Town Marshal Phil Watson. For he wanted to be part of the political base Bascome was establishing in Casper. The fact he was wanted back in New York meant his role would be that of a silent partner. Fleming glanced at Barney Cleever.

"We should hear any day from Montana.

"About Rafe Bascome, yeah?"

"Perhaps as Bascome said, he got his start in the mining business. But it doesn't hurt to have an ace in the hole. Watson, damn, had to get caught stealing horses. But we'll leave that problem to Rafe Bascome. And we'll have to put up with the sheriff of Carbon County for a little while longer."

"Think it'll happen, the governor slicing up the county?"

"Yup, Darby, there's too much political pressure

being applied. As for Lon Echohawk, Bascome insists the man can't be bought." Fleming reached for the whiskey bottle. "Every man has his price. But if the governor votes against splitting up Carbon County, we'll have no other choice than to get rid of Echohawk."

The road curved over yet another flowing section of prairie. Hap Fleming shifted his eyes southerly, to the Laramies dimmed by cloud and flanking their line of travel. The air was filled with a clean, feathery scent. Farther on lay Casper Mountain, with gold and silver being plucked out of its ravines and gulches. He'd considered going after coin of the realm but knew the pickings up on the mountain were slim at best. The real gold mines were scattered to the west and north, holding black gold in the form of oil. A frown flickered in his eyes.

"Sheriff Lon Echohawk . . . got to find a way to get to the man, as everyone has some weakness. Otherwise, you're a dead man, Echohawk."

Four

Late afternoon sunlight touched upon Tyler Echohawk as he bent down to pick up a money belt from the rumpled bed. He was bare-chested and deeply tanned high on his forearms, making a habit of wearing his shirtsleeves rolled up. He'd nicked his left cheek while shaving and a small pinprick of blood showed, with the scent of after-shave lotion wafting into his nostrils. A quick count of the greenbacks stowed in the money belt showed he was down to his last hundred dollars.

Strapping the money belt around his waist, Tyler Echohawk slipped into a new dull blue shirt. "Hard cash," he mused. "Before long, this town will be rolling in it."

Of that he was absolutely certain. Something that wasn't all that hard to pick up on, what with the construction going on, the gold and silver strikes, the railroad coming in to Casper. There'd been an offer from Lon to consider pinning on a deputy sheriff's badge. What better place to hide out, he realized, than behind a badge. Only he didn't cotton to the long rides or the miserly low pay, that once-a-month paycheck that would be part of it. In his prowlings around the growing cow town, he'd seen a handful he took to be outlaws. They probably laid low when the sheriff of Carbon County chanced in, and when the law departed, they took to their old haunts again. He didn't envy Lon Echohawk his marshaling job. "Pay's better for bounty hunters," muttered Tyler as he wedged his Stetson low over his forehead. The final ritual, and one he took the most pains with, was buckling on his gunbelt. Strapping the lower end of the black leather holster to his thigh, he drew the Colt 44.40 and checked the loads in the cylinder. Then he eased it into the holster and locked the door on his way out.

Tyler reckoned the letter he'd written last week would take that much longer to reach Oregon. There'd been five of them involved in robbing banks in eastern Oregon, and into Idaho and Utah. They shouldn't have tackled that bank in Pendleton, but when you're young and had been lucky so far, you took your chances. Out of seven, two got gunned down, the cry blazing out that it was Tyler Echohawk's bunch. From there they managed to get into the mountainous reaches of Idaho, splitting up with the promise to hook up again. That had been a long three months ago. But he knew that when Cap Bentley received his letter, there'd be a response one way or another.

Down on David Street, which was the beginning of the notorious Sandbar District, he glanced briefly at the Chandler Hotel as someone came out of the lobby. The man avoided Tyler's eyes

51

and slunk back to where the respectable element lived. Tyler Echohawk had to chuckle, as he knew a few whores lived in the hotel. Now he checked out the street, coming more alive as the last remnants of the sun died away. He didn't expect to be recognized this far from Oregon, as he was sprouting a new mustache. But with folks heading in because of the gold strikes, it didn't pay to be careless.

"Got a match?"

The woman surprised him coming from behind, but Tyler forced a smile and tugged out a wooden sulphur, striking it against a support post of the overhanging porch. When she leaned in to light her cigarillo, the flare of light showed a woman in her mid-thirties, hard of eye and seeking what this cowpoke had on his mind. He threw her a civil nod and strode away.

What Tyler Echohawk had in mind to do was to find some action at a poker table. Not so much for the game, but to keen his ears and thoughts to all the bar talk. He could head for the saloons and gaming houses lining the west side of Center Street. He found this an amusing situation, for respectable businesses stood opposite, and woe be it to any businessman seen crossing over during the day. But the big money games were in the Sandbar, a section of town guarded by the river to the northwest.

For the next couple of hours, Tyler Echohawk drifted around the red-light district. The cribs where the whores plied their trade were small shacks built on log runners, which stood on the sandy land comprising the flood plain. More than once a spring flood had hit, to have a lot of these shacks destroyed. Afterwards, the whores simply hired carpenters to put up more dwellings, and life went on same as before. He ambled down Market Street, returning the bold stares of the whores sitting out in front of their shacks, and Tyler was tempted. But tonight he felt restless, out of sorts with the way things were going. It was there, this undeniable feeling that here in Casper he could make some big-time money, and not as a deputy sheriff or just hiring out his gun.

Old habits died hard, meaning that one of his first chores upon coming here had been to give the banks a once-over. As soon as Cap and the old bunch got here, they could hit one easy enough. But only as a last resort, as some high rollers were coming into town, oilmen, speculators. He reckoned that what these banks had in the way of hard currency was now just the tip of an iceberg.

"Yup, from what I've heard, this part of Wyoming is gonna be some oil patch." To Tyler Echohawk, this meant a man with a gun would be needed, same as teamsters or bookkeepers or wildcatters.

Angling out into the street, he crossed over to step up on the boardwalk, having decided to try his luck at the Birdcage Casino on Center Street. This section of Market Street was cloaked in darkness, and he stole a look into an alleyway in passing. Furtive movement came to him, deep in the alley where some barrels were stacked, then the faint sound of breaking glass. Hesitation glinted in Tyler's eyes, caution telling him to keep going. He turned to look back up the street, where lights were showing, then swung back to gaze into the alley. Now he saw a cone of light, to have it disappear just as quickly.

"Somebody's bein' damned cautious," he said, heading into the alley while palming his Colt. If a robbery was in progress, it had come to Tyler that arresting those responsible would have the law around here see him in a new light. He had in mind those wanteds on him back in Oregon.

Tyler passed the back doorways of some business places, coming quietly onto the stacked barrels and easing around them. Glinting dully below a door was broken glass, and above it etched in black against white stucco, was the legend Western Assay Office. He eased in closer, to discover that someone had placed a blanket over the inside of the back door. Gingerly, he reached in to ease a corner of the blanket aside. He smiled at a dark figure hunkered before a large, square safe, the gas lantern on top of the safe beaming on the safecracker's tools of the trade. Cracking that gingerbox, mused Tyler as he moved away from the door, should be a snap compared to what we've encountered.

He found an empty packing crate just up the alley and settled down in the shadows. Pulling out the makings, he rolled a cigarette into shape, cupping it in his hand when he wasn't dragging smoke from it. Tyler eyed both the back door of the assay office and the two entrances to the alley. He knew that out here safecrackers were a rare breed, and they sure could have used one on that last job at Pendleton. He was on his second tailor-made, when the muffled sound of an explosion brought Tyler Echohawk to his feet. Another couple of minutes found the back door jarring open and the safecracker bolting out into the alley. The man brushed into an empty barrel stacked upon another, to send it toppling down. He labored under the weight of his tools in one hand and the satchel he carried in the other, but breaking into a fast trot, he pulled up abruptly when confronted by a man bearing a six-gun.

"You work fast," Tyler said pleasantly.

He started bringing up the satchel in an attempt to dislodge the revolver, only to have Tyler side-step and say, "Won't be long before they crowd in here. I've decided I could use someone like you."

"Who the hell are you, mister?"

"Right now, a friend."

"Like hell—"

"Like if we don't vamoose suddenlike, both of us will get caught," snapped Tyler.

"Okay, okay, got no choice." He handed the bag containing his tools to Tyler Echohawk, adding, "You're a heap younger'n me, damnit." Then the pair of them were running up the alley and onto a side street.

"My hotel isn't all that far," Tyler suggested as they slowed into a walk.

"No hotel for me," the safecracker snapped.

"Got lodging further west of here, if that's any of your business."

Holstering his Colt, Tyler smiled, "Good a place as any to palaver."

"About what?"

"My share of the take, for one thing."

"Figured as much. I'm no gunslinger, but—"

"Keep your hand where I can see it," Tyler warned. "What I have in mind'll profit both of us. So, you interested?"

They moved into the glow of a street lamp, where the safecracker took a hard look at Tyler Echohawk. The man wore a grey suitcoat and battered felt hat. He had a shaggy, greying beard and his eyes were alert. He tongued the chaw of tobacco around, then hawked out a stream of brown juice, which splattered onto the boardwalk. "Heard about gold being found hereabouts. Figured there might be some easy pickings. Well, come on. My place ain't all that far from here. We can jaw there . . . and you call yourself—"

"I'm Echohawk, first name is Tyler; an' new to these parts, as you are. Been in the same line of work, so to speak."

"They call me J.P., and that don't mean no justice of the peace. Name's John Phillip Dandridge. Out of a lot of places. Same line of work? Banks, I reckon." He returned Tyler's smile. "Cracked a few of them, too, Mr. Echohawk."

The meandering course of the safecracker brought them to where the red-light district fringed upon the river, then along a sandy bank to higher ground. Clustered around a large frame building were a few wagons and carriages. At their appearance, a large dog bounded out from under a wagon. "Easy," the safecracker said as the dog came up to nip at his hand, then to Echohawk, "Rented me a place to live above this machine shop." Lights from nearby buildings, along with a quarter moon, guided them to a staircase going up the side of the building. Opening the upstairs door, the safecracker entered a small room and set the satchel he carried on a chair. As Echohawk came in and closed the door, he lighted the coal oil lamp on the table.

Blinded for a moment by the flare of light, Tyler Echohawk didn't see the safecracker dip a hand into his coat pocket and pull out a handgun, snarling, "I didn't believe you for a minute back there, mister."

"No reason you should have," Tyler said calmly. "This bag is kind of heavy." He set it down by his feet, then brought his arms away from his sides. "I expect you've heard the name Echohawk before. . . ."

"Any reason I should have? Yeah, there's Sheriff Echohawk."

"He's my brother."

"Why you telling me this? I've got a good mind to kill you right here and toss your carcass in the river."

"Same's you, J.P., I got in here a short time ago. Been spending my time out in Oregon robbing banks. Things got hot and heavy after that last job we pulled in Pendleton, so I decided to pay my brother a visit."

"I've heard some whoppers before, Echohawk."

"I had the drop on you back there. Could have just as easy turned you in. So I figure you owe me."

"Like hell . . ."

"All I want is for you to hear me out."

The safecracker swiped his hat off and slammed it down on the table. "What you wanted was half of the take. You look awful damned young to be a bank robber. But . . . maybe I've got this gut feeling you're what you claim to be." He placed his gun on the table. "I always like to have some vittles after I pull a job. How does steak and taters sound?"

Tyler nodded when the safecracker moved away from the gun on the table and opened the lid on a potbellied stove. The man picked up some wood kindling and announced, "I like my coffee syrupy. Oregon, you said?"

"When we came west some years back, had to pass through Wyoming. My brother Lon—"

"That'll be the sheriff here?"

"Yup. He liked what he saw, I reckon. The folks and I kept on a-going. Been thinking, J.P., that a man with your unique talents should be in demand in places like this."

Shaping a crafty smile, the safecracker said, "Word gets around, I reckon. Hired on to do a few jobs."

"Reason I'm asking is that I want to know just who is calling the shots around here."

"Your brother could have told you that."

"Could have. But he just might want to know my reasons for asking. Matter of fact, I could have been a deputy sheriff."

"Why didn't you?"

"Woulda' cramped my style. Or maybe its 'cause I don't want a bunch of city councilmen turning my crank. I sent word to the bunch I rode with."

"There's a few banks hereabouts."

"Oh, yeah, I eyeballed all of them. But I want to work things different this go-around, J.P. Won't be long before this town grows considerable. What I've got in mind is to hire my gun out to the power boys."

"Where do I come in?"

"As long as folks put their trust in strong boxes," smiled Tyler, "you'll be needed. Those other jobs . . . do one for anybody of importance?"

"I know what you're fishing around for, Echohawk," he said. "Could have. So if I tell you, what then?"

"We could work together, J.P. Soon's that railroad reaches Casper, the oil boom and land rush starts. It would sure profit us being in on the ground floor."

"Had plans of pulling out of here. But, Echohawk, I could change my mind. Yup, I cracked open some strong boxes for a man named Lundahl. Nosed around afterwards and found out he runs the Golden West Land Company. What's interesting, Echohawk, is that Lundahl has connections to some land speculator named Hap Fleming."

"I've heard of this Fleming. Comes from Bessemer Bend." Tyler Echohawk removed his hat when he sat at the table, as the safecracker plunked down two cups.

"In the business I'm in, it pays to know something about the people who hire you. As cracking open the wrong safe could see you killed. It cost me some to find out that Fleming owns the Golden West Land Company. He's in thick with a councilman from Casper, man named Bascome. It was Bascome's safe I broke into."

"Coffee's got a kick to it," muttered Tyler, "but it'll do. I've been in Bascome's place, the Silver Bow Saloon. They say he'll be Casper's next mayor."

"The word is that Fleming's money is backing Bascome."

"Just in case Bessemer Bend doesn't become the new county seat," Tyler speculated.

"It'll never happen," retorted the safecracker. He carried two plates over and set one before Tyler, then he dropped onto a chair and picked up his cup. "Found out it's mostly a ploy by Fleming to sell lots over there."

"Should make a heap the way homesteaders are coming in."

J.P. Dandridge threw out a shrugging laugh, commenting, "Once the railroad gets here, homesteaders'll pay hell trying to claim a section of land. Fleming knows this. It don't mean a damn thing to him that he's selling these folks land

60

now. He's got his cutthroats swarming over the countryside buying up mineral rights and land. All because there's a lot of oil hereabouts. Once drilling operations start, Echohawk, or even before, I pity any homesteader dumb enough to buck both Fleming and the oil boys."

"You know, J.P., this Hap Fleming needs a man like me. Whether he likes it or not."

"He's got strong-arm men now, Echohawk."

"I'll be a cut above that," smiled Tyler. "Just got me an idea how to work it."

"Yeah," grunted the safecracker, "so how's that steak?"

"Best I've had in a heap of Sundays. It was my lucky night running into you, J.P."

"One thing, Echohawk, seems to me you wanted part of what I got out of that assay office—"

"A man will say a lot when he's holding a gun on someone. You earned it. I'll be going, J.P. Hope you stick around, as I've a feeling we can make a lot of money working together."

"I don't know how you're going to approach Hap Fleming. But when you do, look out for Fleming's right-hand man. They say Darby Connor's a mean one."

"So am I," Tyler said softly. "I owe you for the meal."

"And I'm obligated you didn't turn me over to the law."

Tyler Echohawk left then, reaching the bottom of the stairway and following the windings of a narrow lane. He knew it was a stroke of luck,

61

his coming across safecracker J.P. Dandridge breaking into that assay office. He judged Dandridge, with his midwestern accent, to be a man with some character, someone who'd keep his word. The next few days he meant to find out more about Hap Fleming and just how big that man's ambitions were. "Got a hunch about this . . . that it'll turn out right for all of us." The way he'd been walking brought Tyler Echohawk back into the red-light district, music blaring from a saloon causing him to quicken his pace.

Five

The quartering wind—a buffeting, damp turbulence coming from the anvil-crowned thunderheads beyond Pumpkin Buttes—kept striking out at four horsemen approaching Salt Creek. They were strung out in a line, with everyone wearing yellow rain slickers except for Deputy Sheriff Raleigh Carr. Every so often rain would flare in from clouds heading their way, then just as quickly let up. In late afternoon, the sun had worked its way behind more clouds far off to the west.

It had been at least two months since Sheriff Lon Echohawk had been up this way. He was surprised by the number of homesteaders who had settled in along the waterways, something that had been brought to his attention a couple of days ago by a man owning a ranch west of here. Rancher Walt Briscoe had also warned there could be gunplay. Lon knew that Briscoe's spread was one of three or four small ranches adjoining the South Fork of Powder River, with a few more hooked up farther south. Being sort of in the middle of things, Briscoe's had become headquarters for the aroused South Fork cowmen.

"I couldn't help noticing homesteaders have torn down fencelines in some places."

"Back there," said Hack LaVoy as he jabbed a thumb over his shoulder, "was a watering hole I seen many a time when I rode for Alf Linder. Now some jarhead of a homesteader is putting up a cabin there. Linder's been pretty sickly of late, otherwise he'd a' been there claiming what's legally his. An' the way some of the land's been torn up with them damned plows, Lon, makes you sick."

Deputy Sheriff Sy Hagen, a large and somber-faced man with two moles marking his face, said, "The truth is, the kind of soil out here won't do for farming. These land speculators working out of Casper know that. Just breeding trouble, is all."

"We won't be much welcomed out at Briscoe's," Lon Echohawk stated. "So don't let what these ranchers say raise your hackles."

"I figure," said LaVoy, "a Winchester is all the law these cowmen need. As it's all they had in the past, in most cases."

A sudden flurry of rain, in the form of large, slanting drops, struck out at them as the group crested a rise, sighting in on a tree line and buildings spread across a creek. A few men were assembled by one of the corrals. The lawmen found the crossing, just a low spot in the banks, and they splashed across. Lon Echohawk could smell the hostility as he came upon the corral, scattering away some geese. He held to his saddle, his deputies reining up behind, picking out Walt Briscoe with a smile.

The ranchers were men in their middle years, their bodies lean from wind and weather, the lines etching their faces speaking of years of hard work. They wore frayed Stetsons, scuffed boots, and worn clothing, yet there was a reserved dignity about them. Echohawk knew he wouldn't want to buck them in a fight.

"I figured water rights," Walt Briscoe said plainly, "was part of the land you settled on."

This, mused Lon Echohawk, was the unwritten law out in these parts. To hold land you had to control the waterways. Otherwise, land lying away from rivers and creeks left a man pretty much at the mercy of the elements. Later on, some of the ranchers had gotten around to filing claim to their acreage. A lot hadn't, and it was these men who found themselves at the mercy of homesteaders. Before coming out here, he'd checked on this at the register of deeds office. But to these men, he realized, it didn't mean a damn who had or hadn't filed on their land, as this new wave of immigrants meant their way of life was being threatened. Lon knew they'd damn well fight, be it homesteader, land speculator, or his lawmen.

"Homesteaders are just part of it," spoke up another rancher, whose name Echohawk vaguely remembered being Brady Carrington. The rancher went on, "Commission men have been coming in wanting to buy up mineral rights to our land. I figure anything I sell will hurt me in the long run."

"Oil!" spat out someone else.

"Now the railroad's coming in to Casper."

"Times are changing," said Echohawk. "I don't know as how for the better, but that's it. You can't blame the homesteader all that much for wanting to begin a new life. A lot of them will pull out once they realize crops won't take out here. You men know that."

"I know this," said a rancher with shaggy grey hair to his shoulders. "One of my hands didn't show last night." His voice held anger and a deep hurt, and he looked around slowly as he groped for what to say next. "Anyway, early on this mornin', I send the rest of my boys out looking for Easton. They found his hoss further west of where Easton should have been . . . that's all . . . just Easton's hoss . . ."

"I know Easton," piped up Hack LaVoy as he shouldered his horse in alongside Echohawk's. "You're right, Mr. Warner, Easton's awful dependable."

"We'll head over to your 22 spread, Mr. Warner, and check it out," Echohawk told him.

"I don't know if it's another homesteader Easton encountered or what, but I aim to find out," the rancher said. "Could be, too"—he lifted a resigned hand to tip his hat back some—"Easton got thrown and is layin' hurt in some coulee. But I'll find out. . . ."

The sheriff of Carbon County let his eyes flick about at faces that had gone stony, and he knew this could turn into a powder keg. Whatever had happened to cowhand Easton wasn't the issue, as it was just a part of the troubles being handed these ranchers. They were fiercely independent men, wanting and able to do it their way, terribly loyal to one another. Lon knew their way was the gun, and he felt a cold chill. How could he turn his guns on them? For they didn't fully comprehend just how quickly a new order was coming into Wyoming. To them that railroad was the same as a lobo wolf taking out some of their cattle. These land speculators and oil men and such were just other carrion coming in to feast on the leavings of the wolf. That maverick spirit again, he pondered, it just won't stay dead.

"I can't be every place at once," he said for everyone's benefit. "First off, I'll head over to your spread, Mr. Warner, and check out what happened to Easton. I've sent word to the county attorney that I want his office to check out these claims filed by homesteaders. These folks simply do not understand what water rights are all about . . . that in most cases they've been sold a bill of goods which isn't going to pan out. We'll do some other checking into these land companies."

"You do that, Sheriff," said Walt Briscoe, "and we appreciate it. The fact remains, a lot of our cattle are being cut off from water. We won't stand for that. No, for the time being, Echohawk, we won't take the law into our hands. But just remember a cow or calf dyin' of thirst hasn't got too long to live."

* * *

The lawmen had passed over prairie crisscrossed with streams, which had been born in the Big Horns. They'd spent an uneventful night camped just outside of Arminto. Clouds were still spread to the east and screening them from the morning sun, the lawmen jogging their fresh horses to the northwest, but Hack LaVoy had to have one final word for the cow town of Arminto.

"That Dixie Cafe sets out a fine line of vittles."

"Hack, I'll treat you to all you can chow down of steak and eggs back at Casper," said Lon Echohawk.

"That include me and Sy here."

"Reckon so, Raleigh. Doesn't that butte ahead mark the southern edge of Warner's land?"

"Yup," said Hack LaVoy. "The 22 ain't all that big when it comes to open range. A lot of arroyos and canyons spread about, which'll make it hard findin' Easton."

They pressed on, heading where the owner of the 22 Ranch had sent his hired hand, the missing Dan Easton. Just east of them lay more rugged land, marked by a long reddish sandstone wall knifing away from the Big Horns. The wall was notched by a lone passageway outlaws had coined Hole-In-The-Wall. Back at Casper, Lon Echohawk had wanted to head up there in search of outlaws, but he realized this was more important. Last thing they needed was a range war, he realized.

They came to a brushy coulee to search it out. Out of the coulee scrambled a grey fox, with Sy Hagen no more than a yard behind and reining his horse back onto the prairie. He watched the fox take a zigzag course amongst sagebrush, before looking back to have the others spur up to him. From here a suggestion by Hack LaVoy brought them angling to the west. Again they spread out, about a hundred yards apart, the clearing sun spearing them from behind. A wave from LaVoy caused them to rein up, the deputy pointing to a sluggish stream cutting off further progress to the west. They spurred on, cutting toward one another, until they'd ridden up on a high bank. "A lot of rocks and pebbles," LaVoy said. "We was told that Easton was supposed to look for cattle up thisaway, then get back afore nightfall, as they were plannin' on headin' for Casper to buy supplies. Be tough going as those rocks spread out, and nothin' else but gravel and pebbles."

"A rider wouldn't leave any track," Lon said. He looked about, at the southern flanks of the Big Horns tapering toward them no more than five miles away and at a shelf of lower land. At the sprinkling of pine trees and brush choking a lot of draws. Back to the water boiling over rocks and murmurously loud. "If Easton got thrown, he could have hit a rock and been knocked unconscious. There's a lot of deep pockets in this stream. So, we'll mosey along it."

"Up about a mile, there's where we can cross and search along both banks," said LaVoy. "Gonna be a scorcher." He began peeling off his sheepskin, and after he'd stowed it away, the deputy rolled a cigarette into shape as the others doffed and stowed their coats. LaVoy inhaled deeply of the aromatic Mex tobacco, then let it stream out of his nose. "Yup, a scorcher, as that rain didn't do much towards cooling it off."

At quiet orders from Sheriff Echohawk, they spread out along the stream running to the southwest. The farther they got from higher elevation, the trees thinned out but the rocks held, making the ride difficult. Sy Hagen's horse humped up in protest but he quieted it down, and then he called out.

"Found me some tracks!"

Deputy Sheriff Sy Hagen brought his gelding around in a tight circle while staring intently at the hoof-chewed ground. Here there were scattered tufts of shortgrass and sandy patches and several pines. Quietly, the other lawmen came in around Hagen, with Raleigh Carr gesturing at boot marks. "How many do you make out?"

"Hosses; I'd say five."

"Yeah, at least that."

The lawmen swung down and ground-hitched their mounts. They quartered out, trying to find the route the horsemen had taken. Lon Echohawk was the one to come across ground that had been chewed up, with boot markings and sand strewn onto tufts of grass. His eyes landed on a flat grey rock marked with dried blood. He whistled to his deputies.

Hack LaVoy said, "I found where they came in from the southeast."

"Town of Powder River's down that way. Beyond that, Hell's Half Acre."

"The way to Casper, too," speculated Lon. "I

70

make out there was a fight. This blood . . . the way the ground is chewed up."

"You're right, Lon," said Raleigh Carr. "But they didn't turn around and head back the way they came. Must have swung up toward that creek. Could be we'll find their trail, I figure, to the west. Easton, he must have stumbled across them . . ."

"Outlaws?"

"Men ghosting through here," said Lon. "Outlaws know they won't be bothered by ranchers long's they don't rustle any cattle. Just don't know. But let's go find out, if we can." He didn't want to elaborate to his deputies on what conclusions he'd drawn, but Lon Echohawk was worried. Was Dan Easton occupying another shallow grave? "There weren't any tracks left by cattle," he remarked. "Just by four riders."

"Meaning they might not be outlaws—"

Nodding, Echohawk swung into the saddle and squinted skyward. "It'll be noon in less'n hour. Clearing off more. Hack, take the point."

From here on, nothing more needed to be said as the lawmen from Carbon County fanned out behind Hack LaVoy, just coming onto the outbound trail of five horses. His hand signal alerted the others. Soon it was evident the trail they were following would be lost in the rocky ground spreading away from the creek. At a walk, LaVoy let his horse pick its way among the varied-colored rocks and stones, while the other two deputy marshals, at Echohawk's orders, were keeping pace farther away on grassy ground. They kept at it for about an hour, hoping to pick up on the tracks left by five horsemen, until Lon Echohawk pulled up to his deputy LaVoy.

"Hack, you and Carr cross over and try to pick up on their trail. It's been raining; could have wiped it out."

Farther along, about fifty yards, the two deputies managed to get across, Carr going downstream and Hack LaVoy riding the opposite way, but veering to the north to get out of the rocks. Soon he found sandy ground littered with sagebrush, which he rode over. There was plentiful sign left by grazing cattle, pronghorns, deer, a sudden gust of wind causing his eyes to take in the way of it up on the Big Horns. To his dismay, he saw that mottled grey clouds were coming out of Montana, not all that far away, clouds that had been shielded from the lawmen by the mountains. And he knew rain was in the offing.

"Just our luck," he groused worriedly. "Lon said they might not be outlaws, those we're after. But they know enough to hide their tracks. Come on, hoss, pick up the gait a mite."

He came to a low hump of ground, only to be confronted by a short drop-off, and with a jab of Hack LaVoy's spurs, the horse leaped forward to land easily. And here he found what they'd been seeking. "Seems they headed north, then came back this way again." He veered to the north and went on for at least a half-mile to make sure. Now LaVoy unleathered his six-gun and triggered it three times. As he holstered his side-arm, he gazed uptrail toward the mountains. He couldn't be certain, but the tracks he'd found seemed headed for a ravine. LaVoy held his ground to wait for the others.

"Five of them headed into that ravine; only four rode back this way. Easton didn't deserve this."

Hack LaVoy's horse whickered a greeting, and he swung it to the west and nodded at his companions coming up at a fast canter. They reined in around LaVoy, with Sheriff Lon Echohawk being told the facts of what his deputy had found. Quickly, Echohawk headed on, to the faint rumbling of thunder. Three miles of hard riding, and with a cooling wind brought on by the approaching thunderstorm sweeping around them, the lawmen brought their horses laboring up into the mouth of the ravine. In some places the grass was reedy and high, having been pushed down by those who'd been here before. Otherwise, the floor of the ravine was narrow and sloped upward to either side.

Palming his six-gun, Echohawk pulled the hammer back and fired at a turkey vulture that was just skimming inward over some pine trees, the creature veering away in surprise, scaring other carrion birds from a brush thicket. Lon Echohawk knew they'd found the missing cowhand.

Anger flaring his eyes, Lon murmured, "Seems they didn't even take the time to bury Easton." Closing in on the thicket, he swung down as his deputies rode up to dismount. Together they found openings in the thicket and a few rocks spread carelessly over a body, the spurred boots telling them all they needed to know.

73

Carefully, they lifted the rocks away, and then Raleigh Carr exclaimed, "Lordy, they hammered the hell out of Easton. His face . . . all black and puffed up . . ."

Lon knelt down and brushed some flies away from the dead man's upper body. The hat was missing and the shirt torn asunder, and there were more purplish bruise marks on the dead cowhand's stomach and chest. And a few slashing cuts, which caused Lon to say, "Not the kind of cuts a knife would make. Don't see any bullet wounds, either." With the help of Raleigh Carr, the body was rolled over.

"Easton wasn't backshot, Lon."

"No bullet wounds? I figure Easton was held while a third man worked him over." Lon Echo-hawk looked at his deputies. "A man accustomed to using his fists did this. Man wore a ring, too . . . those cuts we found."

"What do ya figure? outlaws?"

"Easton's hoss was found," said Lon as he rose. "An outlaw wouldn't leave that. As for this bein' a robbery, all Easton had was probably a couple of quarters burnin' a hole in his pocket." Worried eyes took in the lowering clouds. "Even if they left a trail, what's coming will wipe that out. You knew Easton. Did he have any enemies?"

"None to speak of," said Hack LaVoy. "You figurin' it could be someone out of Casper?"

"About all we've got to go on," said Lon. "They could retrace their route through Powder River. First we'll bundle up Easton's body, then

74

I'll take it over to Warner's place. You boys scout back along the settlements leading toward Casper."

Through a frown, Raleigh Carr said, "Hate to have you bear the brunt of going to Warner's alone, Lon."

"Better that way. I don't want word of this getting out. Maybe Warner'll do some jawing . . . or take off against some homesteader." Lon brought his horse in closer before he swung into the saddle, his deputies lifting the blanket-wrapped body over the saddlehorn, Echohawk's bronc picking up its ears at the smell of death.

Sheriff Lon Echohawk veered away from his southerly-bound deputies, bringing his bronc to a canter over prairieland. Around him short grass was bending with the wind and a few raindrops were falling. By his reckonings, it would be long after dark when he reached the 22 spread, but he figured he had no other choice.

"Easton had to stumble upon something," he pondered. But just what is up there close to the Big Horns, other than stray cattle and shelfing land? Only thing I can figure is oil is involved."

After a while and when a curtain of rain struck, Lon Echohawk halted to don his rain slicker, then went on, a man burdened down by the law, his own worries, and an unlucky cowhand named Dan Easton.

Six

Even cattleman Hy Akers was letting the notion get fixed in his mind that the comely woman from back east was cheating. A glance around the table by Akers, through a pallor of cigar smoke, revealed how the others felt. A work-hardened hand toying with a couple of poker chips, he allowed a smile for the deft hands of Sylvia Valcourt dealing out pasteboards in a graceful rhythm. The jack dealt Akers was shaded by an ace sliding in front of a whiskey salesman from Peoria.

"Your pair of aces are high," Sylvia murmured to Kingsley, the whiskey salesman. Willowy and somewhat tall at around five eight, she had on a green satiny jacket cut wide in front to show a lot of embroidered blouse. Auburn hair was piled up under a matching green hat. She wore just enough makeup to highlight her cheekbones and green-tinted eyes, with a splash of red dusting her full lips. Piled before her were three stacks of chips and some paper money.

Sylvia Valcourt had learned the rudiments of gambling from her father and his somewhat dubious acquaintances, even before she'd entered her teens. One of the players had dropped out when the conductor had come into the club car to announce they'd be pulling into Denver in a couple of hours. Sylvia's ready smile masked what she'd learned about the other players. The westerner, Akers, wasn't all that concerned about the outcome of the game, while the businessman from the Windy City considered this merely a social diversion. She'd dismissed the whiskey salesman as nothing more than a sore loser, and another player, he of the rumpled grey plaid suit and bowler hat, was too far into his cups to give a damn whether he won or lost. That left the man decked out quite handsomely in a three-piece suit, whose quiet but scorning remarks had begun questioning the fact she'd been winning most of the hands.

They'd been playing since early last night and on into the morning. The conductor had tipped her off to the game after that worthy had palmed a five-dollar gold piece. Then her intrusion into the club car had turned to acceptance when Sylvia bought a couple of hundred in poker chips. Now she figured she was ahead around two thousand dollars, the winnings secondary to her thoughts.

The handsome one called himself Rudolph Becker, the accent a thick Germanic. Which Sylvia had figured out was as phony as the smile flickering in Becker's light blue eyes. Count Rudolph Becker; another bit of malarkey. She'd finally pegged the count as a hustler and con man, and quite adept around a poker table.

Becker's not-so-veiled remarks she could be double-dealing had turned the attention from his nimble fingers to her. And though it didn't show, a hot flash of resentment gnawed at Sylvia Valcourt. She let it run its course, allowing a calmness to turn her eyes to the hand she'd just dealt herself. This particular game was five card stud, with two cards dealt facedown and, in this particular variation of the game, two others showing, with one more to be dealt out.

Without warning but with a gurgling sigh, plaid suit fell backward in his chair, to simply lie there in a state of drunken bliss. A few smiles broke out. This left a gap between Sylvia and Becker, seated across the table. She knew he'd been skimming cards from the bottom whenever he had dealt, being quite good at it, with Sylvia suspecting that the cattleman could have picked up on this. So to divert attention from himself, the good count had turned suspicions upon Sylvia. He'd even dealt winning cards to her, just a few hands during the long night to add weight to his caustic remarks, which were getting uglier now that Denver was looming over the horizon.

"Your aces are high," she said.

"Yeah, yeah." The whiskey salesman hesitated, then he pitched in a couple of chips.

The cattleman responded by doubling the ante, and as his weathered face turned to Sylvia, he drawled, "You've got a pair of deuces showing."

"Can't beat a pair of aces," she replied. What the cattleman meant, she knew, was that no other deuces were showing around the table, that she could have one as a hole card. Her eyes flicked to Becker, knowing he'd picked up on the byplay.

And as a matter of fact, one of Sylvia's hole cards was the deuce of hearts, which had come to her by an honest deal. Becker's chastising remarks could cause gunplay to erupt before they pulled into the train depot, despite the fact she was a woman. Or, if they believed him, he could have her arrested. Sylvia was aware of the two-shot Derringer tucked in the purse snuggled on her lap beneath the table, and ever mindful, too, of Becker's disdainful grimace as she flicked a card in front of him, which turned out to be the king of spades. From the way his hands snaked out to it, she knew it had filled a spade straight.

She finished her deal, and all eyes swung to the whiskey peddler casting uncertain eyes at what he'd been dealt. "Damnation," he cursed, "gettin' this close to hittin' is like kissin' your gramma." Still flinging out his resentment, he pushed his cards away.

The cattleman said, "That leaves my three queens as boss on the table. I'm bettin' . . . two double eagles."

Folding his hand was the businessman from Chicago, who cast a rueful smile Sylvia's way as she matched the raise of the cattleman. Her three deuces, she realized, were no match for what the cattleman had been dealt. Sarcastically, Rudolph Becker spat out, "Miss Valcourt—if that's your name—you must have dealt yourself a damned good hand. But . . . I'm doubling the last bet." His challenging eyes took note of the cattleman matching the bet, even though his gaze was fixed on Sylvia.

"Three queens," Hy Aker said quietly as he turned his hole cards over. He looked at Sylvia folding her hand, and at the German smiling triumphantly. "So, your straight takes the pot." He shrugged and took out another cigar. "What part of Germany are you from, Count?"

"Ah, Hamburg. And you, sir, where do you call home?"

"Wyoming."

"The home of the Sioux and Shoshone, so I've read," said Becker as he began shuffling the cards. "A little seven card stud, gentlemen, ladies," he sneered.

Syvlia let it slide, the cards flicking to her over the green felt cloth, conscious of the fact the bottom card she'd caught out of the corner of her eye was the trey of hearts. All five players with the exception of Count Rudolph Becker drew cards that showed a lot of promise, with the betting matching what they'd been dealt. A series of blasts from the trail whistle told everyone this poker session was about to end, Sylvia noting the passing buildings as she glanced out the window. Then her attention went back to the game and the deck of cards held by Becker.

Finally, it all came down to the last card, which would be dealt facedown. The betting had been heavy, nobody dropping out, the cards on the table telling of hands shaping into winners. Cards, Sylvia knew, that had been manipulated by the skillful hands of the bogus count. She had three nines, the other nine either a hole card or still buried in the deck. Somehow she knew it would be dealt to her, as the whiskey peddler shoved all the money he had left into the mass of chips making up this last pot.

"Damn, best hand I've had tonight."

"It's morning, my friend."

"So what? Just finish dealing."

"Certainly," came Becker's thick-voweled voice, his hand flashing away from the deck he held to lay a card before the cattleman.

Sylvia Valcourt brought a hand beneath the table to flit into her handbag. She was dealt a card, leaving it there as she suddenly reached across the table to grasp Rudolph Becker's right hand and, at the same time, point her Derringer at him.

"That bottom card you just palmed better be the trey of hearts, my German friend!" she lashed out.

Though he stiffened, Becker made no move to pull his hand away from her grasp as he fixed her with a scorning smile. "How dare you accuse me of cheating!" he said haughtily, though he'd paled. With everyone's eyes stabbing at his right hand, held atop the table by Sylvia, he somehow managed to bring his other hand down to his coat pocket.

Only now the bogus count found himself staring down the barrel of a .44-.40 Colt drawn by cattleman Hy Akers, who said, matter-of-factly, "That hand comes up with anything 'asides that deck of cards, Count Becker, you're a dead man. Let's see that trey of hearts you palmed."

At this, Sylvia withdrew her hand, and now Becker's hand trembled slightly as he slowly turned it over to reveal the ace of spades. He stammered out, "She . . . she's been cheating. I . . ."

The cattleman's six-gun bucked, to have crimson slash across Rudolph Becker's cheekbone, the sound a harsh staccato of accusation in the club car, the bullet passing on through a closed window to the shattering of glass. Gun smoke, acrid and blending with the scent of cigar smoke, drifted upward as Becker pressed a stunned hand to his cheek.

Calmly, Aker said, "We'll split this last pot. All except you, Becker. Then we'll divest you of whatever you won, unless you take exception . . . that means, Becker, all of it."

The con man pushed up from the table amidst the cards scattering from his left hand. The core of his anger wasn't for the cattleman but rather for Sylvia Valcourt, who was smiling up at him. Gamely, he blurted out, "Denver isn't all that big that we won't run into one another, you—" Becker left it at that, turning quickly as the cattleman thumbed back the hammer on his Colt and fleeing the club car.

"Here . . . here," stammered the whiskey peddler as he gained his voice, "we was led to believe you'd been cheatin' us . . . Miss . . ."

"Don't sweat it," countered Sylvia in a sweet monotone. "So, Mr. Aker, if you'll divvy up the pot and what our friend the count left behind . . ."

"You're a cool one, Miss Valcourt, awful darned

82

cool," smiled the cattleman. "Thought I was the only one spotted what the German was doing."

"You had me going, Mr. Aker, by not letting on. You're awful cool yourself."

"Yup," he agreed, "I've had my days. Reckoned for a minute there you'd be needin' a lawyer."

"I am a lawyer, sir."

Hy Aker broke into laughter, the others joining in, as he said, "Got no argument with that, Miss Sylvia. But I figured you studied for the bar in bars as much as from books, no offense meant, ma'am."

"None taken. Gentlemen, I thank you for making this long journey west necessary, for the money you most graciously let me win." She rose to a swirl of long black skirt, leaving a smile behind.

Departing the club car, Sylvia Valcourt hurried through some passenger cars until she found her sleeper compartment, only to discover the woman she'd shared the compartment with was gone. As she went to stand before a wall mirror, Sylvia smiled at how she'd first encountered Megan Randsley back at Chicago's boisterous, bustling Union Station. First of all, there'd been Megan rushing through the crowd, pushing toward the gates opening onto the train platform, laden down with luggage, her darkish red hair flailing about her shoulders. Then there was Megan followed at some distance by a redcap, pushing a cart laden down with more luggage, the Negro calling out plaintively, "I tell you, ma'am, the train won't leave w'out yo."

The passenger train, the Santa Fe Special, pulled out a half hour later with everyone securely aboard, and Sylvia facing a compartment jammed with luggage and Megan Randsley. Somehow they made do on the westward journey, in the process becoming friends, learning they had fellow acquaintances back east. Whenever they appeared in the dining or club car, heads turned, and Sylvia knew it was all because of Megan Randsley's seductive beauty. Megan's quick laughter and flashing gold-flecked green eyes were magnets that drew a great deal of attention from men passengers. Though she had a special beauty of her own, this set well with Sylvia Valcourt, in that hers was of a more reserved nature.

What she learned was that Megan Randsley had a beau waiting in Casper, Wyoming Territory, and that she came from a wealthy family. At age twenty-one, Megan wasn't very experienced when it came to men, and Sylvia felt the young woman possessed a restless, devil-may-care spirit. She's vulnerable, was Sylvia's final assessment—and not all that in love with this Irish barrister waiting for her out in Wyoming.

Hefting her twin pieces of luggage, dark leather valises, Sylvia came out into the side aisle and brushed into the wall as there came a sudden lurch in speed, the passenger train finally gliding the last few yards to come alongside a platform crowded with waiting carts and porters. The rest of her luggage, a trunk, would be delivered to the Centennial Hotel. She made her way with others down the vestibule and, spotting Megan Randsley, called out to her, "Megan, wait up."

Turning slightly, Megan waved back at Sylvia Valcourt, then continued her conversation with a man wearing an eastern-cut suit. "But, Mr. Davis, I shan't be tarrying in Denver all that long, as I have to catch a stage for Casper."

He was in his mid-thirties, possessed of a handlebar mustache and bold eyes, the head of a family of five residing back in Chicago and out here on business. Any scruples he felt were being pushed aside by this seductive woman's coy smile. Huskily, he said, "Back on the train, you told me you've never been here before. My dear Megan, I'd be delighted to show you around this enchanting city. And afterwards, there are any number of dining places . . ."

"Megan, glad I caught up with you."

"Oh, Sylvia, this is Mr. Davis. You weren't around when we started pulling in, but now you're here."

"To say goodbye. But not before I find out if you've made arrangements to encoach for Wyoming."

"It shouldn't be all that difficult to arrange for transportation. Mr. Davis knows where the stagecoach office is located. I believe you told me you're staying at the Centennial Hotel . . ."

"Yes, if you need me, Megan."

"I can stay over," she said to Sylvia, but with an eager smile for Davis. "Yes, I'll have my luggage sent to the Centennial. Sylvia, could you make arrangements for me there, as Mr. Davis wants to show me about?"

"I'll handle it, Megan, but . . . take care . . ."

The afternoon had passed quickly for Sylvia Valcourt after she'd checked into the Centennial Hotel, located along Alameda, a wide boulevard choked with traffic. To the west, the mountains knifed up against a darkening sky, the day wind cutting away. The room she'd acquired for Megan Randsley lay across a carpeted hallway, vacated a couple of hours ago by Sylvia as she'd left the hotel to begin looking for her father.

Consigned to memory were names given to her back in New York. She had also encased in her purse a small framed picture of disbarred lawyer Harold P. Fleming. The names she recalled were mostly of people, but they also included a few clubs and gaming casinos her father might have frequented. She could think of other cities her father might have fled other than Denver. What those in the know back in New York had told her about this Mile High City was its reputation of being a haven for bunco artists and petty thieves. Sylvia suspected Hap Fleming certainly had greater ambitions than getting involved in these scam games again.

"So," she mused silently, "Hap would only frequent the higher places to find amusement." Her orders to the hack driver had been to head for the Aristocrat Racquet Club, one of the names on her list.

86

Within the half hour, Sylvia left the hack and passed along a canopy that carried her into the foyer of an elegant brick building. She tapped the handle of a dark red parasol down on a bell on the counter, and within moments a clerk appeared. "I've just arrived from Manhattan," Sylvia announced.

"We . . . we don't allow ladies in the barroom."

"I shall take my ease out on the veranda. Some sherry will be fine . . . and one or two Denver newspapers."

"Why, yes, I—" He stared after Sylvia Valcourt sweeping down a tiled corridor, then shrugged and went to carry out her wishes.

When Sylvia reached the end of the corridor, instead of going out on the veranda, she made an abrupt right toward one of the screened doorways leading into the clubroom. Inside the clubroom the lights were subdued, as was the talk among the tables and from other men taking their ease at the curving bar, while the chinking of cue balls came from farther back in the room. A few women wearing evening gowns were seated with their husbands, and Sylvia felt more sure of herself. Settling down by a table close to the bar, she put her purse and parasol down while gazing about, one of the waiters hurrying over.

"Brandy . . . I'll take it straight."

"Certainly, ma'am."

What had her contact back in New York told her about the Aristocrat Racquet Club? Yes, that it was a place frequented by the affluent and the grifters. She spotted some of the latter type sprin- kled among the tables, then her drink arrived.

"Perhaps you can help me."

"If I can, ma'am."

Opening her purse, Sylvia took out some money and the picture of her father. "I've just arrived from back east. Perhaps you've seen this man in here before." There was a quick smile as she placed some silver dollars on the waiter's tray. "He's my father, if that will help."

A spark of recognition danced in the waiter's eyes, disappearing just as quickly as he said, "Could be I've seen him in here."

"Please, I haven't all that much money. It's been three years since we've since him last. His name is Harold Fleming, but he likes to be called Hap."

"I guess I've seen him in here, ma'am. But that was weeks ago. Does that help any?"

"You've been most gracious," she smiled as the waiter took his leave. Sylvia watched as he eased back among some tables to confer with a man clad in a plaid suit. She brought her eyes down to the picture of her father, the feeling growing in her that Hap Fleming wasn't in Denver. Per- haps it was just as well she head back east. Be- cause she knew that her father would never try his hand at honest work, could at this very mo- ment be involved in some scam. Perhaps her com- ing out here on this venturous journey was to try and save Hap Fleming from his larcenous nature. Now she became aware of the man in the plaid suit making his way toward her table, at the same time she was being watched by another man taking a place at the bar.

"So, you're Fleming's kid." A chair scraped and the man in plaid eased down to Sylvia's right. "I'm known hereabouts as Kid Duffy." His dark brown hair was parted in the middle and combed to both sides of his narrow head, his nose pushed to one side, his eyes lidded and expressionless. He twitched a finger at his nose and glanced at the picture that Sylvia had placed by her purse. "That's Fleming, awright, but a lot thinner."

She'd been informed by a bunco artist friend of her father's that Adolph W. Duff, better known as Kid Duffy, was Lou Blonger's Denver con ring manager. Which meant that anyone chancing in here couldn't operate without Kid Duffy's approval. Sylvia had also learned that Blonger had a direct line to the police chief's office. From the bristling and cold attitude of the intruder at her table, she realized she could be in trouble, and she smiled.

"I'm Sylvia Fleming."

"You can forget the con act as to being Fleming's daughter. He tried to horn in here; got drove out. You . . . you're kind of sharp-lookin'." He lifted a hand and snapped his fingers to summon a waiter. "What kind of hustles you been operatin'?"

At the moment Sylvia knew she wasn't in any danger, but she also knew that if she didn't play along with Kid Duffy, she'd have the proverbial twenty-four hours to leave town. "True," she said pleasantly, "I'm from New York."

"With that accent, where else?"

"Seems an education's been wasted on me."

"You, a college dame?"

"Sort of. What do you do, Mr. Kid Duffy?"

"I'm what you call a manager of things. A lot of things."

"I get your drift."

"Then you interested in working this town?"

"Can I sleep on it?"

"You can if you make it a catnap. Waiter, give the dame a refill. Two days, you've got until then to decide." He rose with the set to his face still intact and strode away.

When Sylvia Valcourt left a few minutes later, it was to hop aboard another hack. She realized without a doubt that she'd be followed, that every con artist in Denver would be informed of her presence. But in her burned the hope of finding Hap Fleming. "Driver, where can I purchase some newspapers?"

"At this hour? I'm sure they sell them at your hotel."

Now Sylvia sank back against the seat cushion. She kept thinking about recent gold and silver discoveries farther west in the mountains that hacksawed their way through Colorado. New towns would be springing up in gulches and ravines where pay dirt ore was found. The same thing was taking place farther north in Wyoming. "I know him," she mused. "My father'll head for a mining town. I only hope he'll hang up his shingle again, or . . ."

She blinked the pensive look from her eyes as

the hack pulled in to stop before the Centennial Hotel. Sylvia paid the driver and eased onto the sidewalk. Hurrying into the lobby, she looked about before veering over to a counter on which newspapers were piled. She selected two local papers, the *Denver Post* and *Rocky Mountain News,* along with the *Cheyenne Gazette.* Dropping the required coins into the newsboy's hand, she recrossed the lobby and went up the staircase. Though she'd stayed up playing poker last night, Sylvia wasn't all that ready to go to bed. There would be an early supper in the hotel dining room, then after retiring to her room, she'd pore over the newspapers. There could be an item in any one of them that would give her a clue to Hap Fleming's present whereabouts. And if not, at least she'd learn more about this territory. Approaching the door leading into her room, Sylvia's stride faltered at a sudden outcry that was choked off.

"That . . . seemed to come from Megan's room," she said aloud.

Sylvia veered closer to the door and rapped urgently.

"Megan? Are you in there?" She tried the doorknob; the door was locked. A faint creaking of a floorboard echoed through the threshold, which gave way to a heavy silence. To mind came the lusting eyes of a certain Mr. Davis, and Sylvia dipped a hand into her purse to dig out her two-shot Derringer. She cocked one of the hammers while aiming at the doorknob and squeezed the trigger, and the Derringer bucked in her hand. The door opened a little, with Sylvia throwing herself at the door and then into Megan Randsley's room.

The man spun away from where he'd been pawing Megan Randsley, who was sprawled across the bed. Sylvia took in Megan's disheveled clothing and bloody lip. The man's white shirt hung out of his trousers, and his coat and hat were tossed on the floor.

"You old, bald sonofabitch! She's young enough to be your daughter!" Sylvia shouted.

"Easy . . . easy with that gun, ma'am." He edged away from the bed and crabbed backward, until the pair of front windowsills nudged against his buttocks.

"Easy, my ass!" Sylvia blurted out as she cocked the other hammer and brought up the Derringer to just below waist level.

Sensing Sylvia Valcourt's intentions, the man known as Davis spun about and launched himself through one of the windows a split second before flame belched from the Derringer. He landed hard on the outside balcony, running around the second floor and crying out in pain, before he managed to gather himself and scramble away. Sylvia dropped her hand to her side, staring angrily at Megan Randsley as the young woman tried to piece together her torn blouse.

"Lucky I chanced in," said Sylvia.

"He just wouldn't leave me alone," Megan said through her tears.

"It just might be you egged him on a little."

"Did you hit him?"

"In the butt, yup. But I had a different part of

his anatomy in mind. Megan, I'm getting you on that stage for Casper tomorrow morning. Now, you tidy yourself up while I go explain all of this to hotel management." Going to the open door, Sylvia hopped around while dropping the handgun in her purse. "And, girlie, the damages will be billed to your room, though I'm springing for supper."

Through sleepy eyes, Sylvia Valcourt pushed aside a copy of the *Denver Post*. Both the *Post* and the other Denver paper had let her put a finger on the pulsebeat of the business community. She'd learned this city had every intention of becoming the business center of the West. Though a lot of articles in both newspapers detailed what was happening up in Wyoming.

She pulled over the *Cheyenne Gazette,* the front page filled with more articles about a land boom that would hit territorial Wyoming once the Fremont, Elkhorn, and Missouri Valley Railroad's new line reached Casper. Farther down she read about the mining camp of Eadsville, and there were other articles telling of the coming prosperity. Leafing through the *Gazette,* Sylvia saw that it contained one advertisement after another telling of land for sale, as well as a long article about the feud going on between Casper and Bessemer Bend over which town would become the new county seat.

"Young towns," she mused, "filled with just the right ingredients to interest someone like my father. But I hope Casper's ready for a man like Hap Fleming." There came a sudden smile from Sylvia Valcourt, followed by a worried frown.

"If he's there, will he want me around?"

She rose and strode to look out a window, at downtown Denver snuggling in for the night, a young woman wrapped in a white robe and the worry of her own thoughts. Here she was, a fledgling lawyer, which to the powers that be meant she had sworn to uphold the law. If he was there, how could she turn her father over to some western lawman? With a sigh, she turned away from the window and moved toward her bed.

"Well, Megan, you'll have company on the way to Casper."

Seven

Tyler Echohawk had settled onto a bench out in front of a hardware store on south Center Street. The porch afforded him protection from a noon sun, with once again the wind getting stronger. Folks involved in the building trade had been drifting into the store. A homesteader had arrived in his wagon, the work horses tied out front, the stench of horse droppings pricking at Tyler's nostrils over the tangy aroma of his tailor-made. He kept gazing across the street at the facade of the Golden West Land Company.

Tyler could have gone over to the land company and discussed with Ole Lundahl the kind of business he had in mind. But the Golden West had seen a lot of people dropping in this morning, which meant Lundahl wasn't about to let a drifting cowpuncher into his office. Tyler had checked out the fact that Ole Lundahl was like clockwork when it came to having a noon lunch at Plow's Diner. The sight of Lundahl pushing out through the front door served to remind Tyler Echohawk that he hadn't eaten today, and he rose to trudge after the stocky, bespectacled Lundahl.

"I just hope Lundahl doesn't lose his appetite after I talk turkey with him. Likely not, as he doesn't seem like someone you can bluff out."

He followed Ole Lundahl around a corner onto B Street, to have both of them pass along in the shade cast by a wooden frame building. Just opposite and about in the middle of the block, carpenters were laying roof shingles on a large two-story building, the thudding of their hammers part of the noonday clamor. Flicking his cigarette stub away, he stopped a moment as Ole Lundahl went up the two steps that carried him into Plow's Diner, then Tyler picked up his ambling gait. Through the plate glass window, he sighted in on Lundahl settling into a booth. Tyler entered the diner and beelined over, quickly seating himself across from the manager of the Golden West Land Company.

"Nice day, Mr. Lundahl."

Having just removed his felt hat, Lundahl held it cradled in one arm as he studied the intruder, then answered, "It is. I assume you're in search of some land. . . .

"Not exactly." Tyler smiled up at the waitress setting down a glass of water.

"The special's—"

"I'll have that," Ole Lundahl said irritably.

"Whatever it is," agreed Tyler, and the waitress took her leave. "I ran into a friend of yours, a gent liking to pry things open."

"Cowboy, just what is your game?"

"Same's yours, Mr. Lundahl, money."

"Well, I could use another land salesman."

Tyler sipped from his glass. "For the record, you hired a safecracker to break open a strongbox belonging to Councilman Rafe Bascome. The Golden West, it's owned by Hap Fleming. You boys have a sweet thing going, selling worthless land to homesteaders and the like."

Tight-lipped, the anger simmering in his eyes, Ole Lundahl picked up his hat and started to rise, only to have the cowboy pinion his arm to the tabletop and tell him softly, "I'll let you know when I'm done, Mr. Lundahl."

He sank down again, saying tautly, "Yes, let me hear all of what you know." He set his hat down. "You do have a name?"

"Echohawk; the sheriff is my brother. Tyler Echohawk. 'S'matter of fact, I was offered a job as deputy sheriff. But I'm not here on behalf of the law of Carbon County. What I've been doin' is nosing around. Found out you eastern boys don't know how to handle the rowdy element out here. Which is where I come in."

"Is that so?"

"Yup," Tyler said in a voice gone deathly cold and whispery low. "You will set up a meetin' with your boss, Hap Fleming. For tonight, as I know Fleming's in town. Say, over at your land company. But pull anything, and that mutual friend of ours gets word to the county sheriff. Make it for seven o'clock." He smiled at Lundahl easing out of the booth as the waitress arrived holding two plates.

Ole Lundahl placed some money down on the table. "Seven will be fine, Mr. Echohawk. Don't disappoint us and not show up." Then he walked away.

"Ain'tcha gonna eat, Mr. Lundahl?"

"Long's he paid," grinned Tyler, "leave both places right here, ma'am. And you might fetch some Arbuckles to wash this beef stew down."

"You're in it up to your ears now, Mr. Geologist!" raged Hap Fleming.

"But . . . this wasn't suppose to happen," protested Cyril Barkley, the geologist. "Things just got out of hand." He was somewhat tall, had a horsey face, and had been hired out of Denver by Fleming.

"A lot of things," Hap Fleming agreed, "have gotten out of hand lately." They were gathered in an office at the Golden West Land Company. The others present were Ole Lundahl and Fleming's strong-arm man Barney Cleever. It was becoming evident to Hap Fleming that Cleever was in over his head. The story brought back by the geologist was pretty much echoed by what Cleever had said, that of accosting a cowpuncher up north someplace. First they'd overnighted at Powder River and, Fleming suspected, loaded up with whiskey, before heading out the next day. They'd been in search of possible oil sites, having in fact found some promising land just this side of the Big Horns. The geologist, Cyril Barkley, had been using the equipment he'd brought along to take soil samples, when the cowhand had ridden in. From here on, Fleming knew, Barney Cleever had taken charge of things.

"You're sure he's dead, Barney?"

"I broke his neck."

Hap Fleming stared from behind the desk in the small office at his henchmen clustered before him. Finally, he nodded, as if the matter of the dead cowhand were closed. He leaned forward to steeple his fingers on the desk, looking at the geologist. "A pity there's no oil around Bessemer Bend."

"A remote possibility," the geologist said. "If you don't need me anymore . . ."

"Mr. Barkley, I'll tell you when you can leave. What I'm about to say next involves you very much. Land buying has tapered off over at Bessemer Bend. We need a gimmick to draw more folks in. Which, my friends, means that we're going to start drilling for oil just south of town, out on the flats there."

"But you won't find any oil."

"I know that, Mr. Barkley. I don't care if cow piss gushes out of that well. The sight of that drilling rig will bring potential clients swarming in to Bessemer Bend. I want operations begun on that tomorrow, Barkley. Hire a drilling crew, whatever, but see it's started. Now you may go."

Ole Lundahl waited until the door closed again, then he said, "Man's running scared."

"I know," said Fleming as he leaned toward a side table and picked up a bottle of whiskey. "But pull out? Not our honorable Cyril Barkley. He does not . . . ah . . . that went down smoothly . . . want to spend the rest of his days rotting in some jail. Nor do we, for that matter."

Lundahl dug out his gold-plated pocket watch and said, "Going on seven."

"Echohawk, you say?" Hap Fleming poured more whiskey into his glass.

"I don't like the smell of it," retorted Barney Cleever.

"Like it or not," said Lundahl, "Echohawk knows about that safecracker. I asked around this afternoon. Seems the sheriff of Carbon County has a brother matching Echohawk's description."

Around a derisive wave of his hand, Hap Fleming said, "I don't think this Echohawk can out-con con men of our caliber. What Echohawk knows could mean a lot of trouble for us. The least we can do is hear him out."

"Before I get my hands on him?"

"Yes, Barney." They heard someone rapping at the back door, and Fleming added, "It seems the honorable Mr. Echohawk has gall enough to show up."

Rising, Ole Lundahl said, "I'll show him in." He left the office door open on his way out, re-appearing with a grinning Tyler Echohawk in tow.

"Evening," Tyler said, a nod from Hap Fleming beckoning him over to take a seat, Tyler shifting around in his chair to keep everyone in sight. He tipped his Stetson back, then took the proffered glass of whiskey from Fleming.

"So you are the sheriff's illustrious brother."

"And you're Hap Fleming."

"You do have a first name?"

"Just call me Tyler. I've a business proposition that should profit both of us, Mr. Fleming."

"Just what would a cowpuncher have in the way of equity, Mr. Echohawk?"

"My guns."

"Pug-uglies are a dime a dozen."

"Those type generally have too much muscle between the ears," grinned Tyler. "I'll get to it. First off, you're hoping to expand your operation. And it doesn't include land, but the oil that's under it."

At that moment, Hap Fleming realized he was facing something other than a run-of-the-mill cowhand. He shaped a pleasant smile. "Go on, Tyler."

"I was offered a job as deputy sheriff. The offer's still open."

"Interesting," said Fleming. "Does your coming to us mean there's been a falling out between you and your brother, the sheriff?"

"Nope, we get along just fine. What I have to worry about is a wanted poster coming in on me. Out Oregon way I'm wanted for bank robbery, among other things. I expect the rest of the boys I rode with to show most any time, Mr. Fleming. But this go-around, I don't have robbing banks in mind."

"You realize, of course, I'll have this checked out, Mr. Echohawk. Though somehow your story has the ring of truth to it. So, the rest of your gang is coming here?"

"Be here most anytime. And once that railroad reaches this cow town, it'll swell up like a

101

bloated cow. Folks'll be swarming in, to find land, or work, or get into the oil game."

"This is all very interesting, Tyler, but—"

"No buts about it. The deal I'm makin' is that I take over your roughhouse boys. Any strong-arm work to do here or out in the boonies, my boys do it. The only connection they'll have to you, Mr. Fleming, is through me. The rest of it is I'll take that job as deputy sheriff. What the sheriff tells me, I relay on to you. A sweet setup, Mr. Fleming."

"A helluva setup," agreed Hap Fleming. "The only fly in the ointment is that safecracker. He could sell what he knows to the local law."

"He won't. And that safecracker'll be working for me, as their breed is a rare commodity in these parts."

"Hap, you ain't buyin' all of this, are you?"

He glanced at the scowling Barney Cleever, then he spoke to Lundahl. "Well, Ole, I've always valued your opinion."

"As I've said before, we're easterners, Hap. The ways out here are a far cry from what we know. No offense, Barney, but up until now, my chief worry has been the strong-arm methods used by our land salesmen. What Echohawk proposes is no different than the protection offered by the mob back east. I believe we need to keep ourselves clear of strong-arm activities, strive to gain respectability, so to speak."

"Yes, we must remove ourselves to a better neighborhood. Echohawk, we'll check you out. Then we can talk further."

Grinning, Tyler Echohawk unbuttoned a shirt pocket and pulled out a folded sheet of yellow paper. He unfolded the paper and slapped it down before Fleming as he rose. "A damn good picture of me. But two thousand? A good cuttin' hoss is worth more than that."

Fleming looked from the wanted poster to Tyler and said, "very commendable. But we'll still have to delve further into your bona fides."

"Yup, do so. You can start at Pendleton, Oregon and work your way westerly."

Opening a lower drawer, Hap Fleming lifted out a cash box and set it on the desk. He opened the lid and counted out five hundred dollars in greenbacks, which he passed to Tyler Echohawk, explaining, "Just in case you're short, Mr. Echohawk."

"Obliged."

"If you don't check out, I'll send Barney around to get my money back."

Tyler laughed as he settled his Stetson over his forehead. "Make sure Barney's packin' something other than his fists."

"That's all he needs."

"Out here a bullet travels a helluva lot faster than a roundhouse. See you gents soon, I hope." His hand dipped to his holstered gun, and in one blurring move he'd cocked the hammer and had it pointed at Hap Fleming, the smile gone, a deadly chill radiating out of his eyes. "I expect what was discussed here tonight to stay between us gents. My price'll be high once we get this operation rolling. I can read sign same's the next man. Meanin' that us working together can see us becoming a heap richer than we are now. An' when you check me out, Mr. Fleming, you'll find that Tyler Echohawk is a man of his word. Night, gents." He swung around to turn his back on the occupants of the room as he holstered his gun and ambled away.

The back door slamming shut brought Hap Fleming jerking his hand away from the whiskey bottle. He found there a film of sweat on his forehead, whereas the men that dealt with Hap Fleming were usually the ones to suffer some form of discomfort.

"He was bluffing."

The others looked at Barney Cleever, then Ole Lundahl said heavily, "No, men like that don't bluff. How could one so young be so . . . so bold?"

"Dangerous would be a better word." Suddenly, Hap Fleming laughed, and he clapped a hand down on the desktop. "To have our hand in the sheriff's pocket! I do believe Tyler Echohawk is what he says he is. But, Ole, first thing tomorrow look into it. Echohawk could be just the man to take care of Colhour. Too bad Colhour got so greedy."

"What's to say Tyler Echohawk won't be just as bad?"

"Once we start drilling for oil and bring in some wells, it won't make any difference. Then we'll be dealing in millions. So, my friends, let's make the rounds, as I feel lucky tonight."

"Not me," scowled Barney Cleever. "I just

104

don't cotton to that smart-aleck cowboy. Don't see what good he can do us." Anger carried the burly man out of the room.

"He'll get over it."

"I don't know, Ole. Cleever likes to nurse a grudge along. He could go out looking for Echohawk. Should be interesting if they tangle."

"Said he robbed banks . . ."

"Echohawk said a lot of things," remarked Hap Fleming. He pushed to his feet and moved around the desk to retrieve his hat from a rack near the office door. "If he pans out, he came along just in time. Shall we start at the Silver Bow Saloon?"

"Suits me."

Once ex-pugilist Barney Cleever decided he didn't like someone or something, that was it. The hulking New Yorker would lock his mind in on his hatred, which now was directed at that loud-mouthed cowpoke Tyler Echohawk. What it all came down to was that Echohawk wanted to take Cleever's job away. He'd been brooding about what to do for the last couple of days. Yesterday he'd sent Trammel and some others out to look for this Echohawk, with word coming in today that the cowpuncher was lodged at the Chandler Hotel.

The rigors of training for a prize fight had in-grained a certain discipline in Cleever. Every other day or so, he would get in some sparring and hit the heavy bag at a local sporting club. About him was a certain cunning, along with a tenaciousness

105

that kept him focused on the job at hand but mostly on those he had pegged as his enemies. Though he put away a lot of corn liquor, he never seemed to get drunk. Another of his vices was to head down to the cribs once a week to roust up a whore. Cleever loved to hate, often sitting alone for hours in some dingy saloon, nursing a particular wrong, imagined or real. Tonight he was draped over a back table at the Barleycorn Bar, rehashing what they'd done to that cowpoke up there near the Big Horns.

"Damn fool spoke out of turn," he snarled.

But it really hadn't been that way at all. Actually, cowpuncher Easton had ridden in peaceably to where the geologist had his tools spread out. They'd exchanged pleasantries."

"Funny you'd be interested in that rock formation, mister."

Geologist Cyril Barkley hesitated before saying, "To be truthful, this is interesting country. A lot of prehistoric animals lived here."

Easton looked over at the three men holding to the shade of fir trees, and then it came to him: There'd been a fourth man over there. He began easing his bronc around, only to have a stout piece of branch slam against his head, causing him to tumble from the saddle. He lay there as his bronc broke away, stunned and hurt.

"There was no need for that."

"Shutup, damnit, Barkley. He knows we ain't up here lookin' for some worthless old bones." Cleever lunged a booted foot into Easton's rib cage, his mouth a grim, determined line of rage, as once again he had something to focus his hatred on. "You bums, hustle over here and hold this cowpoke up. That's it . . . hold him tight now, an' don't let go until I'm done."

Barney Cleever shuffled in with his large hands doubled into fists. On his right hand he wore a knuckle-duster of a ring that was adorned with a red garnet. The inset holding the stone had jagged edges. It was more cutting tool than ring, and Cleever knew it. Like the rhythmic pistons of a locomotive engine, his massive fists tattoed away at the hopeless cowpoke. Every time his right hand landed, it left a welt or tore away flesh. There was a loud pop as a fist broke the cowpoke's nose, blood gushing out to splatter onto Cleever and spill across Easton's face. In his agony the cowpoke groaned, but he was too far gone to know what happened.

The geologist cried out, "For heaven's sakes, man, he's had enough!"

He could just as well have shouted at the wind to let up, for Barney Cleever had worked up a sweat. In his eyes was this animal glitter, as when a grizzly smells blood. Humping his shoulder, he sent a vicious left hook into the cowpoke's rib cage, a snarling smile emanating from Cleever when a rib snapped inwardly. "Hold 'em up, damnit!"

"He don't seem to be breathing."

"Just hold 'em still," rasped Cleever as he shook his arms down at his sides and did a sideways shuffle, then pounded his right hand at the cowpoke's right eye. The ring seemed to push into the eye socket, and when he pulled his hand away, it was difficult to tell what was red garnet and what was blood. Winded now, Barney Cleever stepped back to stare at his handiwork. He felt good, the unmerciless beating wearing off the ragged edge of his hatred. He knew the cowpoke was dead, not so much from the way his chest had stopped heaving air into his lungs, but from the way his head was tilted to one side.

"Broke his damned neck," said Trammel, who'd been sipping whiskey under a nearby fir. "You ever think of gettin' back into the ring, Barney?" Admiration played in his eyes, and his quick laughter cut the tension away.

"You, geologist," barked Cleever, "you're just as much a part of this as the rest of us. Anyway, noboby'll know we were ever out here."

Cyril Barkley, who'd found he had to sit down to steady himself, said lamely, "You just can't leave him here."

"You've got some digging equipment," said Trammel.

"No, not here," snapped Cleever. He nodded to the north, past the low confines of a creek. "Country's too open around here. We'll cross over and dump the body in some coulee. Unless, Barkley, you don't agree . . ."

Cyril Barkley read the quiet fury in Barney Cleever's voice and remained silent. His thoughts still centered on the geologist, Cleever let the remembrance of what had happened a few days ago ebb away. He lifted his eyes from his table to the front of the barroom, as one of his men, Trammel, elbowed through the batwings.

Trammel paused at the bar, muttering, "Bardog." A silver dollar flashing down to pay for the bottle of whiskey, he continued on back. "Right now, Echohawk is escorting a whore around the Sandbar. Sonofabitch must be heeled." He slopped whiskey into Cleever's glass, then he brought the bottle to his coarse lips and guzzled down the liquor. He had on a grimy shirt and Levi's, and a week's growth of beard stubbled his hawkish face. He passed gas, just another fetid odor tingeing the smoky air in the Barleycorn Bar.

He had taken it all in, yet Cleever held to the table. It was still early, around ten, he reckoned. He knew, too, that it never got late in Casper, as the Sandbar conducted its illicit trades around the clock. The place suited him, and he felt easy now that they'd found Tyler Echohawk. He knew that Trammel had some of his henchmen tagging along after Echohawk. And it was Trammel he'd confided in as to Echohawk wanting to work for Hap Fleming. He didn't trust Trammel at all, but sometimes a man had to spill his guts to somebody, especially when it concerned his livelihood.

"Echohawk really is brother to the sheriff," Cleever began. "Some of that lawman crap has gotta rub off."

"Way I figure it, Barney, the way Echohawk is heading through the dives and such, he should wind up at Curly's place in about an hour. From there, he could head for the fancier places over on Center Street. Next to Curly's is this lumberyard. Nice and big and got a wooden fence around it."

"That'll keep the sonofabitch from running away. This oil stuff, Trammel, been around drilling operations before. That damned sulfuric stench . . . like the gates of hell have opened . . . but Fleming says it's oil what'll make us rich."

"Yeah, selling land to homesteaders don't cut the mustard worth a tinker's damn. This rotgut, want some more, or should we head over to Curly's for somethin' better?"

Heaving to his feet, Barney Cleever went ahead to the bar. He'd been keeping a tab for the whiskey he'd drank, going on a bottle and a half now since mid-afternoon. He always paid his bar bills, not so much for the sake of his reputation, but because a man in his line of work needed a favor from time to time or a place to lay low.

"Here, Ben, keep what's left of this double eagle," Barney said gruffly. In turning, he deliberately shouldered the man who'd been slouched at the bar engaged in conversation with two others. The man's curse died in his throat when he realized just how large Cleever was, the latter unmindful of what had happened as he trudged after Trammel, who was beelining it for the front door.

Curly's was actually the Hideaway Saloon, a rambling log structure built on higher ground near the North Platte River. It was located about as far out as the town went, partially in the western fringes of the notorious Sandbar. Everyone knew

Curly LaClarre, and some wished they didn't. A French-Canadian, he located in Casper about three years ago, running some of the biggest games in town—poker, faro, just about anything a man wanted to wager on. He was a debonair, ruggedly handsome man, who could always be seen decked out in a handsome black suit underscored by a white shirt. This was one reason he attracted the downtown crowd. Another was that the customers could take his skimpily clad bargirls upstairs to avail themselves of the bedrooms.

This was the temptation plaguing Tyler Echohawk, as the woman he'd picked up earlier tonight seemed more interested in getting him upstairs than watching him try his hand at craps. He hesitated before betting that a flannel-shirted miner wouldn't hit his point, a nine. More betting went on around the table, the woman, a whore named Dora, flicking a suggestive finger against his cheek. He grinned through the film of smoke and said, "Thought you liked gambling?"

"Not all night, Tyler honey. A gal's got to earn her keep."

"I'll see you do."

The miner spun the dice, which dashed across the long green table to bounce against the far side rail. Tyler grinned when they came up sevens. He picked up his winnings and swung away from the table. "All told, I won a couple of hundred; not bad for a country boy. Not all that late, but it's awful wild in here. I've got a nice, quiet hotel room. . . ."

Moving with him toward the front of the large

gaming room, she thrust her arm through his and said huskily, "About time. Stock any whiskey up there?"

"We'll get some on the way." They brushed through the batwings and came off the boardwalk, to follow the downhill street that ran into the Sandbar District. The moon was full, just hanging over Casper and beaming on the nearby mountain, where if one looked, flickering lights could be seen near its summit. The air had a dead feel to it, with Tyler taking note that this could be a sign of an approaching rainstorm. He'd learned that clouds generally came in from the southwest to pass over the mountain, but a lot of times the mountain would shoulder a storm out of the way, breaking it into scattered cloud.

She was a bosomy brunette in her mid-twenties, who had been in the trade since her late teens, the voluptuousness of youth giving way to a jaded indifference. But to Dora there was a special excitement to waking up in late mornings, for a new day meant a new adventure, what had happened the previous night being washed out of her conscience. So this afternoon she'd agreed, for a fee, to tour the town with this handsome cowpuncher. Soon he'd leave, but there'd be others. She snuggled in closer, and then he drew her into his arms in a rough embrace.

"So, smart-mouth, we caught up to you at last."

Tyler Echohawk pushed the woman away as several men encircled him. There were no streetlights, only the faraway trace of yellow pouring out of the Hideaway. Then he made one of them out to be Barney Cleever, and Tyler knew what this was all about.

"I'm scared," she said, and Tyler replied, "They're not after you. See that big hunk of donkey meat; that's the one wants a piece of me."

"Cleever held up a restraining arm and grunted out, "He ain't goin' no place. Echohawk, you made a mistake going to see Fleming."

"Did he send you?" asked Tyler as he realized the man standing next to Cleever was holding a handgun. Looking about, he noticed the others were riffraff, and he felt a little better. He studied Barney Cleever's scarred and pitted face, knowing what the ex-pugilist wanted was to hammer him into the dust. Something that he wanted no part of, and Tyler smiled and said, "Well, you're here, Cleever, so spit it out."

The burly man gestured to a long wooden plank wall enclosing a lumberyard just a short distance up the street. "You said that a bullet is faster than a fist. We're going in there, Echohawk, to duke it out."

Tyler grabbed the woman by the arm and walked her along the street, the men keeping pace. When they got closer, he saw that the front gate to the lumberyard was ajar. He whispered, "Dora, you know where my hotel is? Good. I'll meet you there, in my room."

"Are you sure they'll let me go?" she whispered back.

Nodding, he glanced over at Barney Cleever keeping pace on the edge of the narrow street, and Tyler said, "She's out of this. Anyone try to stop her, Cleever, and you're the first to die."

"Bold talk when someone's holding a gun on you," Barney sneered.

"You mean that hunk of dog meat really knows how to handle that six-gun?" snickered Tyler.

Trammel, the man holding the gun, cursed, but then Cleever said the woman could go. She threw Tyler Echohawk a last look before hurrying off into the darkness. "So, she's out of it," Cleever stated. "But we can find her when this is over."

Altogether there were eight of them including Echohawk, and a couple of the men pushed the gate open wide. For Tyler Echohawk it was just another tight spot he chanced to find himself in. The danger lay with Trammel, who was armed, and with Cleever, who depended solely on his fists, Tyler Echohawk was of the opinion that the others couldn't afford the price of a bottle, much less what it took to buy a .44-.40 Colt. Four went in ahead of Echohawk and fanned out, with Tyler knowing that once he entered, all the ingredients needed for a pine box would be here in this piney-scented lumberyard. But he ambled in like a man taking a stroll with some friends, followed by Trammel and Barney Cleever, as the last man scampered over to close the big wooden gate.

Quickly, Tyler took stock of what lay close at hand and the aisles running through high piles of board lumber. The main building lay off to the left, the moon seeming to hang over the slanted roof. There were scrap heaps of discarded pieces of lumber, kegs that he figured held nails. He

114

moved over to a makeshift rack, where some short pieces of two-by-fours were stacked, and propped a spurred boot on a keg, smiling at Cleever who was holding a few yards away. Between them lay a space large enough to hold a boxing ring, and he knew it was here that Barney Cleever meant to come at him. Tyler was careful to keep his hand away from his holstered gun, even though he figured he could draw and take Trammel out before the man could pull the hammer back on that six-gun and pull the trigger. But he had something else in mind, a hand draped carelessly over a short piece of two-by-four.

"You're a damned big man, Cleever. Fought professionally, too, I wager. What say me and Trammel go at it first. Just to warm me up before I take you on."

An ugly laugh boiled inside the thug known as Trammel, and he snarled, "I can take this loud-mouth without workin' up a sweat."

"Sure, Trammel," Echohawk said pleasantly, "we're about the same size." He glanced around to check the position of the others, even as he slipped the top piece of two-by-four off the pile and let his hand fall to his left side. Then it grew darker, and Tyler realized the moon had passed behind an approaching cloud.

"No," spat out Cleever, "he's mine."

"Damnit, Barney," protested Trammel, as for the briefest of moments he took his eyes away from Echohawk easing toward him, "it won't be no big chore."

Then it was Tyler Echohawk who was taking a

long stride that brought him much closer, grasping the heavy board with both hands and in one swift movement clubbing Trammel across the right temple. The gun fell one way, Trammel another, with Cleever seemingly stunned by what had happened. But he recovered quickly and made a move for the gun lying on the ground, only to find himself looking down the barrel of Tyler's Colt.

"Back away," Tyler said. "Now, damnit!" Sensing danger to his right, he spun sideways, letting the Colt buck in his hand. He'd been wrong; one of the others did have a gun. But the bullet from the Colt had ripped into his throat, and he fell, strangling and gasping, and died.

Tyler picked out Cleever again, then yelled angrily, "All right, clear out of here! Everyone but you, Cleever!" He watched them pull out, and then he had a wicked smile for Cleever. "You picked the wrong man to buck."

"Toss that gun away and—"

"I'm no damn fool like you. What I figure is that Hap Fleming doesn't know about this. You felt threatened by what I could offer, which is a helluva lot more than you've been doing."

Despite the gun trained on him, Barney Cleever felt his anger boiling over, and he muttered bitterly, "This ain't over by a long shot, Echohawk."

"That so," jeered Tyler. "You should have brought the 7th Cavalry. A wise old man once told me that anger can kill a man. That there's only one cure for it. You've got to beat it out of a man. Found out a lot about you in the past couple of days, Cleever. That chiefly you're a mean, miserable bastard. See this two-by-four? Like I said, only way to cure a temper is knock it out of a man. You lift one arm now and this Colt talks."

Tyler took a firmer grip on the heavy board, slamming it into Cleever's face. The blow was a sickening thud, but even so the burly man managed to keep his footing, though he fell back a step. Blood streamed out of a nose that had been broken before, and there was a deadly fury in his eyes, but Barney held there, knowing that Echohawk was too damned good with that six-gun. Again the board slammed into his head, and he gasped in pain and went to his knees, the shock of the blow ringing in his ears. He didn't see Tyler holstering the Colt, nor would it have mattered now, as Echohawk, grim determination twisting his face, used both hands to wield the two-by-four like a venging weapon.

"Anger," panted Tyler, "can sure as sin cause a man a lot of pain." He hit Cleever in the face again, and the big man was down but still conscious, groaning in pain but still with some fight left.

Echohawk dropped the board, but this time he brought the tip of his boot snaking hard into the downed man's crotch, to have Barney Cleever's agonizing scream cut through the lumberyard. "That was from Dora, my woman of the night, Cleever." He came around to kneel down and grasp a hunk of greasy hair, then pulled Cleever's bloodied head up from the ground and twisted it

117

around so he could see into the man's pain-racked eyes.

"I want you to tell me all about Fleming's little operation," Tyler said viciously. "Both of you are from back east, so I've been told." Unleathering his Colt, he let Cleever take note of the dry husking sound of the hammer being thumbed back, before he placed the muzzle close to the burly man's blackening left eye. "Now out with it."

Staring up at Echohawk, it came to the battered man that his life hung in the balance. Inwardly, Cleever felt this frenzied hatred, which he shoved aside in his pain, but then it surfaced, and he hated himself, too, the fear of what had happened and his fear of this damnable westerner. A loathing filled Barney Cleever at this weakness, and he knew he'd never be the same man again. Bile began rising into his throat and he spat it out, along with broken fragments of teeth, most of it spilling onto his heaving chest. Cramps came from his lower stomach, that kick he'd sustained seeming to drive his testicles up into his intestines. Despite the warm night he began shivering, but there was that Colt requesting an answer to the question posed by Echohawk.

In a mumbled voice, Cleever began a rambling and sordid tale of all Hap Fleming hoped to accomplish out in territorial Wyoming.

Tyler Echohawk stiffened into wakefulness as a possessive hand stroked the hair on his chest. He was reaching to the nightstand for his Colt when

118

the whore got to snoring again, and disgust twisted up his face. A whiskey stench wafted out of her open mouth and her makeup was smeared, with Tyler licking the faint odor of her lipstick from his mouth. Easing away from the naked woman, he was about to drop his legs to the varnished floor when someone rapped sharply at the door.

"Mr. Echohawk, if you're in there, you've got someone a-wantin' to see you."

"Yeah, who?" Again his hand had gone to the six-gun.

"A Mr. Lundahl."

"Oh . . . okay."

"What time is it?"

"Goin' on noon, Mr. Echohawk."

"That late," he groused. "You tell Lundahl I'll be down after I've had a hot bath and shaved."

"Yessir, I'll tell him that. And see to filling the tub with hot water, yessir, Mr. Echohawk."

Running a hand through his tousled hair, he closed his eyes to let the sleep drain away. It would be like Fleming to send someone else, which could mean they were willing to make a deal. Pushing up from the bed, he tossed an empty whiskey bottle away and stretched, letting a luxurious yawn bring fresh air into his lungs.

"Barney Cleever . . . probably crawled into a hole someplace . . ."

He doubted if Cleever had gone to tell Fleming or Ole Lundahl of the beating he'd sustained, or now that Lundahl was here, if they knew of Cleever's coming after him. After Cleever had spilled his guts about Hap Fleming's plans, Tyler knew he was into something a heap bigger than robbing a bank. Out of it had come a greater respect for Fleming. The man may be a disbarred lawyer and bunco artist to boot, but to buck the big oil boys took a lot of moxie. The deal Fleming had made to have the Fremont, Elkhorn, and Missouri Valley Railroad slow down rail-laying operations was probably costing a lot of money. Fleming's land companies alone couldn't finance everything. And then there was the geologist Fleming had hired, as well as the money paid out in bribes. Could be some oil company is backing him, Tyler mused.

But Tyler knew this was just speculation. The fact that Fleming was wanted back east wasn't much of a threat to hold over both Fleming and Ole Lundahl. So Tyler figured his ace in the hole was what he'd wormed out of Barney Cleever—the murder of a cowhand up near the Big Horns.

A lot of other thoughts filtered through Tyler Echohawk's mind as he put on the clothes he'd worn last night. Then he slipped out of the room and headed toward the only bathroom on the second floor. After a hurried soaking in a brass tub, he went back to the room and donned fresh clothing. He let the whore snore on, hoping that when he got back she'd be gone. "They all look jaded as hell in the morning," he said as he buckled on his gunbelt and headed downstairs for the meeting with Ole Lundahl.

He found the meeting wasn't to be held at his hotel but over at a saloon on Second Street. From the guarded but polite way Lundahl had greeted him, Tyler knew there'd been no word from Cleever about what had taken place last night. Nor would there be, since Tyler figured it wouldn't be Barney Cleever telling that he'd been beaten up by a smaller man, as the ex-pugilist had all that pride along with that stored-up anger. Was me, Tyler reflected, I'd latch on to a gun. And he also knew it was just beginning between him and Cleever, that one was going to kill the other. He shrugged this away, a cocky smile creasing his lips as he glanced at the man walking alongside him.

"Well, did I check out, Mr. Lundahl?"

"I wouldn't be here if you hadn't. Nor would you still be alive."

Tyler laughed quietly. "Who'd you have do the job? Barney Cleever?"

"You are a very rash young man, Mr. Echohawk. Hap Fleming seems to like your rather crude style. But I suppose that's the way of it out here. Back east, if a man packs a gun, it isn't seen or noticed."

"A lot out here wear hideout guns, too." They now approached Center Street, the sun directly overhead, Tyler aware of the hunger pangs and of the fact the noon stage had arrived, the driver just swinging down to help his passengers dismount. As was their habit, a few townsfolk had gathered around to glimpse just who was coming in and, in some cases, as grist for the gossip mill. Coming abreast of the stagecoach office, Tyler went ahead to thread his way through the crowd, slowing his pace when an attractive woman emerged from the stagecoach.

"Comely enough," he mused silently, noting another woman about the same age standing in the open door, gazing anxiously about as if someone should be there to meet her. He took in the full, rubied lips parted in a half-smile. Tyler felt a certain pleasure in watching the graceful way she held out her hand to the driver and emerged from the coach. Her auburn hair was swept back and caught up behind, falling away in glossy, shoulder-length ringlets. The satiny green jacket rose with the swell of her full bosom, the full skirt swirling around her. And then Megan Randsley was staring back boldly at Tyler. Somehow he knew those gold-flecked eyes held smoky womanly secrets, even though he judged her to be younger than him. It seemed as if they were alone, her mere presence arousing something in him, and she knew it, he realized. He wanted her bad.

"We're late, Mr. Echohawk."

"Oh, yeah," grunted Tyler, resenting the intrusion of Lundahl's voice. Reluctant boots carried him forward, and then the shorter man caught up to match Tyler's stride. This business with Hap Fleming came first. But afterward, he aimed to find out just who this woman was. The whore Dora and other women he'd known before all paled in comparison.

"She was a looker."

"Uh-oh," he muttered offhandedly, "I've seen better." But Tyler hadn't, and he knew it. He hadn't seen a ring on her left hand, either, but that didn't mean anything. And the woman knew it, too. Be a pity if she turned out to be just another whore. But not gussied up like that, he knew. Tyler shrugged thoughts of Megan Randsley away as Lundahl nodded to a saloon kitty-corner from them.

"We'll cross over and go up the alley," Lundahl told him.

"Was me, I'd find another place to have this meeting," Tyler remarked curtly.

"I own the Silver Lady. Which only the man who runs it for me and now you know, Echohawk."

"Fleming?"

"Yes, of course, Hap."

Stepping with Lundahl out into the dusty street, Tyler Echohawk realized there was something vaguely familiar about the brand marking the flank of a bronc tied farther along the street, idling with four other horses out front of another saloon. In the last few months, he'd covered a lot of territory, seen a lot of varying brands on both cattle and horses. Approaching on the boardwalk, he was about to dismiss ever seeing this particular brand before, two diamonds side by side separated by a double bar. But something jogged in his memory. He knew, as the alley opened up to them, that Cap Bentley and the others had arrived. A warm feeling spread through him. Cap had gotten in the same day as that red-haired woman had; about time my luck got to changing, Tyler mused.

But luck, he knew, had a way of backsiding a man. He'd been torn last night about snuffing out Barney Cleever's lights. It had been Cleever coming after him. If it had been the other way around, Tyler knew he'd be dead right now. And besides Cleever, there were the others to worry about, especially the one called Trammel. They'd learn about what had happened to Cleever, and just like a pack of timber wolves, they'd look to Tyler Echohawk for leadership.

"There was some trouble last night," he said as Ole Lundahl swung over to open the back door of the saloon. "Between Cleever and me. Was me, I wouldn't stand between us if Cleever's in there. But that'd be highly unlikely, from the beating he took. Most likely, Cleever is someplace nursin' his wounds about now."

"You," questioned Lundahl, "had the better of Barney in a fistfight?"

"Soon's Cleever gets the splinters out of his teeth, he'll tell you all about it."

Tyler's uncertainty as to whether Hap Fleming had been told of the altercation was answered when he was ushered into the back office of the saloon. "Echohawk, I just came from where a doctor has been tending to Cleever. According to Barney—"

"There was just the two of us," Tyler interrupted pleasantly.

"Yes, that you got the drop on him someplace over in the Sandbar."

"Was more like Cleever and a mess of others against me and a whore, Mr. Fleming. The

124

whore'll testify to that. Did Cleever tell you one of his boys got killed, which I admit to?"

Fleming looked at Ole Lundahl easing the door closed, and he gestured for Echohawk to use one of the empty chairs. Indecision played across Fleming's face where he sat behind a cluttered desk. Removing his felt hat, Lundahl set it down on a cabinet and stood there without speaking, a bland look on his face. Anything he would have to say would be spoken after Tyler Echohawk had left. And he was still uncertain about Echohawk's role in their scheme of things out here. Now Lundahl decided he had something to say and spoke crisply, "Hap, I was told about this, just before we got here. I can't believe you, Echohawk, or anyone else can match up to Barney in a fistfight. But I'm inclined to believe what I was told, Hap."

"Barney can go off the deep end, we know that," snorted Fleming around the cigar wedged in his mouth. "Tyler, he acted alone and without my permission when he came after you. But what the hell did you use on him? A—a crowbar?"

"Just a little sapling called a two-by-four." Tyler nodded at the offer of a drink, then he related to them just what had happened last night. "I expect Cleever was of the notion I was going to take his job away. By the way, did Trammel show at the doctor's office?"

"Should he have?"

"I used that sapling on him first. Saplings aside, the way I got it figured, neither Cleever nor anyone else you've got on your payroll is up to handling your rough work, Mr. Fleming."

"And you figure you are." Hap Fleming smiled as he handed a glass of whiskey to Lundahl.

"Mind you, I figure you need Cleever, Trammel, and others. But kept away from both of you, gentlemen. Same's me. Which is why I'm taking that deputy sheriff's job. Now here's the way I figure we can work it. . . ."

Eight

It took Sheriff Lon Echohawk the better part of an afternoon to brief his new deputy on just what was expected of him and to discuss some cases under investigation. Lon had agreed to one of the stipulations under which his brother would take the job, that Tyler be allowed to work out of Casper. He'd told Tyler that Sy Hagen would remain in charge of the Casper office.

"Sy's out checking on some complaints filed by a homesteader. But he'll like having some help up here."

"This cowhand that was killed up north . . . Easton. Got any leads about that?"

"Not too much. He was beaten to death, Tyler. Hammered something fierce. Man who did it wore a ring."

"You know, Lon, if they get around to hacking another part of Carbon County away, Casper'll be out of your jurisdiction. Reason I asked about that killing."

"Just because I asked you to become a lawman,

127

Tyler, was it to work with me? As it's a thankless job."

"Partly that. Tired of long winters spent at some line shack." A smile tempered the lies Tyler Echohawk was telling. "At least being a lawman, you get paid steady and see the sights of a cow town more often."

"Sometimes you get paid on time," smiled Lon. He sat slumped behind the desk he shared with Sy Hagen. The report he was holding concerned a murder that had taken place here in Casper, the body being found in a lumberyard. Though the town marshal's office didn't like it, the circuit judge had ordered that all murders be handled by the county sheriff. This particular murder, mused Lon, could be just a falling out between some petty thieves. "Went over to Amberson's Funeral Parlor to look at the body of this gent"—he passed the report to Tyler." Judge him as a hard case."

"He wasn't carrying any identification?"

"Just some change and dust in his pockets. One slug from a .44-.40 took him out. I'll let you handle it, Tyler."

"See what I can come up with."

Lon Echohawk moved with his brother to the open front door. "It'll get worse once the railroad gets here."

"Any idea when that will be?"

"One of the reasons Circuit Judge Albert Childress wants to see me tonight. The judge came in on the afternoon stage. I hate to see you out there alone tonight, Tyler. So don't take any chances. Later on, I'm going to write a letter home to let the folks know you arrived okay, unless you've already written."

"Took care of that chore last week, Lon. But they'd like to hear from you, too."

Lon's nod meant that he would drop their parents a line, and at that, Tyler Echohawk left to head north on Center Street. Back at his desk, Lon rubbed his fingers at the nape of his neck to ease some of the tension he felt. He wouldn't admit it, but he needed a few days off, fatigue etched in the weathered grooves and angles of his hollow-cheeked face. Another thing he needed just as badly was a shave and haircut, which was a priority now that the circuit judge was in town. Tyler's decision to pin on that badge sat easy with Lon, even though he still experienced some unease.

"That haircut, best see to it before the barber shops close."

Along with taking care of that visit to a barber shop, Lon Echohawk had decided it was about time he got a new rig—a cattleman's light brown leather coat, western trousers, and striped cotton shirt. His frugal nature stepped in from there, as tonight as he left the rooming house where he and his deputies were boarding, he had on a spare Stetson and the other pair of Justin boots he owned. Again the moon was making its presence known low in the east. The early evening was balmy, with Lon going on foot down a narrow lane, which he knew in the not-too-distant future would be staked out as a wider street.

Deputy Sheriffs Carr and LaVoy would be reporting back tomorrow or the day after. They'd left three days ago for the Birds'-eye Stage Station, to rendezvous with the sheriff of Sweetwater County. What Echohawk wanted was to set up a network of lawmen passing on information to one another. He believed it was the only way to keep track of the outlaws passing through these parts. It could be, though Lon doubted it, that some outlaws had passed easterly through Sweetwater County and on their way to the Big Horns about the same time Easton had been killed.

"What about Joseph Baldwin?" That silent thought accompanied Lon onto a side street lined with a few houses. Beyond this was where most of the business places were located. The man had worked for a Bessemer Bend land company known to hire men who were more strong-arm specialists than they were land salesmen. Could the murders of a cowhand and an accountant have some connection? To set the record straight, he couldn't lay everything that was happening in the vicinity of Casper at Hap Fleming's doorstep. Other land companies had moved in, surveyors and assayers had set out shingles; the number of saloons and gaming houses had just about doubled. Farther west along Second Street, he picked out banners in windows and on telegraph poles telling everyone to get out and vote on the county issue. He would welcome not having to come up here, as southern Carbon County wasn't all that gentle, either.

Closing on Center Street, Lon got to remembering it was Saturday night, as there would be no other reason for so many buggies and wagons to be holding by the curbings. Here the boardwalks were threaded by more people on foot, and horsemen loped by in search of a livery stable or to just tie up in front of some saloon. No doubt some of them had come in from homesteads and ranches in response to the announcements in the local papers that Circuit Judge Albert Childress would be holding court commencing Monday morning. He knew there'd be some sort of trouble, the kind the new town marshal could handle, along with those new policemen the city council had hired.

"Howdy, Sheriff."

"Ben," responded Lon, tipping his hat to a rancher and his wife.

"Want to thank you, Sheriff, for finding those stolen cattle. Figured they'd drift them up onto Casper Mountain."

"One's still at large."

"So I heard. Me and the missus thought we'd take our ease in town next week until we're called to testify. You take care, Sheriff Echohawk."

Ambling on, Lon swung north on Center Street, wishing that other ranchers would be as amiable. But they were being pushed away from prime grazing land by the new wave of homesteaders. On the downgrade street, he sighted in on the

Wyoming Hotel ablaze with lights. It occupied more than half a city block, with four floors, brick walls, and three entrances, two on Center Street and another around the corner on First Street. There were three barrooms, a billiard and dining room, and up a flight on the second floor the largest ballroom in the city.

Lon couldn't recollect the last time he'd taken a filly out onto a dance floor, much less squired one down to the millpond for a Sunday afternoon picnic. Plenty of women gave him the once-over, and there were always invitations to social events both here and down in Rawlins. Back about five years ago, he'd actually gotten half serious about a rancher's daughter over in the Sweetwater. Lon eventually discovered that what she wanted was someone she could see more than every other month or so. He didn't lament her getting married, a parting word from her of his being wedded to the law. There'd been no argument from Lon Echohawk, but it had gotten him to thinking hard about his future. Finally, after some soul-searching, Lon concluded sheriffing was about the only trade he knew or wanted. Though lately there were gaps in his reasons for staying with the job.

He looked back, then started angling across the wide, rutted thoroughfare. When he got closer, Lon Echohawk began checking brands on saddle horses, and it wasn't long before he saw that some of the ranchers holding land up where Easton had been murdered were here. They were all aware that Judge Childress would be holding informal court up in his hotel suite, but they were mostly here to swap tall tales or cigars and share a bottle of whiskey. Even renegade outlaws had been known to call upon the judge during these evening sessions. They all knew, too, that the gloves were back on once Childress eased behind the bench over at the courthouse. A few who considered themselves to be more respectable than the others had filed complaints with the District Appellate Court, citing the judge's bawdy behavior. But much to their chagrin and Lon's relief, nothing had come of it. Though he wasn't vindictive, Childress had a long memory about such matters.

The judge remembered, too, just how the sheriffs under his jurisdiction handled their offices. To be verbally chewed out while court was in session, as had happened to Lon once, made a lawman take a backward step. This particular time Judge Childress had been informed by an overly zealous clerk of the court that Sheriff Echohawk had padded a bill he had submitted for transporting prisoners to the territorial prison. But the charges proved to be false, Childress making certain the clerk of the court was defeated in the next election and made a public apology to Lon Echohawk.

"Say, Lon, are you here for the dance?"

"Ah, Lawyer Fitzpatrick . . . ma'am."

"With pleasure, I introduce the woman I'm going to marry. Here from Boston, the charming and beautiful Megan Randsley. Our illustrious Sheriff Lon Echohawk. Protector of the people, defender of the truth; a paragon of virtue and honesty."

"No wonder you became a lawyer," Lon

grinned. "Miss Randsley, Sean, actually I'm here at the behest of the circuit judge."

"I, too, shall pay court to our honorable judge."

"Or is it just to get a taste of that imported whiskey he fetches along?"

"Please, Sheriff," chided Sean, "Megan might get the wrong idea about me."

"I know you like a book," she said in a melodious voice. "You, Sheriff Echohawk, are the epitome of what a westerner really is, I might say. I did surprise Sean by coming out here. As . . . we're so in love. But some Irish can be foot-draggers. . . ."

"I haven't a chance," moaned Sean Fitzpatrick as he brought Megan on toward the hotel's south entrance on Center Street, with Lon trailing behind.

He'd been about to ask if Fitzpatrick would be representing cattle rustler Ben Rafferty in court this coming week, a thought that had been shoved aside by the other worries flooding through Lon's mind: musings about murder, how his other deputies were faring, as well as his new deputy marshal out someplace in the Sandbar District.

The lobby being appraised by Lon ran the entire length of the building facade, and it had a deep red velvety look. In the middle a darkly stained oak staircase ran straight up to the second floor, the side railings burnished a dark brown. The tiled floor, decorated with intricate patterns, rang hollowly under the thud of Lon's boots, a sound swept away by people gathering in circles to talk or go up to the ballroom. What Lon sought was a barroom and a sip of whiskey before he called upon the circuit judge.

Another Echohawk had already consumed a few shot glasses of whiskey, chased down with cold beer, in the company of some old friends. Tyler Echohawk's new deputy marshal's badge was tucked away in a pocket. He had an expansive glitter in his smiling eyes now that Hap Fleming had come through with some money.

"That money I handed out is just chicken feed compared to what we're gonna make out of this."

"Oil . . . saw signs of it during my lifetime. Foul-smelling stuff when the wind is right to push it out of some sinkhole. Now it's become more important than gold or silver out here." Cap Bentley had a raspy baritone voice and the respect of everyone seated around the table. He was an old-time bank and stagecoach robber. One would guess him to be in his fifties, as Bentley had a grey beard cut close to the sunken planes of his cheeks. The gist of it was that Cap Bentley had just turned forty, spending half of his adult life in prisons in Oregon and Idaho having left its mark. The beard blended with Bentley's sideburns and thinning hair under the round cowboy hat wedged squarely on his head. He wore a somber grey corduroy coat that came down to his knees. Cap had gotten this bunch together, the first one to join being Tyler Echohawk. Though he planned how each bank was to be held up, right from the start he'd let

135

Echohawk ramrod the others, as Cap Bentley was a man who knew his limitations.

"You still sure you want me to be bossman of this new operation?" asked Cap Bentley.

"Without you, Cap," said Tyler, "it won't go. Wasn't for you, none of us would be here today. Probably be strung up or confined to prison for life. You've sure got our respect. Commencing when I leave here"—Tyler Echohawk looked around the table to add weight to his words—"we don't know one another."

"So Fleming'll get word to you, Tyler, and you us." Cap Bentley scratched at his long nose. When he drank, he did so sparingly, as he didn't want his thoughts clouded no matter where he chanced to be at the moment. One never knew if some lawman had a particular saloon staked out. "Coming in, I saw some places we could bunk at. One in particular, down by some willow trees guarding this creek. About three, four miles out, northwesterly."

"Place has been abandoned," said Tyler. "But I agree, Cap, that it could prove risky finding lodging here in town or over in Bessemer Bend."

"This place has got an old corral and a log cabin with two rooms. Some land salesman might be itchin' to sell it to some homesteader."

"I'll talk to Fleming. The smart move is to have him buy the place. I did mention one of Fleming's boys, Barney Cleever."

"Maybe the smart thing to do would have been to take Cleever out, Tyler."

"Reason I didn't, Cap, is that if I had, Hap

136

Fleming might consider me too much of a risk . . . just another trigger-happy gunfighter." Saying this, Tyler gazed about at the rest, men he'd ridden with for over a year. From up front in the saloon, the tinny sound of a player piano cut into the subdued din of a few idling over cards and another handful standing over drinks at the bar. Nobody was paying any attention to what everyone considered some cowpunchers in for a Saturday night on the town. But they were dead wrong, especially about the Haskell cousins.

First there was Emmet Haskell, no more than a younker until one really took a second look. From the bottom up, Emmet had on scuffed boots, faded-out trousers, and a patched shirt. Riding high at his hip was a holster with a button-down flap, with Emmet's choice of weapon a Remington single shot pistol. By choice, he was no fast draw artist, but once he palmed that Remington, he went for the killing shot. He had downed three men, two more than his cousin, Sandy Haskell. He was fair-complexioned, as was Emmet, but Sandy was a lot larger. Lawmen from back in Oregon were after both Emmet and Sandy, threatening to either hang them on the spot or drag them back to do it proper.

Mitch Olander had run out on his wife and three children. This happened to be his third wife, the fact that he was still married to his first two not having mattered too much to Olander. He was lazy, self-centered, and blessed with a roguish handsomeness. If they stayed here for any time, he'd find some woman to defray his expenses, just so she could enjoy the pleasure of his company. He threaded warily around Echohawk, as he didn't consider himself a gunhand. But to Olander's credit, he had stayed to help the others when things had gone wrong at Pendleton. There'd just been an open alleyway to rein his horse up and get away from all those guns that were yammering at the others coming out of the bank. Just reining his horse around had taken grit, but he had, to come in and draw away some of the gunfire. This setup, as just outlined by Tyler Echohawk, was more what he wanted to do. He'd already spelled that out, and now Mitch Olander was just content to sit there and get his full of whiskey.

Nursing a bad hip wound ever since the fracas at Pendleton, Slater Moore considered himself a lucky man. Manhood had come a month ago when he'd turned twenty-one. He had a shock of wheat-colored hair and buck teeth that devoured most of his chin when he smiled, which was often. He hung around with the Haskell cousins, mostly because Olander was always off chasing some skirt and Cap Bentley preferred his privacy. Unconsciously, he'd been copying some of Tyler Echohawk's mannerisms, a man whom he greatly admired. Just to ride with this bunch, even though some of them were gone and buried, had been the highlight of his life. He was tall, a shade over six feet, but gangly and thin as a rail. But working on an Oregon farm since he could barely waddle had firmed up his muscles, and in a fight he packed a mulish punch. He'd taken off and left farming behind, overwhelmed by the drudgery of having a mule pull some damn plow, as well as having to shock grain filled with bits of cacti and thorns, which could tear the hell out of someone's hands. Like everyone here, charges of murder and bank robbery were hanging over Slater Moore's head. But as long as he had his matched pair of Smith and Wesson Schofield's hanging at his hips, along with his friends, the law could kiss his backside. Damn, at the moment he felt like hurraying someone, but he stayed silent as he felt a twinge of pain coming from his hip wound as he shifted in the rickety chair.

Echohawk noticed the way Moore had grimaced, and he said, "Been a hard ride for you, Slater. I hope it'll be worth it."

"Doggone it, Tyler, this is where I belong. Can't believe we'll be doin' more or less respectable work for a change."

"You boys'll be the core of my operation," said Tyler. "Fleming's got land salesmen out in the field. Got others doing nothing but check out oil rights. Oil, that's us. The paper boys will go in first, try to get someone to sign over their oil rights. If this don't pan out, we follow up with a more serious sales pitch. As I told Cap, we'll have to take on more men, roughhousers. Fleming's got a few now. This Trammel and—"

Emmet Haskell grinned. "The one you walloped with that two-by-four. That I woulda' paid to have seen."

"This Barney Cleever will be a worry," cut in

Cap Bentley. He signaled for a barmaid to come back.

"Won't be if Hap Fleming takes my advice," said Tyler. "In having Cleever work strictly for him an' out of our hair." He pushed up from the chair.

"So, you're leaving?"

"Yup, Cap. There's this dance over at the Wyoming Hotel, I've found out. Where the uppity-ups congregate on Saturday night, which this is."

"Reason you're all duded up in new clothes?"

"One has to play the part of deputy sheriff," Tyler answered softly. "Once I walk out that back door, the badge gets pinned back on my vest."

"Which means," warned Cap Bentley, "any of us see Tyler out on the streets, we don't know him. I still think we should do something with Cleever, Tyler."

"Man holds an awful hatred, for damn sure. So, have a quiet drunk tonight, then head out to camp. Be a pity we mess this up right away, considerin' what's involved." He left some more money on the table, along with a quiet smile, then silently Tyler tramped out the back way.

What Tyler Echohawk had in mind ever since he'd seen that auburn-haired woman arrive on the stagecoach some two days ago was to track her down. But talks with the old bunch and private meetings with Hap Fleming about how to set up this new operation had consumed a lot of time. Now it was Saturday night, and as good a place as any to begin looking for her, Tyler reckoned, would be over on Center Street.

* * *

"Tell us, Judge Childress, who're you favorin'
to become the new county seat?"

"Being a federal judge, both towns have my
vote."

"So it's vote early and often," laughed Milt
Sundby, the editor of the *Wyoming Derrick* and
one of half-dozen men clustered around Judge Albert Childress. "Seriously, Judge, how do you see
it? A new county being formed?"

"Afraid it's inevitable," said Childress as he
took note of Sheriff Lon Echohawk putting in an
appearance in the judge's third-floor suite. The
judge was an apparition of blacks—highly polished
boots, the sturdy gabardine suit, and the string tie
dangling over the boiled white shirt. He had pep-
pery coal-black hair and a drooping mustache
much like Mark Twain had made fashionable. But
unlike the famous writer's nasal twange, Judge
Childress's voice had a baritone richness, which
got a lot deeper when trouble cropped up. His
hands were bony and seemed too large for a man
his size, his fingers large-knuckled and wrapped
around a Havana cigar. He fluttered his cigar in
Echohawk's direction, then keened his ears to a
joke being told by one of the ranchers.

". . . upon closer inspection, it proved out to
be a bull after all."

"That's a salty one," remarked Childress. He'd
been receiving visitors ever since sundown, but tonight, despite the outward appearance of joviality,
business of a criminal nature had cropped up in

the form of two men keeping to themselves at a window opening onto Center Street. One of them, Nathan Fry, worked for the Crown Oil Company, and Childress could tell that oilman Fry hated to be kept waiting. Fry's companion was a Pinkerton operative, whose name escaped Childress at the moment. The trouble they'd spoken of involved the railroad laying track toward Casper.

"Gentlemen," he said, "I have some business to discuss with the sheriff."

"Judge, before you go, I'd like to set up a meeting for next week. Some of us ranchers believe the homesteader situation is getting out of hand. Those who didn't show up . . . well, Judge Childress, I reckon they believe in a different brand of justice. Can't say that I'm not worried, as bloodsheddin' isn't the answer."

"No, it isn't, Gordon, and I appreciate your coming in. How does early Tuesday morning sound, over at the courthouse? That's right, you live out a considerable distance, so make it around five Tuesday afternoon. I was briefed about that killing up north of here, this Easton. A terrible thing. G'night, gentlemen."

Once the ranchers left, others began drifting out of the suite. But still remaining with Judge Albert Childress were his worries over this killing and reports brought to him of other men being gunned down. In his opinion, Lon Echohawk was a better-than-average lawman. Too bad, mused Childress, Sheriff Echohawk doesn't have the biblical gift of omnipresence. Something that would come in handy if this wave of lawlessness continued. He'd had it in mind to have Echohawk accompany him down to the hotel dining room for a quiet talk over supper. Coming in behind Echohawk, who was talking to Milt Sundby, Childress said, "Sorry to break this up, Milt, but there's some urgent business I have to discuss with the sheriff."

"Anything I dare print in the *Derrick?*"

Around a smile, the judge told him, "It has nothing to do with the Sandbar."

Reading the note of dismissal in Childress's voice, Sundby said, "Okay, but promise me I'll get first crack at this. Lon, we'll talk later." He turned and walked away, even as Judge Albert Childress's traveling secretary was clearing the few stragglers out of the suite.

Once the outer door had closed, Childress motioned the Crown Oil man over. "Mr. Fry, was it? Yes, I believe we ran into one another over at Cheyenne. Seems to me your oil company was trying to get some legislation passed."

"The vote came out in our favor."

"Seems money carries considerable weight," murmured the judge. He sought the comfort of an overstuffed chair, where a side table held an ashtray and a box of cigars. He crunched the stub of his cigar out in the ashtray as the others settled in around him. Pulling out a big blue bandanna, he took a swipe at his forehead while fixing lidded eyes upon Nathan Fry. In the composed demeanor of Fry, he couldn't help noticing a smug arrogance, and there was a stir of resentment in Childress over this Saturday night intru-

143

sion. On the other hand, the Pinkerton, a chunky, sallow-faced man, sat off in the sidelines a little with his hands folded in his lap over the bowler hat, like someone who knew his place.

Nathan Fry gave off the faint scent of cologne. He seemed to think his height of a little over six feet and some two inches gave him a commanding aura. He sat on a padded straight-back chair, having eased his trousers up a little so the sharp creases wouldn't get wrinkled, but there was a little street dust on his black low quarters. A diamond pin in his wide tie twinkled back at an overhead lamp. His hands were soft, the nails manicured, his right hand possessed of an expensive ruby ring. His eyes centered in a long, haughty face, had dropped to the sheriff's badge pinned to Echohawk's vest; a high-minded, dismissing glance. On the floor by the chair stood a black briefcase, on which he'd placed his hat, his attention going to the judge in the guise of a quick smile of apology.

"Unfortunately, Judge Childress, this could not have waited until Monday morning."

"I expect not," sighed the judge, whereupon he reached for the box of cigars. Lifting out a cigar, he rolled it around in his fingers before he bit the end away. "Mr. Fry, just who are you representing tonight, your oil company . . . or the vested interests of the Fremont, Elkhorn, and Missouri valley Railroad?"

"Mr. Prater is here on behalf of the railroad."

"That so, Mr. Prater?"

"Yessir, Your Honor," responded the Pinkerton.

"Doesn't the railroad have its own investigators?"

"When things happen, they call us in."

"So"—Judge Childress motioned at his secretary to bring him some brandy—"I judge whatever's happened took place in Wyoming."

"Actually," cut in Fry, "we're just getting into the tip of it. My company has invested heavily in this new line being laid toward Casper. We knew something was wrong to cause all of these delays . . . that more track should have been laid."

"We'd been keeping an eye on the man in charge of laying track. Couple of days ago, we confronted Colhour with our suspicions. Colhour's line superintendent for the railroad. Took some time, but he confessed to taking money under the table. From someone in business here in town. Didn't say who it was, Your Honor, as he feared for his life."

"We want Colhour brought here," said Nathan Fry, reaching down to take some papers out of his briefcase. "I suspect another oil company has got to Colhour."

"Seems to me that's the way a lot of these companies do business," said Childress. "Where are you holding Colhour?"

"Presently, he's under guard in his Pullman car out where they're laying track."

"Guess, Sheriff, this is where you come in. Come sunup, take some of your deputies and Mr. Prater out there, and bring in this renegade line superintendent." Childress took the glass of brandy from his secretary, a droopy-eyed, rotound man named Henry Witland. He watched oilman Nathan Fry unfold a large map, then at Fry's suggestion, everyone rose and clustered around a table.

"Here's where the end of the line is now," Fry pointed out. "Should be at least another thirty miles closer to Casper. You can imagine what this has cost my oil company."

"Oil won't spoil, Mr. Fry. Heard, too, the cheapest place to store oil is in the ground. What are these markings up north of Casper?"

"What I'm about to reveal is secret information, gentlemen. Crown Oil has spent a great deal of time and money in these sections—what'll come to be known as the Salt Creek Oil Field. There is no doubt in my mind that in the not-too-distant future you'll see hundreds of oil derricks up there . . . and very few dry holes once drilling commences. But as I said, gentlemen, without the railroad to haul in our heavy equipment, our hands are tied. I expect, Judge Childress, once we haul Colhour in here he and everyone else involved in this plot will be prosecuted to the fullest extent of the law."

"Fry," snapped Childress, "let me handle the law in these parts. I expect Mr. Colhour won't say anything further until he gets proper legal representation. Just a reminder, but none of this must leave this room. Whoever has been paying off Colhour has to be backed by big money. Which means that no expense will be spared to see that line superintendent Colhour is murdered. So, that's enough excitement for one day. Good night, gentlemen, but you, Echohawk, hold on for a moment."

Moving with the Pinkerton operative to the door held open by the judge's secretary, Nathan Fry paused and swung back to say, "My reasons for showing you the map were obvious, Judge Childress. The same people who are trying to buy up oil rights around the Salt Creek field area could be involved in this."

"Impertinent jackass," Judge Albert Childress muttered as his uninvited guests passed out of the suite. He moved with a wearied gait over to a side table and poured a little more brandy into his glass. "One way to get rid of competition is to speak badly of them. If Crown Oil knows about oil being up there, other oil companies aren't all that far behind. Seems Casper is to become the center of a damned nuisance of an oil patch, Sheriff Echohawk. Roughnecks'll come flooding in, a horde of others wanting to wash their sins in black gold. Been my experience oil fields stink, as they're no holy river of Jordan, either. You take care tomorrow, Lon. Chances are if this Colhour has sold out, the people who've been paying him off have some of their confederates up there laying track just to make sure Colhour plays along." The judge burped and laid a tired grimace on the sheriff.

"I reckon that's all, Your Honor."

"When you leave, take this ulcerous stomach along."

"I'll leave before sunup," Lon informed the judge, then departed to find the staircase.

Down on the second floor, he found the wide double doors leading into the ballroom were open, the sound of fiddle music coming his way. Smokers stood out in the hallway, a sprinkling of townsmen and cattlemen. He wanted to go in and watch a couple of dances, but the old habit of staying aloof held him at bay. A couple of young women came out and skipped down the staircase, and Lon felt a lonely aching take hold of him. Maybe he'd made a mistake in not going after that Sweetwater rancher's daughter. Too late now, came a silent lament. And with his boots thudding hollowly on the staircase, Lon Echohawk shifted his thoughts to first getting hold of his deputies and planning how they'd handle heading out to where track was being laid toward Casper, breaking into a half-smile when he spotted his brother Tyler just coming into the lobby.

"Hey, big brother, I didn't figure you as going to dances."

"Wasn't dancin' that fetched me over here, but the territorial judge. We'll be doin' some ridin' Sunday morning, early Sunday morning. Come on, that barroom'll do to fill you in."

"I reckoned Sunday was a day of rest," Tyler protested halfheartedly.

"Not according to Childress." Lon's voice softened to a whisper. "Seems the railroad is having some trouble. . . ."

Nine

The image in the full-length mirror stared back boldly at Sylvia Valcourt. The dress she had just put on rode low over her bare shoulders, boldly revealing the cleft between her creamy breasts. The robin's blue ribbon in her upswept hair matched the color of her dress. Indecision brought her nipping at her upper lip, as she considered the dress too flauntingly bold. But not as bold, she realized, as the note she'd had delivered to her father, asking him to come to tonight's dance here at the Wyoming Hotel. She could at least have signed her own name to the note, she thought, murmuring to herself, "To come all this way and then to weaken at the last moment."

Soon after pulling into Casper, Sylvia Valcourt had started looking for Hap Fleming. Much to her surprise, his name had been mentioned quite prominently in some local newspapers. They also told of her father residing in nearby Bessemer Bend. And so she'd gone to see about making arrangements to rent a horse and buggy, only to discover the very man she'd come all this way

149

to find suddenly emerging from a business place on Casper's Center Street. It was here all of Sylvia's resolutions fled. Her legs started trembling, refusing to go on down the boardwalk. Self-doubts flooded through her mind. It had been seven years since they'd seen one another. Standing there with her eyes fixed on the man striding toward her, she realized Hap Fleming had changed, while she herself had blossomed into a young woman. Somehow she found herself pirouetting over to stare into the window of a haberdashery shop, panic over what to do written on her face. Then the moment passed, as her father tramped by to go round a street corner, and Sylvia fled back to her room at the Wyoming Hotel.

A bittersweet smile tugging at her mouth, Sylvia turned away from the mirror. She would wear this dress, and if her father so boldly showed up at the ballroom dance, she would confront him. "Daddy always said women aren't overly bold. Yup, gal, here you can play a mean game of poker. Travel halfway across America . . . and then find you don't have the courage of your convictions." Reaching to the dresser for her gloves, Sylvia pondered another lingering doubt involving her father: the possibility that she hadn't wanted to confront him with his past. Perhaps Hap Fleming had no desire to see his daughter, didn't love her after all.

"Gal, there's only one way to find out."

She put on the gloves and the satiny jacket, leaving behind any uncertainties as she vacated her room. Sylvia thought about Megan Randsley, with whom she'd kept up her friendship. Though Megan was all excited about her upcoming marriage to Sean Fitzpatrick and had even asked Sylvia to be one of the bridesmaids, something told Sylvia Valcourt there would be no wedding.

As for Megan's fiancé, here was a man, in Sylvia's opinion, who seemed as solid of character as Casper Mountain. Sean Fitzpatrick had shown her and Megan around town, and she'd found the Irishman to have a unique sense of humor, as well as the respect of the townspeople. She hadn't asked Sean if he knew her father. Perhaps when Sean found out that Hap Fleming was a disbarred lawyer . . . But that was her worry.

At supper one night at the Plainsmen's Club— she'd gone along at Megan's insistence—the sheriff of Carbon County had been beckoned to their table by Sean, to have a spark of interest flare up between Sylvia and Sheriff Lon Echohawk. But ruminating over it now, Sylvia realized the show of interest had been decidedly one-sided. In the club had been other lawyers, businessmen, and local politicans, their talk split between what would happen to Casper when the railroad finished laying track and the fight with Bessemer Bend to become the new county seat. The food had been delightful, if not surpassing even what the best restaurants served back east—saddle of veal with dressing, asparagus with cream sauce, French coffee, and strawberry pie for dessert. Through a few business acquaintances of Sean's, who'd dropped by their table, Sylvia had learned that a certain element headed by Councilman Rafe Bascome wanted to make Casper a wide-open city, as Dodge City had become with the arrival of trail herds from Texas. The plan of those opposing Bascome, though Sean Fitzpatrick had made no comment, was to run him for mayor in the fall elections.

, Passing down the staircase to the second floor, a pair of cowhands and a woman snuggled up to one of them reeled past Sylvia. Through a low whistle, one of the cowhands spilled back, "Lady, you're right pretty. I reckon four of us can have a right smart party."

Sylvia turned slightly and looked up at them, the cowhands recklessly drunk and not even in their twenties. Judging from their wide grins, they meant no harm, then the woman with them got an offended look in her eyes and tugged the cowhand onto the third-floor landing. With a silent laugh, Sylvia strode somewhat anxiously down a wide hallway leading to the open doors of the ballroom.

When she entered the ballroom, Sylvia recognized the tune being played by the string band as the Virginia reel. The dance floor was crowded and chairs encircled the walls. High windows were open to let in a night breeze; red, white, and blue bunting was draped around paintings depicting the West. Her presence drew a few speculating glances from women seated close to the walls, before their eyes went in search of something more interesting. At the far end of the ballroom and in one corner stood a young man who at once reminded her of Sheriff Lon Echohawk. Even more remarkable was the badge pinned to his striped black and white shirt. Sylvia kept staring at him, her puzzlement growing over the naked intensity flaring out of his eyes, which were fixed on the dance floor.

Sylvia followed the slant of his stare, until she, too, homed in on Megan Randsley being spun about by Sean Fitzpatrick, the band swinging from the Virginia reel into a hoedown song without seeming to miss a beat. She brought her eyes back to the starpacker. Smoke from the insolent tailor-made he had gripped in his teeth wafted out a nearby window. He seemed indifferent to everyone but Megan swirling about on the far side of the dance floor. Now when Sean brought them past the low stage occupied by the band, Sylvia caught the sudden glint of lustful passion rising in Tyler Echohawk's eyes as he dropped his cigarette, crunching it out with the toe of his spurred boot and striding onto the dance floor.

"Ah, pardon me, Miss Valcourt . . ."

"Uh . . . oh, I'm sorry . . ." Sylvia swung sideways and smiled back at one of the businessmen she'd been introduced to at the Plainsmen's Club. "Mr . . . Hackett? . . ."

"You do remember. I saw you come in. There's punch over here, Miss Valcourt."

"Yes . . . yes, that would be nice," she replied, taking a fleeting glance toward the dance floor in search of Megan Randsley. Then she was close to a long table covered with a white tablecloth and the businessman was pouring punch into a clear glass cup.

"Sean seems to have a high regard for you, Miss Valcourt."

"He does?"

Please, call me Wilbur. I'm middle-aged and widowed, which means I can treat lovely ladies to punch and manage to eke out a living at my hardware store." Hackett had a round head adorned with a fringe of brown hair and pleasant features. "Did Sean mention any mayoral ambitions to you?"

"That he didn't. By the way, Wilbur, who's that young man dancing with Megan . . . over there by the north wall?"

"Of course . . . that's Lon Echohawk's brother. Seems he's wearing a badge, too."

From where he'd been surveying all that was taking place in the ballroom, Tyler Echohawk had scarcely dared believe the woman would be here tonight. That she was with Sean Fitzpatrick, a man known to him, was of little consequence. He hadn't been able to tear his eyes away from Megan Randsley swirling by out on the dance floor. He felt kind of giddy-headed, as when he'd first bedded a woman. But that had been just a dispassionate coupling of two people destined never to set eyes on one another again. On the other hand, Tyler had felt a tightness in his chest when he'd taken in Megan's flaming head of burnished hair, the creamy shoulders and pale cameo face brought vividly alive by the splash of red lipstick, and those large, luminous eyes swimming with laughter. To Tyler Echohawk, her deep red velvety dress seemed more fit for a bedchamber than for this place. Damn, but she was a desirable bundle he aimed to possess. That was when he'd stomped out his tailor-made and had gone out to claim her.

"Sean didn't seem all that pleased that you cut in, Mr. Echohawk."

"Are you pleased?" had been his first words to Megan Randsley. He spoke boldly, with a possessive arm hooked around her slender expanse of waist, their hands touching as they began dancing. He kept gazing into her eyes, knowing without a shred of doubt that she was more than pleased. He danced her away from Sean Fitzpatrick, mingling with others near the south wall and around to the opposite side of the dance floor, the heady scent of her perfume sweeping over Tyler like the welcome heat of his bedroll.

"How—how long have you been a lawman?"

"Not all that long, Megan. What's Sean' to you?"

"We're engaged to be married."

"That so?"

His arm tightened to draw her closer, to have her come willingly, her lips parted to show the tip of her tongue. In her eyes he could read what was in his: a lust to possess one another. "I ain't never met a woman like you before, Megan, nor wanted one so bad."

"Mr. Echohawk, I—"

"Yeah?"

"I told you I'm getting married."

155

He brushed this aside with, "Got myself lodging at the Chandler Hotel. What about you?"

"Please, Tyler, I . . . this isn't right . . ."

"What about you?" A reckless smile lidded Tyler's eyes. He could feel her fingers tightening on his, and he added in a husky, teasing whisper, "Unless . . ."

"No . . . I . . . I'm staying here . . ."

Then Sean Fitzpatrick was there to cut in, and a gracious Tyler Echohawk bowed slightly before murmuring his thanks to Sean and taking his leave. According to a wall clock it was going on eleven, noted Tyler, weaving around a few dancers on his way out of the ballroom. Just before going out into the main hallway, he felt someone's gaze upon him, and Tyler glanced to his right at Sylvia Valcourt, who was taking her eyes elsewhere. But not before he'd glimpsed the disapproving glint in them. He shrugged this away, along with recalling the woman had arrived on the same stagecoach as Megan.

Still enflamed from his encounter with Megan Randsley, Tyler exited the hotel in search of a saloon and some whiskey. He knew the dance in the Wyoming Hotel could go on for another three, four hours. But he'd be back tonight no matter what the hour, to find Megan's hotel room. Crossing Center Street, Tyler didn't notice that striding along the boardwalk he'd just vacated was Hap Fleming.

For Fleming it was more curiosity than anything else that had taken him out of a stud poker game, though he hadn't minded, as luck didn't seem to be with him tonight. Fleming had all but forgotten the intriguing letter that had been delivered to him over at Bessemer Bend. The handwriting had been definitely feminine, the note touched with a drop of perfume, and so just for diversion's sake, Hap Fleming had decided to humor this woman who'd gone to all of this trouble.

"Let's see . . . what did she call herself? Ann . . . Gordon, I believe . . . But no matter, as she'll pick me out if she's here . . ."

Another reason for his attending the dance at the Wyoming Hotel was that Hap Fleming knew steps had to be taken to cultivate a new image for himself here in Casper. Tyler Echohawk had been right, he knew, in that he must separate himself from the past, at least the past out here in Wyoming. Wedged in amongst his thoughts, too, was the drain on his finances. It seemed land sales had picked up, and as they had, so had the payoffs, continuing in the form of money passed along to Rafe Bascome, along with a heap more to greedy line superintendent Martin Colhour. Though Colhour was buying him time, Hap Fleming felt in him this surge of unease whenever the man's name came to mind.

Inside the Wyoming Hotel, he found a washroom just off the lobby. He doffed his hat and put it on a table, then he poured water from a pitcher into a washbasin. The game had gone on since noon, and Hap Fleming felt the need to wash his hands and face. After drying off, he combed out his thick greying hair. If he had been pursuing this woman, there would have been some flowers for her and a red carnation for his lapel, he mused. Feeling refreshed now, Fleming straightened his tie and reached for his hat, veering toward the staircase.

One of the first men to catch Hap Fleming's eye on the second-floor landing was the new town marshal, and he threw Justin Reed a cordial nod. All he knew about Reed was of his having Rafe Bascome's blessings. To his right and just beyond the bannister, three men were talking quietly, and on benches out in the hallway a few women were taking their ease. Now Hap Fleming paused before entering the ballroom. Coming in response to the woman's letter made him feel like an awkward schoolboy. Through the open doors, he took in the high-ceilinged ballroom. A fiddle cut into a fast melodic tune, a guitar and a bass joining in, and Fleming's foots felt a little lighter when he went in to begin mingling with the crowd.

He vaguely recalled the song as being named "Sugar in the Gourd," many folk clapping and stamping their boots in time to the music. Passing along the north wall, Hap Fleming picked out one or two people he knew, letting his eyes play longest over Circuit Judge Albert Childress up near the refreshment table. Just to keep his hand in, Fleming had attended one of the judge's court sessions here in Casper. And from a back bench he had come to the conclusion that Childress knew his law, though informality seemed to hold sway. Farther on he took in a young woman dancing with a local businessman, and Hap Fleming allowed a frown to show.

"A remarkable resemblance to my daughter . . . but Sylvia's a little younger . . ." Other dancers obscuring his view of the young woman, he turned around with the intention of going to find what refreshments were being served. Sylvia; guess she's old enough for college. Her mother was the stumbling block, with all of her money. Edging around some idlers, he felt a hand touch his left shoulder. He turned around, expecting it to be the mysterious letter writer. Instead, he found himself gazing at the young woman he'd seen out on the dance floor.

"I didn't think you would come, Mr. Fleming."

Taken aback, he blurted out, "You're so young . . . You . . . are Ann Gordon?"

Now that the moment had arrived, Sylvia Valcourt felt her resolve melting away. There was no question but that it was the same Harold Fleming, but to her eyes he appeared harder and a bit more frayed. Still, he was her father. And she had sought this moment. She could see the questions beginning to form in his eyes under those bushy brows she'd known so well.

"I'm disappointed."

"Eh, how is that?"

"You always brought flowers for your lady of the moment."

"You . . ." And then he knew. "Sylvia!"

"Yes, your daughter, Sylvia. Come all the way out to Wyoming seeking you."

"Sylvia!" he exclaimed as his eyes began misting. "Oh, my darling daughter." He brought his arms sweeping around her shoulders to draw her close. Now he held her at arm's length and laughed delightedly. "I saw you out on the dance floor . . . said to myself, she so looks like my daughter . . . but she's so much older. But, my darling Sylvia, it's truly, truly you." Mock sternness deepened his voice. "However did you find me?"

"It wasn't as hard as it seemed," responded Sylvia.

"Your mother . . . she isn't? . . ."

"She's the same, all tied up with society work."

"And you . . . why, you've become so—so beautiful."

"I have a good hairdresser."

"Yes, ever the practical jokester. Come, come, come, we must talk." He placed her hand on his forearm with his usual elegance, and together they left the ballroom to share this moment in the quieter hallway. "You know I ran out on you and your mother. But still, you sought me out. You must also know, Sylvia, that I'm in trouble back east."

"I know all about that, Hap. I guess—I guess I remember how gentle you treated me and all the things I learned from you—poker, craps, how to ride a pony, how to deal from the bottom."

They laughed together, as Sylvia went on to tell her father about seeing stories about him in some of Casper's newspapers. Further details related by her were of her graduating from college, but something kept her back from telling Hap Fleming she'd received her law degree. Perhaps it was because he'd been disbarred from ever practicing law again.

"Well, how long will be you here? Where are you staying?" He reached for her left hand. "And you're not married? I insist that you stay at my place in Bessemer Bend. What a quaint little town but growing every day, thanks in part to my land company and efforts."

"I like staying here at the Wyoming Hotel."

"It has some advantages."

"Hap, I reckon, as they say out here, I'll stick around for a while. Jobs are plentiful."

"Jobs! Your poor, rich mother would have a heart attack if you used that word around her. Jobs, yes, this town is just waiting to explode, as so much is happening out here. I have it, the perfect solution. Come to work for me. I've found good help is hard to get. This way, we can get to know one another a lot better. I have high ambitions, my dear Sylvia."

In the short time Sylvia had been here, she had picked up on stories about her father's land dealings. The jury, at least to the townspeople of Casper, was still out on Hap Fleming, with a lot of people resentful of what Fleming and his land company had accomplished. Sorting through all of this, Sylvia was of the opinion that Hap Fleming was still involved in some crooked activities. She realized he would never change, and it saddened her. Sean Fitzpatrick had inadvertently mentioned the name of Fleming's Bessemer Bend land company in connection with the murder of some bookkeeper. Further checking by Sylvia had revealed that a couple of her father's eastern cronies were in town, men who used to come around back in New York—Barney Cleever and con man Ole Lundahl. She more than suspected that Lundahl ran the Golden West Land Company for her father.

"I'd like to find work here in Casper," Sylvia said.

"Without giving Bessemer Bend a chance. Casper, you said. Say, I know they need office help at the Golden West, a land company owned by a friend of mine."

Sharing a smile, she replied, "I'd like that."

"I know, my dear daughter, I forgot my promise . . . that when you turned twenty-one we'd share a drink together."

"You're three years behind the times, Hap."

"Seems I am, at that. Come then, there's a delightful barroom downstairs where they serve gentlemen and their ladies."

Heading with her father for the staircase, Sylvia Valcourt realized that despite Hap Fleming's pleasure in seeing her, he had definitely changed. It was an awareness more felt than seen. Her love— and truly Sylvia did love her father—had also opened her eyes to all of his character flaws, whereas when she was a pigtailed girl of around ten or eleven, Hap Fleming had seemed larger than the Statue of Liberty to her. The endless swirl of parties . . . the checkered characters he called friends . . . the double-talk and crooked dealings. These were the pages of a book that had yet to see its last chapter written. Somehow she knew Hap Fleming was authoring the greatest con game of his life. Only this time murder had become a part of it, the wanton murder of a bookkeeper.

With a steeliness of mind, Sylvia laid this aside for the moment, the smile she had for her father still holding. She knew she was destined to stay out here until the story of Hap Fleming was told with sweet memories or concluded in territorial court.

Her eyes going to his, Sylvia said lightly, "By the way, Daddy, Mother had my last name legally changed to Valcourt."

"Why, that . . . bitch. Isn't anything sacred?"

"Only filling an inside straight, it seems."

Tyler Echohawk hung around the saloon until well after midnight. He'd been drinking sparingly, his chair placed at the table so he could glance out a front window and down the street at the Wyoming Hotel. Though Megan Randsley was his reason for being in this saloon, what Lon had told him about the Salt Creek Oil Field lay heavy on his mind. Hap Fleming will be pleased to hear about this, he mused, but of more urgency was that Fleming's house of cards would come tumbling down if line superintendent Martin Colhour told what he knew.

Lon had informed him they would leave early tomorrow morning for the railhead in order to bring Colhour back to Casper. And if Colhour got to testify in court, it would probably be back to robbing banks, something that brought a distasteful grimace to Tyler's face. Later tonight he'd ride out and get together with Cap Bentley. But killing railroad man Colhour would cost Hap Fleming a heap.

The urge to go over to the Wyoming Hotel brought Tyler up from his chair. Heading outside, he angled across the street until he reached the hotel, entering through the side door that opened into the lobby. A wall clock read a few minutes shy of one-thirty, and few people filled the lobby. One thing he hadn't gotten was Megan Randsley's room number, which brought Tyler striding to a counter presided over by a slick-haired night clerk. He reached out to spin the register book around, muttering, "Sheriff's business." He flicked a page over to find what he wanted, then strode away.

Hesitating by the wide staircase, Tyler could tell from the music pouring down that the dance was still in progress. Knowing he didn't want to go up and gawk at Megan from the sidelines, he swung about and headed for the nearest barroom located just off the lobby. Inside, he found the lamps were set down low, the only clientele a sprinkling of salesmen. As Tyler's eyes adjusted to the dimmer light, he picked out the woman who'd just risen from a table occupied by a thick-set man, whom he recognized a moment later as being Hap Fleming.

The woman took her leave through another door, with Tyler recalling he'd seen her in the ballroom. Now as Fleming started to shove up from the table, Tyler stepped past the bar and weaved over, to say softly, "Something damned important has come up."

Fleming sank down again.

"Come sunup, we're heading out to the railhead to pick up a prisoner."

Scowling, Hap Fleming asked, "Is that all?"

"Nope." Tyler turned where he stood and told the bartender to bring over a bottle of whiskey. Now he sat down, facing bunco artist Hap Fleming. "There's a helluva lot more, Hap. You ever hear of the Crown Oil Company?"

"About the biggest oil company around."

"There was a big powwow tonight in Judge Childress's suite—the sheriff, the judge, and this oilman. Seems the prisoner we're to escort back here is line superintendent Martin Colhour."

"Colhour," muttered Fleming. "I knew he didn't have the stomach for this." Uncertainties played across his wide face. "The point is, what has he told them about his connection to my operation?"

"What kind of money have you been paying him?"

"Enough," Fleming hedged.

"I expect you want him taken care of. What say later tonight I ride out and get together with men who'll take out this line superintendent? For a price, of course."

"Yes, I expect it'll cost me. There is no hard evidence tying me to Colhour other than the money I've been paying him. In court, it'll be his word against mine."

"Going to court is something neither of us can afford, Hap."

"He must be killed."

"Consider it done, say for five thousand."

"A high price, Tyler."

"Not so high when you hear what I've found out. Ever hear of the Salt Creek Oil Field? Nope? Well, according to what I've learned, it's gonna be the biggest oil patch in these parts. What I was told is it's located north of here, about twenty or so miles. Crown Oil is investing heavily up there, buying up mineral rights and such."

"This, Tyler, could be what I've been looking for, as Crown Oil or any large company wouldn't invest unless they're into a sure thing." He paid for the bottle of whiskey the bartender had just brought over, waiting for the man to drift back behind the bar before he continued. "They have the money to secretly bring in geologists and agents to buy up the land they want. But first come, first serve. This'll mean, Tyler, I'll be depending heavily on your men. One thing, I might have to bring in some investors."

"Do what you have to. My boys'll back up your play."

"So, you were right about putting on that badge, Mr. Echohawk. And Colhour, he's taken care of?"

"Consider him a dead man. Now, I've got to sidle out of here, as I've got other business." Tyler downed the whiskey in his shot glass.

"You'll receive your money from Ole Lundahl."

"That five thousand is just chicken feed, Hap. So is the price of sending flowers to Colhour's widow."

Out in the lobby, Tyler intended to take the back staircase up to the third floor, but first he needed a key to gain entry to Megan Randsley's room, in the off-chance she was still in the ballroom. Crossing over to the check-in counter, he found that the night clerk had gone off someplace, and it took but a moment for Tyler to slip behind the counter and lift a key to room 347 from the pigeonhole rack.

A low whistle accompanied Tyler Echohawk up the back staircase. As he checked off the room numbers while easing along the carpeted hallway, the flames of his expectancy over seeing Megan brought a glitter into his eyes. There was every chance she might send him packing, that just savoring the sweetness of those full lips wouldn't be enough. He found the door to her room and rapped softly, knocking again before he used the key to gain access. From within he locked the door, to moonlight flaring in through the windows as he gazed down upon Center Street. Over by one of the windows stood an overstuffed chair. After opening the window a little more to let in the night air, Tyler settled down and took out the makings.

"Yup, coming here proved to be the right thing to do. Fleming . . . awful shrewd and maybe dangerous . . . and there's Barney Cleever to fret over, too." Striking a wooden match on the arm of the chair, he ignited the tailor-made, then set everything aside but lustful notions of Megan Randsley, the scent of her perfume strong in the room.

The rasping of metal in the keyhole brought Tyler out of a dreamy reverie, along with causing him to snuff out the third cigarette he'd rolled. Quietly, he rose from the chair when he realized Megan wasn't alone, slipping into a closet.

The door swung open and Megan said, "It was such a charming night, Sean."

"You seem to like it out here."

"A lot smaller than Boston," she said. "But you're here." Megan offered him her lips, than eased away, only to pause when he asked; "Are you sure about us? After all, I've been out here for some time."

"Sure as can be, my dear Sean. Tomorrow at noon?" Then she closed the door and turned the key. She lit a lamp before passing into the connecting bathroom to find a hairbrush. Coming back, puzzlement gleamed in her eyes as she wheeled about toward the front windows. Megan managed to smother the scream with her hand when she gazed at Tyler Echohawk smiling at her from where he sat in the chair.

"You . . . you're here? . . ."

He held out the key. "Used this to get in. I had to see you."

"Tonight? At this hour? I . . . I resent this intrusion . . . I . . ."

Shoving to his feet, Tyler stepped up to her and gazed down into her eyes, which registered uncertainty and just a little fear. Slowly, he reached out and touched her cheek, holding one hand there as he brought his other hand to the small of her back and drew her close. She lifted her face, the defiant scowl being replaced by a moan that passed through her lips as they found Tyler Echohawk's. Now it was Megan pressing closer, all of the floodgates of her resistance fleeing her bedroom. She found herself being lifted up and carried over to the bed, wanting him beyond reason, beyond caring.

"Tyler, this isn't right . . ."

"There are some things which are always right."

"Yes, yes . . ."

Ten

False dawn was draped like a widow's shroud over a hump of land marking the eastern reaches of Casper. The fringes of sky close to the horizon still seemed a part of the prairie and mountain range extending southwest, but farther up stars were dimming out of a sky more smoky grey in color. A windless, soulless morning, which about matched the feelings of Sheriff Lon Echohawk.

During the night he'd found himself waking, restless, unable to put a finger on his worry over what tomorrow would bring. It seemed simple enough: ride over to the railhead and pick up a prisoner. Lifting his collar, he shouldered more into the warmth of his sheepskin. To his left rode Tyler, beyond that Hack LaVoy astride a grey gelding, all three horses snorting out streams of whitish vapor, although Lon Echohawk's bay had picked up on its rider's worried frame of mind and was getting in the mood to buck.

"Always these cold mornings."

"But you can't beat breathin' air that ain't all bogged down in humidity. Hot as it gets during the day, a man don't get all sweated up like he does down in Arkansas and such places." Hack LaVoy leaned forward in the saddle, to look past Tyler and at the sheriff. "Three of us to pick up one prisoner . . . an' some railroad man at that. Must have done somethin' tolerable wrong . . . or have a lot of enemies . . ."

"You can blame Judge Childress for breaking up your beauty sleep, Hack."

"Childress, huh?"

In a flat tone of voice, Lon said, "Let's pick up the gait." He set his horse into a lope along the slender ribbon of stagecoach trail knifing due east.

The North Platte River still lay off to the left of the lawmen coming in on the railhead, which they hadn't caught sight of yet. Guiding them in for the last few miles was the continuous sound of hammers striking against steel, along with the sight of smoke stabbing toward a clear sky.

Clearing still another rolling sweep of prairieland, with Lon Echohawk and his deputies taking note of an abundance of pronghorn, they could make out one engine idling where track was being laid and, some distance to the south, black coal smoke roiling away from another work train heading toward the railhead. Their horses went downhill at a canter, Lon looking at his watch and announcing it was a quarter past one.

"We'll water our horses and grub up, then head back."

171

"Look at all them shiny rails: Must cost a heap to do something like this."

"When you think about it, there must be a lot of money floating around these parts," Tyler Echohawk said.

"Maybe," Hack LaVoy threw in, "we should ask the county for a raise in pay."

"Dream on," said Lon, as he spurred up a little to come in between a stack of rails, where several men were carrying another rail just before placing it down on the railbed. Immediately, others with hammers started swinging away at heavy spikes. Passing along the tracks and the cars attached to the engine, Lon pulled rein near the middle of the Pullman car when a man emerged and threw him a casual wave.

"See you made it, Sheriff."

"Not all that long a ride," said Lon.

"Holding your prisoner in here. A shame what some men will do."

"I've seen it all. Like to water our horses and rest them some before we pull out."

"I'll have my men tend to your horses. You'll eat with me in the Pullman; just railroad fare, but it's tasty. One thing, Sheriff, Martin Colhour isn't all that happy about being taken to Casper. But let him tell you."

Dismounting, they turned their horses over to two railroad hands summoned by the new line superintendent. "Sheriff Echohawk, I'm Frank O'Rourke. I guess I have Colhour to thank for being out here in Wyoming. Most of my work for the railroad has been further east." Then Lon introduced his deputies, and they stepped up to enter the Pullman car. Only one man armed with a sawed-off shotgun was guarding Martin Colhour, who sat at a table by an open window. Colhour, in the midst of a game of solitaire, lowered the deck and picked up his coffee cup, regarding the lawmen over its rim. From his appearance, he hadn't shaven in some days and had this sullen set to his face.

"Colhour," asked the new line superintendent, "will you eat with us?"

"A last meal, so to speak," he responded flatly, hesitating as everyone but the man holding the shotgun settled in around a table. "I'd like to talk to the sheriff in private."

Lon pushed up from the chair and said, "I see no harm in that." He moved toward where Colhour was sitting, to ease down across the table. "So, Mr. Colhour, this is about all the privacy you're going to be accorded. I have a warrant for your arrest in my saddlebags, if you want to see it."

"Issued by my contemporaries," Colhour remarked quietly. "I knew . . . well, no sense rehashing this over again . . ." He gritted his teeth, deepening the lines in his cheeks and around his eyes, before he spoke again. "I feel, Sheriff, if I'm taken to Casper, I won't have long to live. Certainly arrangements can be made to take me to Denver. Otherwise, I'm telling you now I will not reveal the others involved in this."

"What crimes you've committed were done in Wyoming," Lon said quietly. "I figure the only way we can keep you alive is by your revealing the names of the others in on this."

"It would be my word against theirs." He brushed a wayward strand of hair from his forehead. "Sheriff, there's no hard evidence, just the money I've been paid."

"Where did they make the payoff?"

"They came out here; before that, we'd gotten together in Denver."

"Seems to me some of your workers could testify as to them coming out here to the railhead."

"But I'm the one who'll be sitting in jail in Casper. For how long until the trial begins? A month? Two?"

"Only the territorial judge and my deputies know we're out here to bring you in. Which I've got no other choice but to do, Mr. Colhour. You'll be guarded around the clock. But as I've said, not revealing who they are is damnably stupid. But, you chew it over."

"I . . ." He gazed up at Sheriff Echohawk coming to his feet. "Yes, decisions have to be made." A wan smile poked through the stubble of beard. "Perhaps joining you for dinner is a start."

They left within the hour, their prisoner astride a horse belonging to the railroad. Even with the temperature in the seventies and a few clouds cutting away the glare of the afternoon sun, Sheriff Lon Echohawk still hadn't been able to shake this vague sense of unrest. On the way to the railhead, Lon kept stealing glances at possible places an ambush might be set, and they were plentiful. There were high, rugged hills and ravines gulching out of the Laramies toward the North Platte River, barren and crumbly rock spires, and flat-topped ridges. Maybe, he cautioned himself, they should have waited until sundown.

Tugging worriedly at the brim of his Stetson, he said quietly to Hack LaVoy, "Just can't shake it."

"You do seem awful fidgety."

"Not all that far to the river. We could head over and loll around a campfire until dusk, and then head in."

"Up ahead a ways, Lon, the country opens up more. Shouldn't have no trouble then, but you're calling it."

"Either way, we've still got about forty miles to cover. Be a full moon tonight, too. Reckon we'll keep stringing out, Hack, keep our eyes peeled."

"This Colhour must have been involved with some mighty big money people, as he's awful darn scared. The kind of scare that can spook us'ns, too, if we let it."

Riding alongside the prisoner and in back of his fellow lawmen, Tyler Echohawk had picked up on his brother's worries on the way over from Casper. A worry he shared in a way, for Tyler knew he could easily fall victim to an errant bullet. He anticipated the ambush taking place within the next five miles or so. His eyes went casually to Martin Colhour humped over the saddle horn of his horse.

"You know, Colhour, you're not helping yourself by holding all of this in. Seems they caught you dead to rights. Was me, I'd be damned if I'd be the only one going to prison. This Judge Childress, awful tough when it comes to handin' out sentences. The judge'd sure go easy on you if you was to open up."

He stared back at Tyler Echohawk. "Deputy, so far I've been deprived of the services of a lawyer. I—"

"Out here most folks can't afford to hire a lawyer, much less pay any fine."

The talk fading away, they cantered to the west, following the stagecoach trail, the sun trying now to edge itself under the front brim of their hats. They stopped once to give their horses a breather and to drink from their canteens, with Sheriff Echohawk commenting that soon the land would open up more. Here Lon held back to ride alongside their prisoner, as his deputies took the point.

About twenty minutes later, Tyler Echohawk had this feeling it was about to happen, the stagecoach trail just ahead of them knifing to the east a shade to clear a long hill crowned with layers of reddish rock. Sneaking a glance at Hack LaVoy, he saw the same pondering look in the deputy's squinting eyes. Tyler knew the ambushers would be Cap Bentley and Emmet Haskell and Slater Moore, with Haskell down tending to the horses.

"What do you think?"

"Just another quiet Sunday afternoon ride," LaVoy replied.

"Tell that to my brother."

"I don't want to get my head chewed off." The wind had picked up, and LaVoy spit grit out of his mouth. He dug a hunk of chewing tobacco out of a vest pocket, then twisted in the saddle to look back just as it happened, their prisoner lurching in the saddle, followed by the heavy recoil of a Winchester.

Another rifle joined in, the lawmen flinging startled glances at the hill off to their left. Even now Lon Echohawk had lifted out his rifle and was shouting, "Up there . . . those puffs of smoke . . ."

Bammity-Bam-Bam!

Sheriff Echohawk was levering another shell into the breech of his rifle, when a slug punched into his shoulder and he sagged in the saddle. Both of his deputies had found their rifles and were pumping shells along the ridgeline. It was LaVoy who became aware that the sheriff had been hit, but even so, Lon Echohawk had dropped out of the saddle and was huddled by the downed prisoner.

"I think I hit one of them," LaVoy shouted.

"They've quit firing," Tyler yelled back. "Stay here and tend to the others." A hard jab of his spurs and Tyler's bronc was into a gallop. He headed for the flank of the hill, to find a place where it sloped out and down to meet prairie. From here he brought his bronc laboring upward, onto the crown of the hill.

He headed to the south, following the lay of the hill, reining up sharply and holding when it began tapering away. First two riders appeared on the flats far to the south; shortly thereafter, a riderless horse came trailing in after them. There was always the risk that one of them would take a bullet. And Tyler hoped it hadn't been Cap Bentley. He brought his bronc down the shoulder of the hill, where more hill rose to screen what lay below. Even from here, he could pick out fresh hoofprints, and he whistled shrilly just in case a rifle barrel was trained in his direction. Then he shouted, "It's me, Tyler! I'm coming down."

"Damnit, Tyler," came a voice from some hidden recess, "I've been hit . . . in the leg . . . tore it all up."

After working off the hill, Tyler saw movement amongst a choke of brush and sagebrush, and he rode there to find Slater Moore trying to stem the flow of blood with his bandanna. He swung down, telling Moore, "You'd be pleased to know you took out our prisoner."

The wounded Slater Moore tried grinning around his pain. "I ain't that bad a horseman . . . but just fell off my hoss. I figure Cap and Emmet'll be coming back. But damned glad to see you, Tyler."

Reaching down, Tyler Echohawk lifted the sidearm from Moore's holster. Though he liked Slater Moore, the reality of it was that the man had become expendable. Also, he expected that Cap Bentley would swing back most anytime, but when he did, it would be to find a dead man. Lifting out his own Colt, Tyler fired Moore's into the ground. Then a slug from Tyler's Colt penetrated into the wounded Slater Moore's forehead, and he folded over dead. Dropping Healy's six-gun, he swung into the saddle and cut away.

It took Tyler about a half-hour to work his way back to the stagecoach trail and the others, who were holding where he'd left them. By this time the body of the luckless Martin Colhour had been loaded aboard his horse, with Tyler having sympathetic eyes for the wound suffered by his brother.

"Got one of them."

"Heard gunfire."

"Seem to be heading for the mountains."

Lon grimaced as he climbed into the saddle. He'd felt the jolt of a slug before and was thankful this one had gone on through. Still, once he got back, he'd have a sawbones swab in there and clean out the wound. But more painful to Lon Echohawk was that he'd lost a prisoner. If any leak had come, he pondered, it could have been from the railroad people. His examination of Colhour's body had revealed he'd been hit three times and about dead center. A marksman out here meant an outlaw sure enough, with Lon sorting through the wanteds he had acquired in Casper. His conclusion was that perhaps a handful qualified for a job of this kind.

"Know you're hurting, Lon," said Hack LaVoy, "but next time I'll listen to your suspicions. If we'd waited as you wanted . . ."

"Anyone this determined to kill Martin Colhour would have tried again in Casper. Colhour's paid for his sins. Now our job is to find out who killed him . . . and hopefully those behind this."

They'd set out a short time, only to have the silence interrupted by Tyler Echohawk producing

179

a pint bottle of whiskey from a saddlebag, which he passed to Lon. "This'll cut the pain."

Though Lon Echohawk disliked the idea of fetching along whiskey, he nodded his thanks and took a long drink. Grimacing, he handed the bottle to LaVoy. "You sorry I asked you to wear that badge?" Lon asked his brother.

"It was awful hairy there for a moment," said Tyler, "but nope. I just want to be there when we catch these killers."

"Highly likely that'll happen."

Eleven

Sheriff Lon Echohawk could remember how when they'd pulled into Casper after dark last night, there'd been this meteorite shower lighting up the sky over the mountain. About the same fiery display had been Judge Albert Childress's response upon finding out one of his sheriffs had been nicked by a bullet and an important prisoner gunned down from ambush. This had been when Echohawk had traipsed into the judge's chambers at the courthouse, not in all that good a mood himself because of the pain emanating from his wound.

Explanations aside, the judge had taken Sheriff Echohawk over to Amberson's Funeral Parlor to view the remains. Just before leaving the courthouse, Henry Witland, the judge's secretary, was sent to fetch oilman Nathan Fry.

It wasn't until mid-morning that everyone concerned about Martin Colhour's untimely death was clustered in a preparation room rank with the decaying odor of old blood and overridden by the sharper tang of formaldehyde. A few horseflies buzzed around tools spread out on a wall table, and a moth that had come in through a rent in the screen door was flitting over the sheet that covered the recently demised line superintendent. Nathan Fry, who had brought along the Pinkerton operative, was gazing at the sheriff of Carbon County as if the lawman had betrayed him.

Judge Childress lifted the sheet away and said, "Awful fine shooting."

Everyone looked at the three puck-shaped holes punching through the chest area. Echohawk knew that any one of those rifle bullets had caused the fatal wound, that the rest of them were overkill. They could just as easily have taken him out along with his deputies. Shortly after Tyler had come back claiming to have downed one of the ambushers, they'd gone over for a look at the body, only to find it had been removed. Lon knew then that he was dealing with professionals.

"So, Mr. Fry, have you told us everything?"

"Judge, we only know that Colhour had been paid to hold back on laying track. He'd be alive . . ." His voice cut away as he glanced at Echohawk.

"I could just as easily have gone down," Lon said acridly. "Only the four of us knew about my heading out yesterday morning. But someone else had to know, too."

"Are you accusing me?"

"Easy," snapped Judge Childress. "Look, Mr. Fry, I've heard about this competitiveness between oil companies. I know some operate outside the law at times; good business, they call it. Morality isn't my job here. What puzzles me is why another oil company—or there could be more than one—would want to keep the railroad from coming in, as oil's been discovered west of here . . . the Shannon Field, Big Muddy."

"I've told you all I know," said Fry. "Crown Oil has no intention of letting this rest, Judge Childress."

"By that you mean"—Childress nodded at the Pinkerton operative—"others like him will come in to muddy things up. Can't stop you from doing that, I reckon."

"You will continue with your investigation?"

"I don't like getting nicked by bullets, Mr. Fry," Lon Echohawk declared. "Take it kind of personal. It would have been more interestin' if you and your shadow there could have ridden along out to the railhead. Just to see how it feels to come under gunfire."

Stiffly, Nathan Fry said, "Judge, I'll drop by." He hurried out the back door, followed by the Pinkerton agent.

A shadow of a grin appeared on Childress's face, disappearing as he drew the sheet over the body. "Lon, here's the way of it. I'm sending U.S. Marshal Joe LeFors over to Rawlins to handle things for a spell."

"Meaning I'm to stay up here?"

"And get to the bottom of this. I sort of have to agree with what you was hintin' at before, Lon. Someone besides the four of us knew about you going over to the railhead."

"Fry?"

"Find out for me, Echohawk."

"A big chore, considerin' the only one knowin' what's been goin' on is dead. Can't be any of my deputies; been through hellfire together." He followed the judge out the back door and around the side of the building to the boardwalk. They talked briefly, then Childress swung away to head back to the courthouse.

As Lon stepped along the boardwalk, he decided that his first order of business would be to call a council of war with his deputies. They would scour through the Sandbar District and other places in town known to be hangouts for lawbreakers. He knew that somewhere in Casper, the men who'd winged him and committed murder were holed up. What he needed most of all was to pick the brains of someone more acquainted with the oil business.

"Money? Yup, what Tyler and Hack were chewing over back when we was headin' for the railhead, that it took a heap of greenbacks to buck the big oil boys."

Somehow Lon knew he'd just stumbled onto part of the puzzle he sought to clear up. Another part of it, though still shadowy in his mind, was a connection to the Salt Creek Oil Field.

Casting a quick glance at his left arm encased in a sling, he muttered, "This darn pain can muddy up a man's musings, too. But . . . got this hunch I'm onto something."

By the time early afternoon had rolled around all of Lon Echohawk's deputies were out looking for the ambushers, while Lon himself had just passed the Liberty Gunshop display window and found the center staircase. He tramped upstairs, retreating a little when a woman came out of Sean Fitzpatrick's law office. "Howdy, Miss Randsley," he said, tipping his hat.

Blindly, she hurried past Lon and bounded down the steps. He turned to see lawyer Fitzpatrick emerging from his office, muttering, "Maybe you can tell me what's troubling Megan . . . so, come in, Lon."

"You two have a spat?"

"I picked Megan up around eleven to take her to dinner. There was something different about her. It was as if I weren't there, as if a wall lay between us."

"Did this have anything to do with Saturday night's dance?"

"No, but anyway, I'll figure it out. Now what was it you wanted to discuss?"

"For one thing, I hear they want to run you for mayor. You go for it; you've got my support." Lon picked up a chair and brought it closer to the desk on which he dropped his hat. Settling down, he smiled at the cigar tendered across the desk by Sean. "Obliged, counsellor."

"How's the shoulder?"

"Healing."

He lit Lon's cigar, then his, and said, "In court this morning, I had to present a case before an unhappy Judge Childress."

"I've been there before. Your wanderings around town at night have given you an advantage other lawyers don't have here. Meaning, folks hanging out in these places will open up to you."

"When you go fishing, Sheriff, you put a little bait on your line."

"Okay, Sean, I have to confide in someone other than my deputies." He laid out the reasons line superintendent Martin Colhour had been murdered. "Holding back on laying track? Those behind Colhour's murder need time, maybe to raise money, but chiefly to buy up oil rights."

"The land office could give you part of what you want to know, Lon."

"I intend going back there. This sheriffing job keeps me in and out of Casper. I do know that no oil company has come in and set up an office. Once the railroad gets here that'll change. The other part of it, as you know, Sean, is that some of our local public officials are mixed up in shady dealings. Reed, the new town marshal, is Rafe Bascome's lapdog."

"This murder out near Bessemer Bend . . . the man who was killed worked for Hap Fleming's land company."

"I was coming to Fleming, as my office has received a lot of bad reports as to how he operates."

"One of his men, a tough named Barney Cleever . . . ever hear of him?"

"Doesn't ring a bell."

"Right now Cleever is recovering from someone working him over with a two-by-four; was told this down in the Sandbar. Your new deputy is reputed to have done the job on Cleever."

"Tyler?"

"Way the story goes."

He hadn't at all considered Tyler as anything but his brother. Skeptism lay heavy in the eyes Lon turned upon Sean Fitzpatrick. "Did this happen after he pinned on a badge?"

"The way I heard it, around that time. Anyway, Barney Cleever likes to hang around cheap dives but keeps to himself. He's no gunman but likes to use his fists, and I gather at one time he was a professional boxer."

"Interesting . . ." Lon tipped the ashes from his cigar into the tray on the desk. "That he is connected to Hap Fleming is even more interesting." There was the cowhand, Easton, beaten to death, and whoever did the job on Easton wore a ring that had gouged out flesh. "Cleever . . . any idea where he hangs out?"

"Lately nobody's seen him. I expect he's hiding out until he looks halfway human again. Why this sudden interest in Cleever, if I may be so bold as to ask?"

"Just that he could be mixed up in a killing. That of a cowhand up this side of the Big Horns. Sean, I don't want you to get involved in this, because if Cleever is one of those we're looking for, it could be dangerous."

"I respect your position, Sheriff, but consider that I've a lot at stake here, too. Nobody wants to become mayor of a town where murder is rampant."

"That means you're running for the job?"

"Until you walked in, I was sort of shying

away. But I guess you could say I am, Lon. Seems this shanty Irishman has some friends here after all, those who want me to run." He laughed around the cigar wedged between his even rows of teeth. "Back to Cleever. If perchance I find out he possesses such a ring, I'll get word to you. But ring or no, without hard evidence you have no case against him."

"My hunch is that a lot of Hap Fleming's land agents are not only selling land to homesteaders, but also involved in buying up mineral rights. Over at Bessemer Bend, a well is being dug just outside of town. Fleming's more or less boss man over there. Could be it's Fleming's well."

"Here in Casper, I do know that Hap Fleming and one of our councilmen have gotten together from time to time. That would be Rafe Bascome. Which brings us to the Golden West Land Company."

"Over on Center Street, I believe."

"When Fleming goes barhopping in Casper, it's often in the company of a man named Ole Lundahl. Is the fact that both Lundahl and the illustrious Hap Fleming are in the land business coincidental?"

"They say drunks seek out other drunks."

"So they do," said Fitzpatrick as he rose.

Lon put out what was left of his cigar before reaching for his hat. Standing up, he said, "The gentleman from Crown Oil revealed where his company is going to start drilling operations once the railroad reaches town. I just wonder, with nobody supposed to know about our going over to pick up Colhour, that word of what Crown Oil intends doing has leaked out. Well, Sean, obliged for your time. As I said, watch yourself around Cleever."

"I also heard that Barney Cleever has stated he intends doing harm to your brother."

"Used a board on him . . ."

"A two-by-four can do a lot of harm."

Idly, Lon said, "A body was found over at this lumberyard about that time." He left it there, along with a grateful nod for Sean Fitzpatrick as he went out into the hallway and down the staircase.

Out on Center Street, Lon Echohawk realized that what he'd learned from Sean shed new light on a lot of things. Especially about his brother, Tyler, a man he'd accepted at face value. Just what had prompted Tyler to leave Oregon other than a desire to see him? wondered Lon. The trouble was, all he could remember about his brother was connected with the wagon train, when he'd waved goodbye to his family and Tyler had continued west. Just a hunk of unruly hair, those worshipful eyes of Tyler's watching him ride away, a good memory relived at night around a campfire.

A spasm of pain tearing at his shoulder was a harsh reminder of this exact moment. All he'd consumed so far today were a few cups of chicory-rich coffee. Added to this were Judge Childress's equally strong comments, as well as oilman Fry's contemptuous opinion of him as a lawman. But fork a saddle for days on end, and a rider's first chore was to see his horse watered and fed. At this notion Lon swung up the street, his eyes darting to the facade of the Demorest Home Restaurant. The hunger pangs clutching at his stomach overrode everything else at the moment, even though Lon Echohawk knew he really should be heading over to that lumberyard where some luckless hard case had been murdered but realizing if he did so he just might find something that would incriminate his new deputy.

A pair of workers were unloading lumber they'd just wagoned down from the sawmill on Casper Mountain. The wood was still rich with the smell of pine. One of them nodded at Sheriff Lon Echohawk ambling by where they were working. After a dinner of stew and brown bread, Lon had gone back to his office. He'd dug out the report on the murder that had happened here at the Uvald Lumberyard. The details of what had taken place had been sketchy.

As for Tyler, his brother was still out, as were his other deputies as they searched for the men who'd killed Martin Colhour. Just because Tyler had used a hunk of wood on someone, he mused, doesn't mean it had taken place in this lumberyard. But the murder and what Tyler had done had happened about the same day. Farther on, other workers were loading up wagons from stacked board lumber lying out in the open, while choicer lumber was stored in the main building. He spotted lumberman Beryl Uvald through one of the windows in the small office and would have gone in, but Uvald hurried outside.

"Sheriff Echohawk, I don't expect your wanting to buy lumber brought you here."

"Sorry to say it didn't, Mr. Uvald. I just want to go over the crime scene again and to see if you might have forgotten something. Let's see, it happened over here; at least that's where we found the body."

"Yes, past these stacks of lumber. Did I mention they'd broken in through the front gate? Believe I did, as I had to purchase a new padlock. Did you ever identify the dead man?"

"Just some drifter. If he's got kin, they'll never find out what happened to him."

Stepping on ahead, Uvald came around the last stack of lumber and gestured at an open area somewhat larger than a boxing ring. "The body lay there, Sheriff, by those old pieces of lumber, short ends and such. We discard stuff here, and sometimes folks come by to pick out what they want."

"Thank you, Mr. Uvald. I'll take it from here." He allowed the smile to hold until the lumberman was gone, then Lon gazed down at the sun-baked ground. Dusty boot prints prowled through it, old lumber, empty kegs, and a sprinkling of weeds making an untidy pile nearby. Beyond that lay a high board fence. Opposite it, lumber was stacked on thick pilings the size of railroad ties, to keep it off the ground.

With his arm bound up like this it felt awkward bending down, but Lon managed to do so as he searched the open places under the stacked lumber, not certain what he was looking for. He got up stiffly and continued his search around the perimeter of the small open area, working his way up amongst the litter and weeds. He scared up a garter snake, which slithered toward the fence, then he toed aside an empty whiskey bottle. What soon caught Lon's eye was a newer piece of lumber some three feet long. He reached in among the weeds to pick it up, discovering parts of its surface were bloodstained. Any lingering doubts he'd held about what Sean Fitzpatrick had told him were now gone.

Could it be, he wondered apprehensively, that my brother is mixed up in a murder? How could Tyler, or any man, use something like this two-by-four to beat up on someone else? Which brought to mind that he knew little about Tyler Echohawk. Tyler, and maybe Barney Cleever, and some others, including the man who was killed, had come in here at night. Cleever works for Hap Fleming, Lon mused. Could be that Cleever was one of those involved in the murder of that bookkeeper. He moved out of the weeds, almost sorry that he'd come here, but through a sigh, Lon said, "Due process of law has to be served."

Twelve

To a whisper of silken petticoats under her dark brown clothes, Sylvia Valcourt passed through the open front door of the Golden West Land Company. She paused, taking in the people occupying the benches resting along the side walls of the anteroom, while more people were being waited on at the long counter running the width of the building. Behind that were several desks and a few wooden file cabinets. Plastered to the walls were large advertisements taken from newspapers, plat maps of the area filling in the spaces in between.

Of the seven clerks, one was a middle-aged woman who beckoned to Sylvia. "If you're the new clerk, just come on back. I'm Peggy Adcock." She opened the door in the counter to permit Sylvia access to the open office area.

"Thank you. Mr. Fleming told me to show up around ten."

"So you're an hour early. You can put your purse and hat back there, the closet to the right. Lundahl—he's the boss—he isn't here right now."

She turned back to finish doing some paperwork for a customer.

Sylvia went to open the closet door, glancing down the hallway running toward the closed back door. There were three more closed doors, the murmur of voices seeping over the transom in one room. From what Hap Fleming had told her, at least a dozen land salesman worked out of here. She'd asked her father not to mention their relationship, and somewhat reluctantly he had agreed. Her remembrance of Ole Lundahl was of someone able to blend in with the wallpaper. But Sylvia wasn't about to underestimate either Lundahl or her father.

Taking in the scene at the counter, she realized the land company had plenty of business. Along with the three clerks presiding over the counter, four more were dealing with customers seated alongside their desks. Sylvia assumed she'd be broken in to handle this end of things.

As she brushed back an errant lock of hair, Sylvia Valcourt couldn't help reluctantly dragging herself back to late Saturday night. After bidding good night to Hap Fleming down in a hotel barroom, she'd retired for the night. The excitement of finding her father had made sleep virtually impossible. Twice she'd gotten up to gaze out at downtown Casper, just about snuggled in for the night, the few stragglers moving away from the hotel and some Center Street saloons or gaming casinos. Perhaps just staring out to the south at the higher darkness of the mountain below a starlit sky had made her realize just where she was.

Once some noise had filtered in from the adjoining room occupied by Megan Randsley—mingled voices of Megan and, Sylvia assumed, Sean Fitzpatrick—the door closing again. Shortly after this, or so it seemed, came Megan's gasp of surprise, cutting away just as quickly. Then the soft tramping of boots, and Sylvia had left it there, withdrawing to her bed. For after all, she'd thought at the time, Sean and Megan were about to be married. Then . . .

It was some time later that night that she was snatched from the fragments of a dream to wakefullness. Darkness still gripped her room. The intruder was again a sound coming from Megan's room, a door clicking shut. She'd lain there for a while, thinking that Sean had taken his departure. Then, for some unaccountable reason, Sylvia had thrust the coverlet aside and risen to cross over to a window. Center Street seemed barren of movement, until a man emerged from the hotel and strode on, approaching a street lamp at the corner. As plain as if he were in her room, Sylvia could see the sudden upward tilt to Tyler Echohawk's face as he grinned up at the third floor. He went on quickly, leaving Sylvia's mind tumbling with the enormity of it all. She stayed by the window, waiting for Sean Fitzpatrick to put in an appearance, Sylvia Valcourt's thoughts drifting to how Megan had behaved in Denver. Several minutes later—and she hated to think this—it dawned on Sylvia that Sean had gone home a long time ago.

"Miss Valcourt . . ."

"Yes?" She blinked the image of Megan Randsley away, a smile helping Sylvia regain her composure. "Please, it's just plain Sylvia."

"That dress—whoeee! Bit fancy for a job like this." Peggy Adcock, somewhat plump and wearing a plain white blouse and long skirt, had an air of easy familiarity about her. "About you, Sylvia, is this touch of class. No offense meant, but working here is a little below your station in life."

"Out here there is little work for women," Sylvia griped.

"Tell me about it, dearie. Once the railroad pulls in, it'll get worse. This is a boiler shop operation: They come in, we flimflam them with fast talk about the glorious virtues of owning land out here. But a gal has to make a living. Oh, there's the Sandbar"—she brought Sylvia over to a table laden with paperwork—"you know, the infamous Sandbar—"

"Sorry, I'm—"

"Our red-light district, dearie. A lot say it's what put Casper on the map. Anyway, here's all this paperwork; each folder has a name on the front of it. There are the files. Well?"

"Can do," Sylvia said eagerly, adding, "And yup, Peggy, I've heard of the . . . Sandbar."

In the days after he'd learned about Crown Oil's discovery of a new oil field, Hap Fleming checked things out at the land office. What he found out, at least in Fleming's mind, justified his hooking up with Tyler Echohawk. He sent word out to his men in the field to return to Casper, which Fleming did from Bessemer Bend, using the back door to enter Ole Lundahl's office at the Golden West Land Company. Accompanying him were Barney Cleever, Trammel, and geologist Cyril Barkley, with Trammel remaining outside by their horses.

It was late Thursday afternoon, a fast-moving thundercloud dumping a heavy rainfall upon the streets. They'd gotten in just before it started raining, the first few drops sleety with ice and hammering upon the roof of the building, then quickly changing to rainwater. Lundahl had closed the window to the south, the summery storm coming from that direction, but the other windows were left ajar to let in the fresh air. Through the windows away from the storm and to the north a lot of clear sky could be glimpsed, and they knew the cloud would soon pass on.

Lundahl hadn't questioned the orders that had come from Bessemer Bend to purchase some new plat maps taking in country north of Casper. One large map lay over a table he'd dragged into his office. Painstakingly, Lundahl had marked off sections of land recently bought up by, he assumed, agents of Crown Oil.

What he wanted most of all was to get out of the land business, as dealing with poor homesteaders and all of these immigrants flooding in here was a bargain basement way of making money. He felt good about this ever since Hap had outlined the way they'd work it. The real problem, as Ole Lundahl saw it, was the initial effort involved in acquiring enough land and mineral rights. His concern in this direction lay with Lundahl's opinion of Tyler Echohawk. He would never voice this concern to Fleming or anyone, since he considered worry and its accompanying illnesses signs of weakness. He had perfected a way of staying in the background, aloof but ever alert to changing trends. Where other bunco artists generally managed to fret their way into jail, the patience of Ole Lundahl had always given him the edge in the past. Echohawk—got to prove that he can do more than hammer the hell out of Barney Cleever with a two-by-four. It would be out of character, but he would voice this concern to Hap when they were alone. For what he saw as he gazed at the map spread over the table was a glittering future.

"Mr. Barkley, on the way over, we pretty much discussed all the aspects of this new venture."

"I have to agree, Hap, that Crown Oil has invested heavily in this new Salt Creek Field." Cyril Barkley was relieved that he'd been ordered to shut down drilling operations over at Bessemer Bend. To get away from that place and out in the field would mean not being around Fleming and that pack of hard cases. He moved closer to the table, as did Lundahl by rising from his desk and walking over, while Hap Fleming took the time to light a cigar before easing down alongside the geologist. Barney Cleever seemed oblivious to it all, keeping to a chair he'd dragged by a north window. His face had regained its shape and wasn't as puffy, but he was more sullen than ever, wounded of spirit and definitely a more dangerous man.

"The scope of what Crown Oil has bought up," marveled Barkley, "shows they mean business."

Hap Fleming indicated acreage that had been claimed by Crown Oil. "Overall, what they've filed on extends about forty miles east to west. Along most of the waterways. Once they move in their rigs, they can pretty much keep others from the unclaimed land."

"What they can't do is stop up any creeks. But yes, they're big. Still, there's plenty of acreage left."

"Which we intend to gain control of. Barkley, soon's you can, I want a list of the supplies, men you'll need, to throw together some drilling rigs."

"We're talking about a lot of money."

"That never stopped me before," Hap Fleming boasted. "In a couple of days, my men'll have filed on these sections of land"—ashes from the cigar he held spilled onto the map—"and here and here."

Ole Lundahl spoke up. "You've more or less encircled what Crown Oil has filed on."

"That's the point," said Fleming. "What me and Barkley discussed on the way over. Crown Oil may have filed first."

"Yes," said Lundahl, "to get in there, they'll have to cross over our land."

"I expect Crown Oil has taken core samples over most of this . . . yeah, Salt Creek Field. Barkley, I want you to stay in Casper tonight and come up with some money figures. Come sunup, I'll need them. Any questions?"

"I'll probably have a few once I get into this," said the geologist as he turned to open the door and left the room.

"What do you think?"

"Oh, Barkley is the same as anyone else when a gold mine is discovered. He'll hang in there, hoping to make a few bucks out of this."

"Only thing you didn't tell him, Hap, is that a lot of land you pointed out is controlled by ranchers. And a few homesteaders have pulled in up here. I expect this all comes down to how persuasive Tyler Echohawk and his men are."

"Won't be too long before we find that out."

"Now, as you know, Hap, paying off these Casper bloodsuckers and Colhour has cut down on our ready cash."

"Don't worry, Ole. Now it all comes down to the time we used that safecracker to crack open Rafe Bascome's safe." Fleming moved around to sit down behind the desk. "I hear ever since, Bascome has been looking for a few personal items that could prove embarrassing to him if they got into the wrong hands—such as Johnny Law."

"He did leave a lot of sins behind in Montana. What kind of money do you think Bascome has?"

"Bascome has friends hereabouts who have a considerable amount of money," smiled Fleming. "I'm sure that our Mr. Rafe Bascome will use his influence to see they invest heavily in our new oil venture. Say to the tune of a hundred thousand."

"Bascome . . . he could sic some of his hard cases on us. He's a hard one, Hap."

"We're just as ornery, Mr. Lundahl."

"I expect you'll have to tell him—that is, if he doesn't already know—about Crown Oil coming in."

"Ole, I do believe you're a name dropper." He consulted the wall clock. "Right about now the honorable Rafe Bascome likes to have an early supper at the Avalon Club. Perhaps a few before-dinner drinks. So, gentlemen, what say we join him." Fleming rose to his feet, then he tucked at the lapel of his coat to fluff it out as he followed Barney Cleever toward the door. "Oh, by the way, Ole, we mustn't forget to take along one or two of the items we obtained from Bascome's safe."

"They're tucked away in this drawer. I hope this works."

"I figure Rafe hasn't got any other choice. The Avalon Club . . . I believe their specialty is prime rib . . ."

Sean Fitzpatrick was surprised that the ground swell of support to see him become mayor had taken root among a lot of the businessmen and clergy of Casper. By the middle of August, the entrenched powers that be had announced that Rafe Bascome would be their candidate. This made Sean more determined than ever to put his full efforts into the campaign. One of those he enlisted to help him was Sylvia Valcourt.

Sylvia had turned up at many of the rallies held at local churches or in homes scattered around town. But Sean had seen little of the woman he was to marry. Megan Randsley seemed aloofly distant, as if a wall had come between them. Tonight there was to be a rally at a grange hall on Second Street. Afterward, the chairs would be pushed aside and there'd be a dance, with Sean very much doubtful that Megan would show up.

It had occurred to Sean that what he needed was the counsel of a woman, which was why he'd asked Sylvia to meet him at noon at the Plainsmen's Club. He'd arrived early, around eleven-thirty, to seek a glass of beer in the barroom and to buttonhole possible supporters for his candidacy. Very much on Sean's mind, now that the newspapers were still carrying stories about the murder of railroad man Martin Colhour, was his promise to Sheriff Echohawk. The arrival of Megan had kept him away from the saloons at night, and even though he'd gotten word out about Barney Cleever, the man seemed to have disappeared.

He knew that if Rafe Bascome won the mayoral election, Casper would become even more wide open. Even though Sean had a lot of support, Bascome was backed by money. He knew some of these men—one or two cattle barons, a meat packer, and a couple of bankers. It didn't seem conceivable for them to want to have a saloon owner as their mayor. But out here, Sean had learned, a lot of respectable men had shady pasts.

"Sean, are you leaving?"

"Just going into the dining room," he told the small group clustered with him at the bar. "I hope we can draw more than flies at tonight's rally."

"I'm betting," said a businessman, "we'll have a full house. Folks are beginning to realize you've got a lot of sterling qualities."

"Such as buying that last round." Sean left a smile behind as he strode out of the barroom. At the far end of the hallway, people were coming in the door facing onto the street and going into the dining room, and when he got there, Sean found that Sylvia had claimed a window table.

"How goes the land business, Miss Valcourt?"

"Tolerable, Mr. Fitzpatrick." She wore a lacy white blouse with a high collar buttoned tight around her neck, a gold-plated locket, and a black pleated skirt. Her elbows were on the table, supporting her hands cupped under her chin, and she wore just a touch of makeup.

Sylvia hadn't been all that surprised when Sean had asked her to dinner, since it was fairly obvious relations were very much strained between him and Megan Randsley. She hadn't divulged to anyone the glimpse she'd had of Tyler Echohawk leaving the Wyoming Hotel that night of over a week ago, having tried to bury it so as not to incriminate Megan or, for that matter, to hurt Sean Fitzpatrick.

Working on Sean's campaign had given her a

new insight into the man. Her respect for him had grown, especially when it came to how he withstood some of the blistering attacks placed in the newspapers by his mayoral adversary. Now the enemy camp had come up with the idea of having a debate. "About the debate, I believe it would hurt Bascome more than help him."

"What I've been led to believe, Sylvia." He refilled her coffee cup from the porcelain server, then trickled coffee into the cup at his elbow. "Someone said that Bascome had actually attended church services last Sunday. The man's getting desperate." He laughed while lifting a sugar cube out of a bowl. "Tell me about Megan . . . when you were coming out here."

"What's to tell? She's a lovely young woman."

"I mean, did she say anything about me?"

"Spoke about you all the time." Sylvia looked up at the waitress hovering over the table. "I'll have a ham sandwich."

"The same."

"Spoke about getting married, how different it all was out here, the usual things."

"I should have gone back sooner, to Boston. Probably be married by now. What I'm saying, Sylvia, is that she isn't the same Megan I knew back there."

"May I voice an opinion?"

He shrugged over the rim of his cup.

"She's out of her natural environment, and for what it's worth, Sean, awful immature. Perhaps she isn't ready for marriage. Which brings up the question, are you?"

"You would have made a wonderful lawyer."

"Perhaps I'll be one someday."

"Immature; she's that. Marriage is something sacred, and to be honest, Sylvia, it does make one sit back and think. But what you're driving at through all of this is do we love one another."

"People fall out of love, Sean."

"You both live at the same hotel. Is . . . well, is there someone else, as Megan rarely mentions any preparations for the wedding. She's been somewhat elusive of late, too, about going out."

"I haven't been keeping tabs on her, so to speak. Maybe the culture shock of being out here has been too much. She might want to go back home." Sylvia knew that to mention the name Tyler Echohawk would serve no purpose, that by doing so would hurt Sean. "She's very lovely, and you have to admit, a lot of young men around here have been taken by Megan."

"Very lovely," murmured Sean as their food arrived. "You said fall out of love. On reflection, if I had loved Megan so deeply, I would have gone back a long time ago to claim her. I knew even back in Boston she needed to grow up more. But love . . . perhaps, as I search my soul, Sylvia, I didn't truly know the inner Megan Randsley."

"Quoting Hume: 'Beauty in things exists in the mind which contemplates them.' "

"Reckon her beauty has been held captive in my thoughts. You'll be at the rally?"

"Of course, Mr. Fitzpatrick."

But will Megan? mused Sean, a thought he carried with him throughout the afternoon. He left his office around six o'clock, making his way to the house he'd rented over on Third Street. The housekeeper he retained on a part-time basis had been in earlier in the day, the note he found in the kitchen telling Sean she'd left some fresh vegetables. After a change of clothing, he took the six block walk back to the downtown sector.

Another promise, and one that he'd halfway honored by contacting a rancher acquaintance, was to purchase some horses broken to the saddle. He'd discussed with Megan their going out and staying a weekend at the ranch, and at the time she'd agreed wholeheartedly. "Now, I'm just lucky if I catch her in," he mumbled under his breath.

Coming onto Center Street, the sight of Sheriff Lon Echohawk entering a saloon brought Sean in the same direction. The fact that Echohawk had publicly endorsed his efforts to become mayor meant a lot, as did a friendship that was becoming stronger. Pushing through the batwings, he found a space next to the sheriff, who was standing at the bar. "Drinks are on me," he said. "How's the shoulder?"

"Supposed to get this sling off most any day now. Obliged, too."

"Sorry there's been no word about Barney Cleever."

"I heard he was spotted in town earlier today. Just between us, counsellor, I haven't braced Tyler about this."

"Expect you've got your reasons."

"One reason is I want to hear what Cleever has

to say first. That'll mean a ride over to Bessemer Bend." He gazed at the back mirror, which reflected the action at the tables. "Had to ride out east on law business yesterday. Won't be long, less'n a month, before the railroad reaches town. That should see your business picking up."

"I'm busy enough as it is."

"You stand a better'n average chance of being mayor."

Sean declined the offer of another drink, then both of them swung away from the bar, as did everyone there when the batwings were flung open and in came the editor of the *Wyoming Derrick,* waving some newspapers. Excitement had flushed Milt Sundby's face as he shouted out, "Boys, Casper is no longer a part of Carbon County." He began handing out newspapers to eager hands, thrusting one at Sheriff Echohawk. "This special edition of the *Wyoming Derrick* is free, as we've been freed by Governor Moonlight's decree."

Lon Echohawk swung back around to lie the paper on the bar top as others crowded in. Below the banner headline and wedged between columns of print was a map detailing the limits of land torn away from Carbon County.

"Seems we've got three months in which to hold a special election and get our house in order," commented Sean.

"After which I'll be heading back to Rawlins." In Lon was this sense of unease, mingled with frustration and maybe a bit of anger. All along this was what he'd wanted, but with the men responsible for these murders behind bars. The special election would see a new sheriff elected, he mused, his worry that it would be a man without any experience. The way this town would expand even before the election occurred, it wouldn't be the most envious place to pack a badge.

"Lon . . ."

"Oh, sorry, just ponderin' over what this'll mean. To the rally. I reckon, Sean, I could show up later this evening."

Turning to push the sawdust out from under his polished boots, Sean Fitzpatrick had a smile for all the excitement the presence of the *Wyoming Derrick* was causing. He exited the saloon, going north along the boardwalk through the darkening shadows of dusk. Though he was elated over the governor's decision, this also meant that Lon Echohawk wouldn't be around anymore. "I suppose there's a penalty we have to pay for progress."

Then he set all of this aside, for across the intersection loomed the Wyoming Hotel, blinking out light from its lobby and a scattering of upper windows. A passing dray wagon blocked his access to the street, and when it trundled on, he became aware of the buggy idling on the side street and the couple who'd just come out the lobby door. The man got into the buggy first, bringing his hand back to help the woman up, with Sean breaking stride a little when he recognized Tyler Echohawk. When the woman loomed above the back of the buggy for a moment before dropping onto the seat close to Echohawk, all

Sean could mutter was, "Megan? . . . I don't believe this!"

What Sean viewed next was even more painful, as Megan placed a hand on Echohawk's shoulder and turned her head to receive the man's lingering kiss. As the buggy reined away to the west, Sean Fitzpatrick shuddered inwardly from the chill still gripping him. He didn't want to believe what he'd seen, yet there'd been the damning evidence of Megan snuggling in close and eagerly giving part of herself to Tyler Echohawk. Almost gropingly, he swung back to stumble up onto the boardwalk, like a blind man reaching out for something tangible to clutch.

"Damnit, if it weren't Echohawk, it would probably be someone else. Guess I've been deceiving myself that I really knew Megan Randsley."

Long after the rally and the dance following it had ended, Sean Fitzpatrick prowled the nighttime streets of Casper. From the more respected places that he'd gone in search of Megan Randsley and pouring down a lot more whiskey than was his habit, Sean had finally approached the Sandbar District. He was sober mad, the liquor seemingly having no effect on him, angry at himself for being played a fool, yet torn apart by the love he'd given the woman, as he now called to Megan.

"Caveat emptor!" he shouted out loud to the dark and unlit street, and to five cowboy hats bobbing under dark silhouettes passing by. "Let

209

the buyer beware," Sean muttered to himself. "That woman is spoiled goods . . . but damnit, it hurts, damned if it doesn't!"

He wasn't here with the intention of trying a woman lurking in one of the cribs, but rather to find Tyler Echohawk, as he'd heard that Echohawk often came into the Sandbar to indulge in his pleasures. A man, he threw out inwardly, who'd take a two-by-four to someone would treat a woman the same way. In a shambling walk, he turned yet another corner of a narrow street, lights from a saloon he'd been in before beckoning to him from the far end of the block.

"That you, Mr. Fitzpatrick?"

"It be me, Mr. Town Marshal, sir. I'm in search of another gent packing one of them tinny badges—Tyler Echohawk."

"Awful late to be out, past two o'clock. But Echohawk . . . seems to me he's got lodging at the Chandler Hotel. Couple of blocks away . . ."

"Obliged, Mr. Town Marshal, sir. By the way, when I'm elected mayor, I'll damn well see they get streetlights out thisaway. G'night."

Sean swung around and made his way back to the east, until he was nearing the Chandler Hotel. He could make out the dim shape of a buggy parked along a side wall, but the horse that had pulled it was gone, all of this conclusive evidence to him that his quarry was in the hotel. Sean crossed the threshold and approached the night clerk, who was stoking a wood stove.

"Does Tyler Echohawk have lodging here?"

"Yes?" the clerk stammered as he spun around

to add, "You sort of snuck up on me. "Yes, Mr. Echohawk is in his room."

"Is he alone?"

Hesitation crawled across the night clerk's face.

He grabbed the man's shirtfront and said hotly, "I expect Mr. Echohawk had a woman with him . . . about this tall . . . auburn-haired?"

"She . . . she went up with him, yessir . . . sometime ago, maybe two hours ago . . . yessir . . ."

Letting go of the man's faded shirt, Sean Fitzpatrick sighed heavily and turned away. He recrossed the threshold, coming in under the porch to hold for a moment while he gathered his thoughts. Gone was the bitter anger over being betrayed by Megan. Ebbing away was this image of Megan he'd carried around ever since coming out here, even though the sadness of the here and now were almost more than he could bear. She's a temptress for sure, Sean mused, placing one boot in front of the other, sobered by being confronted with the truth about Megan Randsley.

"Caveat emptor, Echohawk, caveat emptor . . ."

Thirteen

Once again Lon Echohawk was in the district judge's chambers facing that worthy's wrath. Only this time there was a third party in attendance, oilman Nathan Fry. Now that the sheriff had finally arrived, the oilman had worked himself up into a fine rage, the gist of which was his accusing every damned lawman in Carbon County of violating a sacred trust.

"You've let word get out about Crown Oil's oil interests up at Salt Creek," Fry raged on. "How else do you explain, Echohawk, every man jack in these parts rushing over to the land office? We're being sealed off up there, and Judge Childress, Crown Oil doesn't like it. We might start litigation pro—"

"Simmer down," the judge said in a loud and heavy voice, which seemed to sway the window curtains behind his desk. "As I recall and surely you remember, Mr. Fry, this same betrayal of trust happened when Echohawk went over to bring back that prisoner. I resent, too, Fry, the accusations you people have made against this court. Damnit, I should hold you in contempt."

"Your Honor, a lot is at stake here," Fry tried to explain.

"Sheriff Echohawk almost got killed in the line of duty," snapped Childress. "But we agree, the both of you, that we're being sold out by some Judas. What about your associates, Mr. Fry? Are all of them trustworthy? Never mind, I don't want you gettin' a heart attack on my account. But I can promise you I intend gettin' to the bottom of this. Fry, you mentioned the railroad gettin' in a lot sooner than anticipated."

"Once they hammer that last rail into place here at Casper, Judge Childress, a special train will pull in with Crown Oil equipment. We have local carpenters putting up warehouses to hold all of this."

"I see," said Echohawk, "they're also getting timber ready to form derricks."

As Fry put on his hat, the oilman gave Sheriff Echohawk a cold glance, declaring, "I anticipate there'll be a lot more trouble in the days ahead. But believe me, Judge Childress, it won't be because of Crown Oil."

Both Sheriff Echohawk and the judge looked at Nathan Fry as he departed, then Childress went over and closed the door, telling Lon to sit down alongside his cluttered desk. Childress moved around the desk to gaze out a window, then he turned back and asked, "What have you got?"

"A lot of claims that have been filed were by men working for a local land company. Though

Fry didn't say so, these claims pretty much tie up the Salt Creek Oil Field. I expect Crown Oil'll have trouble getting in there when they get to drilling, as there aren't any roads going from Casper to that oil field."

"No public accessway," grunted Childress. "Knowing the oil business, there could be a shooting war."

"Right now the Golden West Land Company has its agents up in that general area trying to buy out homesteaders and ranchers. Found out a man named Lundahl owns this land company, or seems to own it. Lundahl's got strong ties to Bessemer Bend, in the form of Hap Fleming."

"Yes, his name comes to mind. A pompous ass, as I remember. Now, Sheriff, have you figured out how all of this ties in with the murder of that railroad man Colhour?"

"Somewhat, as I suspect it all comes down to working capital. I've checked over at the land office. Found out that Fleming's interests weren't only in selling land to homesteaders. What he's been doin' is buying up mineral rights at other oil fields."

"Selling land to homesteaders isn't all that profitable.

"Fleming generally uses strong-arm tactics to get what he wants, according to what I found out. Another thing is that Fleming and local saloon owner Rafe Bascome are thick as fleas on a saddle blanket. Could be Bascome is bankrolling some or all of this."

"I don't see how these small operators think

they can squeeze out Crown Oil. No, Sheriff, all of this still doesn't come close to pluggin' that leak."

There were more things Lon Echohawk had refrained from revealing to Judge Childress. Chief among these were Lon's worries about his brother Tyler. He still hadn't received a return letter from their parents living out in Oregon, and in a way, it was with the premonition any such message would contain bad news. The two-by-four he'd found in that lumberyard Lon had secreted away, so neither his deputies nor Tyler could stumble across it. What he wanted when he left here was to ride over to Bessemer Bend, as he'd found out about Barney Cleever's coming in to Casper with Hap Fleming and then heading back the same day. To this end he'd sent Hack LaVoy over to Bessemer Bend on a scouting mission, LaVoy discovering just where Cleever was holding out. Once he had Cleever's side of the story, then he would confront Tyler.

"I see you've gotten rid of that sling."

"Shoulder's still a little gimpy, but I'll manage."

"Now," said the judge as he claimed his chair behind the desk, "Moonlight has signed that county decree. Which gives us three months to clean this mess up."

"I'll try to oblige you."

"You could get killed in the process. Burying you would cost the county a lot of money. So watch your backside, Echohawk."

* * *

Crossing that log bridge over the North Platte River brought anger into Lon Echohawk's eyes. He could almost feel the presence of slain bookkeeper Joseph Baldwin crying out for vengeance. Through the bitter chord of remembrance the wind picked up, and Lon ducked away from the gust eddying up from the gravel road.

Just uphill lay the new settlement of Bessemer Bend. Situated as it was on the crown of a long stretch of hill and not sheltered down closer to the river, he was doubtful that it would survive for any length of time. Which raised the question: Perhaps that was what its founder had in mind all the time?

That founder being the notorious Hap Fleming. Cantering along the upsloping road, more buildings came into the range of his vision, new ones, he noticed, and lots had been staked out toward the outskirts of Bessemer Bend. Backgrounding south of town was an oil derrick. He recalled having seen an advertisement in a Casper paper, which had been placed there by Hap Fleming's land company. COME TO WYOMING'S NEW OIL METROPOLIS. Judging from the lack of activity around the derrick, it was just another dry well, as was Bessemer Bend.

Lon didn't ride in but rather skirted the town, as did most cowhands upon leaving Casper and heading back to the home ranch. Deputy Sheriff Hack LaVoy had told him to look for a place about two miles out, down close to where the river formed an oxbow to the east. He would have ridden his bay out here, but it had a more clippy gait than the grey he was astride. Even so, Lon felt the stiffness settling into his shoulder. Before leaving he'd doctored his shoulder with liniment and was vaguely aware of the acrid stench clinging to his shirt.

By force of habit, he drew up just short of where a worn trail would give him access to the lower parts of the slope, easing out his six-gun to check the loads. Leathering his gun, he surveyed the few buildings stretched along the riverbank and then pinpointed what LaVoy had described: a large pile of wood stacked against a greying shed, the house a sod-roofed affair with the front door facing riverward, and the fact that Barney Cleever forked a claybank.

"The claybank's there . . . and two other hosses."

He detected movement, which turned out to be some chickens pecking away in the barren dirt yard surrounding the buildings and a mongrel dog lifting a hind leg to lick at its testicles. Either manner of varmint, mused Lon, could sound the alarm, even though it wasn't his intention in coming here to arrest Barney Cleever.

But here's what Sheriff Lon Echohawk had suspicions about . . . that Cleever had killed that cowhand, Easton. The body they'd found in the lumberyard was part of it, along with the fact that Cleever had been there when it had happened. The bookkeeper had probably been more of Barney Cleever's handiwork.

He ruled out Cleever being involved in the death of Martin Colhour, however. That was a job handled by professionals, imported and not locals. He affirmed this after bringing in for questioning such known criminals as Driftwood Jim McCloud, Tom O'Day, horse thieves Kid Anderson and Dad Young, chivalrous bandit Bill Carlisle, and Otto "Gentleman Horse Thief" Chenoweth, among others. What Lon feared most of all was that these imports could still be hanging around until the need arose to use them again.

"Those bucking Crown Oil, for instance," Lon spoke out loud.

On the flats across the river, a horseman came around a bend in the road. Closer, he could be discerned as a homesteader aboard a horse wearing a work harness, the leather tracers hooked up to metal ringlets, with blinders attached to the bridle. The patch of ground containing the flats extended the two miles to where Casper Mountain humped back to the east. When the homesteader disappeared behind the scrub trees guarding the bridge, Lon eased his bronc closer to where the trail began cutting down the slanted edge of the hill. About halfway down he lost sight of the buildings where Cleever was holed up, but he'd noted there was mostly open ground along the river road and the lane passing into the corral.

Down by the river the dirt road was soft, as it was firming up from a recent rainfall, the bronc splashing through drying puddles, birds chirping pleasantly in cottonwoods and flitting amongst the brush. Then he got a clear glimpse of the buildings and the two men emerging from the cabin and heading the short distance to the corral. Keeping his horse to a walk, Lon moved onto the lane. One of the men in the corral had swung into the saddle when he spotted the incoming rider, what he yelled echoing past Lon and toward the riverbank.

"Hey, Barney, you've got company."

Lon Echohawk pulled up by the woodpile, holding to the saddle when a big man came out to fill the doorway of the cabin. Barney Cleever had his left hand wrapped around the neck of a whiskey bottle and malice beamed out of his eyes. Malice that was directed at the badge pinned to Lon Echohawk's shirt. He was unarmed, just standing there and glaring, as if that and his immense size would see this lawman turn tail. A double-bladed axe was propped against the wall next to the open door. The mongrel hadn't barked but was just baring its fangs and growling, and it was bothering Lon's bronc.

"Easy," Sheriff Echohawk said as he sized up Barney Cleever. There were still black marks streaking away from Cleever's left eye. A jagged line curled up from his chin, and Lon could make out the faint stitch marks. Something glinted on the hand that held the bottle. A ring of some kind, Lon reckoned, and he snapped out, "Cleever, I want a word with you."

The one called Trammel stood in the corral, weight down with all that whiskey he'd had beginning at sundown last night and continuing until now. The man with him had climbed into the saddle with some difficulty. He was one of Hap Fleming's land agents, and drunk as he was, he smelled danger in all of this. He just wanted to get the hell out of this corral and make tracks back to Bessemer Bend.

"That's Sheriff Echohawk," he muttered softly to Trammel, who merely threw him a sneering grin.

In the doorway, Barney Cleever brought the bottle to his mouth and gurgled down the rest of the whiskey. Then he flicked the bottle toward other garbage littering the hard-packed ground and snarled, "I ain't got nuthin' to say to no bastard of a lawman."

"You heard him," piped up Trammel. "Make tracks outta here or go for that water pistol you're packing."

The planes of his wind-scoured face tightening, the sheriff of Carbon County nudged a spur at the flank of his bronc to swing it sideways some more. He knew Cleever wasn't packing any weapon other than those rock-hard fists. The one astride the grain-fed horse was Ed Ansley, out of Colorado and wanted for trying to rob a Wells Fargo office. The wanted said Ansley had tattoos running down both arms.

"They call you Craze Trammel," Lon said flintily. "There's a heap more AKAs you go under. I won't bother to cite your crimes, Trammel, only to inform you—and you, too, Ansley—you're under arrest."

"Like hell you ugly sonofa"—Trammel had managed to drag out his Smith and Wesson Schofield and hold it down so it was concealed by his shaggy coat. He brought it up in one swift motion, knowing he was about to kill a lousy county sheriff.

When Trammel made his move, his first shot went wild. He was thumbing back the hammer on his revolver, Ansley trying to control his horse and at the same time get out his pocket gun, when Trammel received a snap shot from the gun of Lon Echohawk. The bullet entered Trammel's mouth and exited through the back of his head. But Echohawk wasn't aware of this, only of the hard case toppling down, for Ed Ansley was bringing up his handgun. At the same time, Echohawk caught a corner-of-the-eye glimpse of Barney Cleever springing over to grip the double-bladed axe. Even as Echohawk punched two slugs in the direction of Ansley, the axe thrown by Barney Cleever thudded blade first into the woodpile just to the sheriff's left, and his horse reared up and spun around in a tight circle. He was holding the reins with his left hand, but the sudden jarring motion of his horse caused him to let go and he pitched out of the saddle. He landed heavily, winded, aware of Cleever rushing in.

Lon Echohawk managed to scramble up still holding on to his Colt, but with Cleever looming over him and just about to fling a large right fist. Desperately, he kicked out with his boot, the heel of it slamming into Cleever's kneecap, to have the intended blow miss by inches as Cleever groaned in pain and tumbled down, grabbing at his knee and cursing.

"You damned Echohawks . . . damn you!"

Spinning around, Lon Echohawk zeroed in on

the corral, sagging in relief when he saw that Ed Ansley was down. He turned back, drawing air into his lungs around a painful grimace. "What about us Echohawks?"

"Nothing, you damned starpacker, go to hell."

"Raw hamburger looks better than your ugly face, Cleever. So tell me, did you have a fight with one of my deputies?"

Cleever made a move as if to rise, but held there as Echohawk thumbed back the hammer on his revolver.

"Hold up your left hand. That ring . . . I'll bet it's gouged out flesh from more than one man. Say a cowhand named Easton. You were there, Cleever, don't deny it."

"Cowhands are a dime a dozen out here. If you wasn't holding that gun—"

Viciously, he slammed the gun at Cleever's head, and the burly man folded over. Then still gripped with pain, Lon Echohawk went over to the corral. One quick glance told him both men were dead. With a look in Cleever's direction, Echohawk moved out of the corral and went toward the house. Inside, it was just the two rooms collecting dust and littered with Cleever's belongings. On the unlit stove lay a pair of saddlebags that he rummaged through. Then he checked out the few drawers in a cupboard, coming up with nothing that could incriminate Barney Cleever.

The stench in the place getting to him, he hurried outside to find Cleever stirring and trying to rise. Lon's horse had settled down, and he came up to it without the animal shying away. Unstrapping his canteen, he drank from it as he turned to Cleever, who was gaping up at him. Stepping close, he turned the canteen upside down and let warm water trickle over the man's head. Cleever took it, his muscles tightening but otherwise letting the sheriff of Carbon County have his way.

"That should cool you down. Both Trammel and Ansley are dead. You're gonna load their bodies on their horses, then saddle up yours, as you're under arrest."

"When you opened up, I was just defendin' myself. You got nothin' on me."

"I figure enough to see you do some skydancing. You're awful damned stupid, Cleever. I figure you were involved in three killings, maybe more."

"I won't even be in jail an hour before I'm bailed out."

"There won't be any bail, Cleever. Just you in a cell and some river rats. I know all about Hap Fleming's operation. His turn comes next. Now get a move on before I bust your other kneecap."

Entering the corral, Echohawk picked up the weapons lying on the ground, checking to see if there were any rifles or other weapons stowed in saddlebags. He stood watching as Cleever strapped first one body then the other over the backs of the horses. Then, saddling his, Barney Cleever climbed into the saddle and rode just ahead of Lon Echohawk down the lane.

"I hear someone worked you over with a two-by-four, Cleever."

"You're so damned smart, you figure it out."

"Deputy Sheriff Tyler Echohawk, so I've been told. Well, was it him?"

There was no response from the man, but Lon Echohawk already knew the truth of it, knowing also he would have to brace Tyler as soon as he got back to Casper.

Fourteen

At first Cap Bentley wasn't at all certain they needed to hire on cattle rustler Mo Baxter. After all, they had maps provided by Tyler Echohawk of much of the area around the Salt Creek Oil Field. What changed Cap's opinion, and mighty fast, were the vast number of creeks meandering through the plains of central Wyoming. Out on a hot summery day one looked the same as another. But not to Mo Baxter, the outlaw able to pick his way through this labyrinth of waterways even at night.

What Cap Bentley hadn't told the Haskell cousins and Olander was the exact truth about how Slater Moore had been killed. It still bothered him about Moore going down, as he'd been a good hand with a gun. But both Cap and Tyler Echohawk had agreed that a wounded man was a liability, considering all of them were wanted. Though Tyler was keeping a watch out, any day now wanted posters could arrive from back in Oregon. Cap still worried about this, as well as about their hanging in one place for too long a time.

He let what had happened to Slater Moore ebb away. Cap estimated they were about thirty miles due north of Casper, in more rugged land cut by jagged hills looming over prairie. The sage brush was thicker in low places, and long draws opened onto small valleys fed by creeks. Oftentimes they were able to make their way by guiding onto the Big Horns skying to the northwest.

Before leaving Casper, Cap Bentley had been given a list of names, along with specific instructions, from Tyler Echohawk. Their first stop had been around noon, back ten miles and a new log cabin and a patch of freshly plowed ground along a creek. The sodbuster had seen them coming in, leaving his cabin to hold them at bay under the barrel of his Winchester, figuring he had the edge. A clothesline laden with soggy clothing told Tyler Echohawk's enforcers there were at least three children and the sodbuster's wife hiding in the cabin.

The dialogue went about like this.

"You're Harlon Spivak?"

"Never mind who I am. This is the third crew's been out here pestering me. I'm tellin' you same's I told the others: I ain't selling the mineral rights to my hunnerd and sixty acres."

Bammity!

"Got him!" And Emmet Haskell's sneak draw had, a slug from his six-gun busting the rifle away from the sodbuster.

Next they'd brought the sodbuster into the cabin,

with Cap Bentley detouring over and lifting the axe away from the chopping block. He came in just as Mitch Olander had broken a loaf of freshly baked bread in half and started chomping away. Cap took note of the heat still emanating from the fieldstone fireplace, the woman hovering over her brood of crying younkers, while Sandy Haskell had this sarcastic grin in place. But not so Emmet, who jabbed his cocked six-shooter into the sodbuster's rib cage.

"You damned fool, you coulda' killed my hoss."

"Easy, Emmet," intoned Cap Bentley. He pulled a chair away from the table. "Sit down, Spivak. Emmet, holster that gun and find something to heat up, like that butcher knife over there."

One thing a life of crime had given Cap Bentley was a thorough knowledge of human nature. He knew that every man had a breaking point. Judging by his clothes, Spivak had just come over from Poland or another one of those Eastern European countries. He still had that defiant glare glued to his stubbled face. The man's wife, though, would come unglued in a minute if he were to slap her around. But Cap Bentley felt the sodbuster needed to be taught a lesson in how to welcome company. Reaching beneath the folds of his coat, Cap took out a folded sheet of paper. "I suppose it won't do no good to ask you to sign this, Spivak."

"No!"

Grimacing, Cap Bentley muttered, "Get him onto that chair . . . that's it . . . now stretch his right arm out on the table."

The woman screamed when she realized what Bentley intended to do with the axe.

But he paid her no mind, as hefting the axe with his right hand, he forced the sodbuster's fingers apart. A downward motion of Cap's wrist brought the needle-sharp cutting edge of the axe slicing Spivak's little finger away, with the blade gouging into the tabletop. Gaping at the blood spurting from his hand, Harlon Spivak added his unbelieving scream to that of his wife's. Sidling over to the fireplace, Cap grasped the wooden handle of the butcher knife. Ambling back, he brought the red-hot blade across the wound to cauterize it. Just for a moment there was the smell of burning flesh, and then Spivak's head lolled down to thud onto the table When they roused the sodbuster, it took him but a moment to sign the quitclaim deed.

Now as Cap Bentley rode behind Mo Baxter, bringing them out of the draw, he summed up his treatment of the sodbuster with a silent comment that losing a finger wouldn't cripple a man. And Spivak's wife will damn well make sure they pull out of these parts.

The next place they intended calling upon was of an entirely different nature. It lay about two miles away, as marked by chimney smoke lifting over a tree line. Coming onto an elevation, at a word from Cap Bentley, everyone reined up. They could see the way the home buildings of Toby Sinclair's small ranch were situated between the watery tines of two creeks, the main branch cutting across the floor of the valley. Reeds marked a large marshy area, where waterfowl were floating on a brackish green pond. It seemed peaceful enough to the men watching. But the report on Sinclair was of his deliberating killing one of the horses ridden by a Hap Fleming land agent.

"You said, Mo, there's just the pair of cowhands."

"Them and Sinclair and his wife. Time I came through here, she hazed me off with a shotgun. Mean and old and ugly as her husband. How do we handle it?"

"It'll be a lot easier if Sinclair's hands are out working cattle." Cap Bentley judged by the sun that it was around three o'clock. Plenty of time to handle this chore, then head up to a camping spot Baxter knew about, he figured. As for Sinclair's Double S Ranch, according to Tyler Echohawk, it took up a damned good chunk of the Salt Creek Oil Field. Cap didn't know about oil or how men could determine if the black stuff lay deep underground. Maybe by the varying rock formations encircling him. But if oil made him a lot of money, nobody like Toby Sinclair had better stand in his way. He'd been broke too long, had seen too many good years slide by from a prison cell.

Flatly, he said, "We just might have to take out Sinclair."

"His old lady'll still look ugly in widow's togs," laughed Mo Baxter. "Bedding her would be t'same as taking on a frog. Maybe, Cap, we kill her instead of Sinclair."

The Haskells were grinning but not Cap Bentley,

who was checking out through a field glass, what lay deeper in the valley. Mitch Olander wasn't all that amused by the raspy mannerisms of Baxter, though he couldn't help cracking a smile. It was in the high eighties and all of them were sweating, their horses not all that eager to move on.

"Well, we won't get the job done idling here." Bentley twisted in the saddle and thrust the field glass back into a saddlebag. "We went over it enough times . . . how we're to come in. All the same, if you have to open up, make damned sure it ain't where any of us are riding. How's that shoe, Emmet?"

"About the same, Cap. But when we pull in there, I'm swapping hosses."

Slyly, Sandy Haskell commented, "You mean hoss stealin' don't you?"

"Whatever," Emmet muttered, reining ahead.

They came in on the tree line and from there fanned out. Cap Bentley went in under the trees and held up on the far side in the shade. Closest to him was the rambling log house. A shed cut off his view of the main corral, beyond which were stacks of hay and a small barn. He had a feeling that the rancher was out working with his men, but then Cap heard the faint closing of a screen door. The rancher's wife came out from behind the house, carrying a small basket covered with a blue and white cloth. Bentley was all set to head on in, when the woman suddenly stopped, to bring a shading hand to her eyes. He realized she was taking note of a few birds winging away from scattered trees west of the buildings, then she continued along a path worn through grass spreading around the marshy area.

"Goin' berry picking?" Cap Bentley wondered as he rode toward the ranch buildings.

Ida Ruth Sinclair knew that something was out beyond the trees, either a coyote in search of prey or—and at this thought a frown lifted her thin eyebrows—it was some more of those troublesome land agents. Last Sunday she had celebrated her sixty-seventh birthday by attending church services over at Chimney Butte. The sermon the Reverend Scovil had preached was from the book of Corinthians, about neighbor loving neighbor. But Ida Ruth, a slim and erect woman of five seven with a coif of greying hair, resented the intrusion of these land agents more than she did the homesteaders starting to edge in on their ranch, realizing these sodbusters would scatter away once they'd had a taste of a Wyoming winter.

She reserved her greater worries for the man she'd married over thirty years ago. Though younger by two years, Toby Sinclair wasn't about to admit he could no longer handle a spread like the Double S. He couldn't see, as she and their friends could, just how fast he was aging. An iron-willed shrewdness had helped her husband wrest this place away from Indians and white interlopers. Now it seemed to Ida Ruth Sinclair that the kind and able man she'd married so many years ago had turned into a cantankerous old coot. There'd been no need for Toby to kill that land agent's horse. But that violent act had seen the pack of land-hungry men beating a track through the trees and away. After he'd dragged the dead horse over to the boneyard, Toby Sinclair had sought the sanctuary of the pond and his fishing rod.

She drew up again to just where the pathway began trickling down through the reeds to the small wooden dock. "Could be Gus and Emory heading in," she murmured questioningly. She took in the tree line to the south and around the northern bend, noting how the birds were still lifting away in too many places for it to be just a couple of riders. Beyond the trees and the encircling hills, not all that distant, lay the main trail heading up to KayCee. Sunbeams cloud-danced down from the lowering sun, a view that she never grew weary of. If Ida Ruth had taken the pains to gaze back toward the house, she would have called out to Toby that a stranger clad in a long, unkempt coat was drawing near. But, with a fretting hand lifting to brush away a lock of hair, she went down the path.

In the basket was a jar of lemonade and some homemade chocolate chip cookies, which were Toby's favorites. Before her lay the dock jutting out about eight feet into the pond, which was about three acres in size and held sway over the surrounding wetland. The boat Toby had made—had it been ten years ago?—was tied to one side. And there was her husband on a chair without legs, judging from his posture sort of nodding off, the rod held slackly in his hands. The old basset hound lay beside the chair on the hot planking of the dock, one ear cocked at her approach but otherwise making no effort to get up.

"The pair of you . . . lazy as all get-out . . . Toby, I brought something cold to drink."

Flexing his shoulders to drive the sleep away, Toby Sinclair squinted to the west. "From the looks of it, it'll be more of the same tomorrow."

"I see you caught some."

"Four; maybe two more and there'll be enough for the boys." Slowly, he pushed to his feet. Then he hooked the fishing rod to the chair, and when he turned to look at his wife, he found she was staring back up the pathway at the shoulders of a rider framed by the sky.

"Birds were really acting up," she said without looking at her husband. "I don't reckon he's by his lonesome."

"Appears," he said indifferently, scrunching his shapeless hat back to get at an itch along his hairline, "to be just another cowpoke lookin' for some free vittles. Toby was thinner than he'd been a couple of years ago, and somewhat lanky and slow-moving. But he had a dignified way of holding himself and of speaking. He stepped past Ida Ruth and came off the dock with the intention of going up the path, but held as the horseman keep easing on in.

"You be Toby Sinclair?"

233

The man's voice stung at his ears, and he replied back just as curtly, "Could be."

"I expect you are Sinclair," Cap Bentley said. From astride his bronc, he could see the four with him easing their horses along the reeds guarding the pond. Staring back at the rancher, a quick assessment told him Sinclair would be a hard nut to crack.

Whereas before Cap Bentley had been in a hurry to get this over with, just the smell of this wetland and the water rippling as a fish jumped had taken hold to slow his frame of mind. He envied the rancher having all this to himself, though this came without rancor. The presence of the waterfowl, some canvasbacks taking flight, brought back other memories as well. Some go a lifetime without having a setup such as this, he thought.

"I see you caught some—"

"Trout," responded Toby Sinclair. "Just what is it you want, stranger?"

"For one thing, to get paid for that hoss you shot."

"So you're one of them," said the rancher. "As from the looks of you, you ain't no lawman. I'll tell you as I told them others: Get the hell off my property!"

"Toby, look!"

He snapped his eyes to where his wife was staring, at one rider, then to his right around the pond to three others observing what was going on by the dock. Anger took hold of Toby Sinclair, despite the presence of his wife and the possible danger to her. The dog had come up to brush against his trousers and was sharing the rancher's feelings by snarling between barks. Somehow Sinclair got a grip on his temper, knowing he was in a bad spot as he'd left his rifle up at the house and wore no handgun.

"Awright, mister, speak your piece."

"You always this hospitable to company?" spat out Mo Baxter. He spurred toward the path, his teeth gritted in a mocking jeer. "You remember me, don't'cha, Sinclair?"

"Yup, now I do. Yup, Baxter, you're a lousy cattle rustler. Got no cattle on the home ranch. But I expect you thieves will take what hosses I've got in the corrals."

"What we aim to do, Sinclair, is palaver," Cap Bentley said pleasantly, as he swung down and ground-hitched his reins. The others came in now, crowding in on the pathway and dismounting. Bentley added, "Before you turned down a mighty fair offer for the mineral rights to your place, Mr. Rancher."

"I'll sell none of what's mine, damnit."

"Easy with the damnits, Sinclair, as I offend easily." He eased onto the dock creaking under his added weight, with Bentley lifting the cloth away from the basket the woman held clutched to her chest. He removed a cookie. "Freshly baked; you are a lucky man, Sinclair." Chomping on the cookie, he gestured with the hand that held it toward the small body of water. "Got all this, too. I've searched all my life, it seems, for a place like this. Or maybe my expectations of what I want are too high. Peaceful . . . way out from any town . . . game a-plentiful, too . . ."

"How about us gettin' some of them cookies?"

He turned slightly to glance at Mo Baxter. A smile split Cap's lips as he declared jestingly, "Thought you told us Sinclair's wife was a toothless old gnome. Seems pleasant enough to me, Baxter. Can sure cook, too. You see, Mr. Sinclair, if you want to keep on enjoyin' your missus's cookin', you'll have to sign this paper I packed along." His gaze went from the rancher to the woman, with a demanding hand taking the basket from her, which he tossed to Emmet Haskell who was just coming in on the dock. Now Cap Bentley produced a folded piece of legal paper. "This here paper, Sinclair."

"Never, you pack of thievin' wolves!" Toby Sinclair took a step that brought him to his wife, the dog hesitating, but before it could snap out at Cap Bentley, a savage kick to the animal's rib cage sent it spilling into the reedy water by the edge of the pond.

Palming his six-gun, Sandy Haskell let go a slug that drilled into the dog's head, the sudden report of the gun causing waterfowl to lift away from the pond. With a smile for his handiwork, Haskell claimed the basket. The cry of protest from Ida Ruth died in her throat as her attention swung back to the man in the shaggy coat, who was lashing out to strike her husband across the face. Though Toby Sinclair reeled, he managed to keep from crumbling to his knees.

He spat blood out of his mouth, then shouted, "Cattle rustlers or sneak thieves, you're all one and the same. You come in bunches, 'cause one of you by himself ain't even a man!"

"That mean you ain't signin' this paper, Sinclair?" Cap asked in a mild rebuff.

"Want me to work him over, Cap?"

"Be like tryin' to make honey out of hossshit. That boat gives me an idea." He stepped back a little to give him room to turn and look at Olander. "Mitch, you and Emmett shuck your gunbelts, as you're takin' Mrs. Sinclair for a little boat ride."

"Leave her out of this. Just leave us alone, damn you."

"Name's Cap Bentley, out from Oregon way. Same's the others, except for Baxter there. We're wanted men, Sinclair, for such heinous crimes as robbin' banks and gunnin' down unarmed men and a lawman or two." He drew his sidearm and brought the rancher a short distance away from the dock, but with them holding to the path as Haskell and Olander moved in to do Cap's bidding, forcing the woman into the boat. With the boat untied from its mooring and Mitch Olander handling the lone oar, it was brought out into deeper water, Olander ceasing to row when Cap lifted an impatient arm.

"Ida Ruth can't swim," protested Sinclair. "Please, why don't you people leave us alone. All my life I've lived in these parts. I—"

"I ain't interested in hearin' the sad tale of your life, Sinclair. But you'd better believe you don't

237

sign this here paper, your missus will soon lose hers."

"I'm enjoyin' this," chuckled Mo Baxter. "Only wish I was in that boat."

"See how she likes to drink pond water," Bentley called out. Now he brought the barrel of his gun nudging into the rancher's ear, as out in the boat Emmet Haskell forced the woman's head under the water, with her arms flailing and the boat in danger of tipping over.

"You inhuman monster," yelled Toby Sinclair.

Out on the pond, the pressure behind her head went away and Ida Ruth Sinclair came up coughing out pond water. "Toby, please, help me . . ." she cried out. Then her upper body was forced under the rippling surface of the pond again.

Cannily, Cap Bentley said, "This time I might let her drown. So you've got less'n a minute to keep this from happening, you damned fool."

"Please, I'll—I'll do as you want." Without warning, he stiffened in the shock of what was taking place, his mouth forming an O of surprise and kind of choking, as if his wind had been cut off. He clutched at his chest, but just for a moment, the eyes of Toby Sinclair going to those of Bentley's one final time. And then the rancher sank down onto the path to lay eerily still.

"Sinclair . . ." Cap Bentley stooped down quickly, with a quicker glance spelling out that the rancher was dead of a heart attack. "The woman! Emmet, give her some air."

Emmet Haskell knew even as he brought the

woman's head out of the water that something was wrong. Cradling her upper body in his arms, he took one look at her face, and then he shouted across the water to the others, "Damned if she didn't up and drown on us."

Fifteen

"Luck's still holding," muttered Tyler Echohawk from where he stood staring down at a bunch of wanted posters spread out on the desk. One in particular held Tyler's attention. He picked up the wanted and smiled at the drawing of himself, the big bold letters beneath it stating that whoever brought in Tyler Echohawk could claim five thousand dollars. Every morning he'd assumed the chore of going over to the post office and picking up the mail. Now he lifted the lid on the potbellied stove and dropped the reader onto burning hunks of wood. He did the same to the readers out on Cap Bentley and the others.

Replacing the lid, he set the coffeepot on the stove top to let it heat. Fatigue was etched on Tyler's face, caused by his trying to juggle all he'd undertaken. Ramrodding that surly bunch hired by Hap Fleming to prowl the territory buying up mineral rights was part of it. Lately, Fleming had been acting like a caged puma, fuming about these oil derricks being put together and the lack of men hereabouts qualified to drill for oil, as well as his being tied up some with this battle still going on about which town would become the new county seat. Tyler had stood aloof from all of this, having last seen Hap Fleming about a week ago. One happy note had been Tyler's stumbling upon the connection between Fleming and Councilman Rafe Bascome, which Tyler braced Fleming about. Out of it had come more money for Tyler Echohawk, along with the news that Fleming would soon cease all operations over at Bessemer Bend.

"Fleming's damned well suckered that town," Tyler muttered aloud.

He found a cup on a side table and poured some coffee, the steam rising from it bringing him back to late last night and the fog ghosting in along the river. Through a smile he sipped from the cup, for he'd been out with Megan Randsley. It seemed he couldn't get enough of her, as of someone craving opium. She was just as willing to have him spend the night at her hotel or his. In a way he had expected to be confronted by Sean Fitzpatrick, something that hadn't happened. As for Megan, it appeared the lawyer was a part of her past now. Footsteps sounding in the back cell block area swept his smile away.

A naked worry flared in Tyler's eyes. The charge brought against Barney Cleever had been the attempted murder of a peace officer. The circuit judge had proclaimed that Cleever would not be released on bail. Ever since his arrest, the ex-prizefighter had maintained a stoic silence. But whenever Tyler Echohawk had gone back into the cell block, he'd seen the hatred stamped on Barney Cleever's face. Tyler wasn't sure if this had been noticed by the other deputies or by the sheriff. It rankled him, too, that he was only allowed into the cell block when another lawman was present. Did Sheriff Echohawk know about the fight he'd had with Cleever? Perhaps he did, from the stories circulating around the saloons.

"But lately, Lon's been kind of . . . distant."

In that shoot-out over at Bessemer Bend, two men had been gunned down. As far as Tyler knew, the dead men hadn't been tied to Hap Fleming's operations. But close at hand was Barney Cleever, someone in on the ground floor from the beginning. Can't take the chance of Cleever going to trial. It might be that the friendship between Barney Cleever and Hap Fleming went back a long way, but commencing with his arrest, Cleever had become a liability. Vaguely, Tyler Echohawk considered how he'd cold-bloodedly killed Slater Moore. Slater had known the risk, he mused, and young as he'd been had never expected it to happen that way. Whereas Cleever was a crafty old river rat, a breed that took a heap to kill.

"Prisoners are restin' easy," proclaimed Raleigh Carr as he closed the door leading into the cell block. "I see you've fetched the mail again, Tyler."

"Nothing much there," he answered off-handedly. "Where's Lon off to?"

"Out investigating unsolved murders," Carr said politely but somewhat distantly. It was plain as dust roiling along the stagecoach road during a windstorm, this tension between the Echohawks. He hadn't formed an opinion about Tyler, but Carr did know the man liked to work by himself. This was something the other deputies resented. Carr knew that young Echohawk had stolen that lawyer's woman. He eased down behind the desk while flicking a glance at Tyler Echohawk strolling out onto the boardwalk. Then he set about the task of looking over the mail.

Through the settling dusk, Tyler Echohawk could make out a man he knew slouched against a support post in front of the Chandler Hotel. Tyler had gone to a back-street saloon to wile away the afternoon, and he'd gotten engrossed in a game of stud poker and poured down just enough to make him reckless. Still heavy on his mind was what to do about Barney Cleever.

"Didn't expect you back so soon, Cap."

"Way it goes sometimes. Let's find a place we can talk private."

"Not my room," scowled Tyler around his dangling cigarette. "Bar just down the street." He looked back toward Center Street before falling into step with Cap Bentley. "Trouble, huh?"

"Depends if they find that dog." Cap Bentley lapsed into silence until they were huddled around a bottle of whiskey at a back table in the saloon. Plainly, he told Tyler what had transpired out at the Double S Ranch. "Never expected that rancher to have a heart attack."

"Out by that boat and all, it'll appear both of

243

them drowned. Trouble is, Sinclair died before he could sign that paper."

"Got in couple of hours ago, at which time I paid a visit to the land office." He slid a hand under his coat, the folded sheet of paper he produced touching down by the whiskey bottle. "Pretty fair imitation of Sinclair's signature. Trick is to date this thing back a month or two."

"You old fox," grinned Tyler, shaking away the feeling of despondency. "This'll sure as hell please Fleming."

"Couple of more weeks at the most, we should be done with this business. Then I expect like you said, Tyler, there could be trouble between Fleming's wildcatters and the Crown Oil people."

"Crown Oil's got a helluva lot more muscle and money than we have. So far. That'll even up a heap when we bring in that first gusher. Now, what's to be done with Barney Cleever?"

Claiming his horse at the livery stable, Tyler Echohawk set it into motion along Second Street. He knew Hap Fleming wouldn't be at the Golden West Land Company offices, Tyler's hunch being that he'd find him down at the new warehouse built along the railroad right-of-way. That was another issue, the main line of the Fremont, Elkhorn, and Missouri Valley railroad being no more than ten miles from Casper.

He kept the bronc at an easy lope, but once the business places fell behind his gait picked up some, with Tyler leaving the rutted street for a lane cutting up north. Here surveyor's stakes marked out lots that were for sale. Three houses were under construction, all one-story dwellings with brick chimneys. He couldn't quite picture himself or Megan Randsley occupying any house as small as these, nor could he imagine her as a common housewife. As damn, about her was this wanton recklessness. When he'd first sighted Megan over at the stagecoach office, he'd known she was something else. But to let her get under his skin like this, to let any woman dominate his thinking for that matter, was something that could lead to trouble. Her face still sort of sticking in his mind, Tyler Echohawk wasn't aware that trouble was following him in the form of a horseman just turning onto the lane.

Less than a hundred yards to the north, warehouses and new holding pens formed a long line along the railroad right-of-way. The warehouse he sought was guarded by a high board fence shielding the activity within from passersbys. He headed that way, along a sort of road that had been gouged out by wagons laden with building material. Lumber piles loomed on either side. Most of the warehouses were still under construction, and he knew more would be erected once the railroad came in. He'd never been part of a boomtown before, and in Tyler was this sense that he would become an important part of things to come.

As he approached the main gate, a man with a gunbelt strapped around his waist came out of a shack and threw Tyler a casual wave. "Sorry, but no visitors allowed."

"I'm not exactly here for the pure pleasure of it."

"Oh, yessir," the guard muttered as Tyler Echohawk thrust his vest aside to reveal the badge pinned to his shirt. "You here to see Mr. Barkley on some law business." The guard threw the bolt and swung the gate open, receiving no response from Deputy Marshal Echohawk as he rode on in.

Tyler had been here just the one time, after the workers had gone home, when he'd conferred with geologist Cyril Barkley, Ole Lundahl, and Hap Fleming. A lot more had been done in the sections of derrick stacked around the large yard encircling the warehouse. He could see at least twenty workmen moving about, but his interest was centered on the geologist just emerging from the warehouse, and Tyler spurred that way. Farther along the side wall of the warehouse stood a black surrey that belonged to Hap Fleming. "Seems you're really going to town here," Tyler said over the din of saws cutting into pine and the more solid thud of hammers.

"The place is a madhouse," agreed Barkley as he turned and shouted an order to a passing worker. He turned back and framed a wry smile. "You here to see Mr. Fleming?"

Nodding, Tyler slid down to move on, until he came up to the surrey, where he tied the reins around a wheel spoke. He went back and followed Barkley into the warehouse, which was starting to fill up with drilling equipment. "How tough has it been to get this stuff shipped in here?"

"An impossible task at times. All of it by wagon trains. The railroad . . . you know Crown Oil has a say in what they freight in here."

"I reckon competing with that oil company won't be easy. But once we start drillin' and hit oil, things'll damn well change."

"What Fleming keeps assuring me," said Barkley as he gestured to a small corner office. He started to say something else, then a wave from a worker carried him away.

"Worries too damned much," grunted Tyler. He followed a rap on the open door into the small office, where he found Hap Fleming sipping from a flask of whiskey and peering down at a blueprint.

"Echohawk, is something wrong?"

"Got good and bad news. The good is that we've obtained mineral rights to Sinclair's spread. No, no whiskey. Some of the bad is that Sinclair and his wife are dead."

"Couldn't have been handled any other way?" Fleming snapped.

"I expect it could have," Tyler retorted heavily. "It was made to appear as if they'd drowned." He went on with some sketchy details of what had happened. "Remember, Hap, Crown Oil had their agents out in that oil patch too. They wanted Sinclair's place even more than we did. But thanks to Cap we've got it, and some more lined up."

"Your man Bentley forging Sinclair's signature. Not dating that paper will help." The large man sipped thoughtfully from the flask, his eyes flicking from Tyler to a large topographical map adorning a wall. "Yes, we had to acquire Sinclair's place. At any cost. I'll find out if they had any children, close relatives. Possible Sinclair filed a will. But despite what happened, Tyler, I'm overwhelmingly pleased."

"When I left the office this afternoon, early on, nobody had come in to report what happened out there. But they will. The sheriff'll head out to investigate, and I'm hoping find no indication of foul play. What we can do, Hap, is to try smearin' Crown Oil's reputation. Have Cap claim to be workin' for Crown Oil next time he calls on a sodbuster."

"I like the idea. After all, nobody has much use for the big money boys."

"Which you hope to be shortly, Mr. Fleming. But it won't happen unless we do somethin' about Cleever."

"The rest of the bad news, Tyler?" Hap Fleming fluttered a hand as if in agreement. "What a stupid thing to do, open fire on a lawman. But Trammel was like that . . . dull-witted. If Barney had been alone . . . well, he's rotting in jail."

"So far he's clammed up."

"Maybe that beating you administered to Barney took the heart out of him. In any case, if I were to be brought to trial for attempted murder, I'd be looking for avenues of escape. Barney's sly as they come, Tyler. Along with that, he's rotten to the core inside."

"I reckoned he was your friend . . ."

"Business acquaintance, really. You can learn a lot about a man when he's in his cups. I wanted to visit Barney, but your brother the sheriff wouldn't allow it. We could get word to Barney that an escape attempt is in the offing. Which might serve to see he doesn't open up to the circuit judge about us, Deputy Echohawk."

"All the same, he's got to be killed."

"So be it." Hap Fleming drained the flask. "You will take care of that little detail, I expect."

"Personally. As I don't want any slipups. What about Ole Lundahl? He's one of your old bunch, too."

"I expect if you hadn't suggested this remedy, Ole would have, and probably done the job himself. Sympathy is for widows and orphaned children. And clouding up Crown Oil's reputation, that we'll do, Tyler." From an inner coat pocket, he pulled out a manila envelope. "You'll find five thousand in here."

"Obliged," said Tyler. "I'll pay my men. As for Cleever, that job'll be done free . . . gratis. Catch you later, Mr. Fleming."

When Tyler left, it was to ride along the rutted road going west. He had expected some opposition from Hap Fleming when he brought up his notion of getting rid of Cleever. "Should know different by now when high stakes are involved. To a man like Fleming, even you're raw meat, Echohawk. Meaning, I need some kind of insurance policy."

And to Tyler Echohawk, this meant availing

himself of the services of safecracker John Phillip Dandridge. "If Fleming is contemplating a move to Casper, it just might be he's already got some papers stowed at the Golden West Land Company. Pick it up, hoss."

Sixteen

Around two o'clock, rain poured out of clouds that had been coming in from the northwest. The rainwater came down slanting and cold, a reminder that fall wasn't all that far away. Only an occasional thunderclap could be heard, the front of the storm moving slowly over the higher ground guarding Casper to the north. At this hour only those seeking the pleasure of a saloon were out on the dark streets, the rain driving them to shelter. Even the pickpockets and thugs lurking in the Sandbar District had called it a night.

While the rain proved a curse to other petty thieves, it was the perfect cover for safecracker John Dandridge, slogging through the mud. He was wrapped up in a heavy raincoat and whistling tunelessly, his alert eyes sweeping ahead. Strangely enough, his thoughts were on Deputy Sheriff Tyler Echohawk. There was this feeling that Echohawk was about to pay him a visit.

"Rumors are that the new deputy sheriff has something goin' on the side. Somethin' damned big."

Ever since that chance encounter with Echo-hawk about month and a half ago, the safecracker had seen to it that a lot of Casper strongboxes had been examined as to their contents. City newspapers and the new town marshal kept saying this had to be the handiwork of a gang of safe-crackers. There'd been some close calls for Dan-dridge, but a long dry spell with the pasteboards was the chief reason he was out tonight and hom-ing in on the Stordahl Freighting Company of-fices.

Now he stayed closer to the buildings, to shuf-fle along a little slower. At a corner he cast a wolflike glance along Collins Avenue, which speared back toward the business section. It lay quiet and dark, but even so the safecracker held like a coyote, smelling out the way of things. He picked up on a few night sounds muffled by the downpour. Pushing on, he took in the buildings and large yard and corrals of the freighting com-pany. In the last couple of weeks, he'd drifted by to get acquainted with the layout. Some of the teamsters had boasted of how business had really picked up, and from one of the clerks he'd learned that a lot of ready cash was kept in a strongbox.

"Be a heap easier than takin' on a Hopkins' safe," he muttered, at the same time checking out both ends of the street.

The main office had its front entrance opening onto the street and set back in a recessed door-way. He came up on the steps and picked out a pry bar, before lowering the tool kit he carried onto the wooden porch. Quickly, he brought the flat blade of the bar in between the door and the frame, and with little effort the lock sprang open. Then he was inside and quietly closed the door.

He made his way back to a large office, and there as the clerk had told him reposed the strongbox. Closing the office door, he lit the lamp on the desk. There was in John Dandridge this faint sense of excitement that stirred his blood. It was mostly his anticipating just what the strongbox would contain, which might very well be enough money to help him get out of these parts. Money he'd spend lavishly until it was gone, as there would always be another safe to crack. Viewing the strongbox, he allowed a smile to crack through the stubble of beard.

"Be like openin' a sardine can."

Shrugging out of his coat, he shook the rain from it before dropping it on the desk. He rubbed his hands together and flexed his fingers to chase the chill away, then he hunkered down by the strongbox. Something began banging, and he paused to listen. Just the wind playing night tricks, he mused. From his tool box he removed a chisel and hammer and a thick piece of cloth, which he placed over the chisel to help deaden the sound. The age lines weaving across his thin face were deceptive. For under the unkempt clothing, corded muscles rippled across the chest and the wiry arm that plied the hammer. The flaw in John Dandridge was his lungs, about eaten away from tobacco smoke. He got winded easily, but what he feared most was that this freezing rain might cause a cold to settle in his chest.

Another source of worry was of his being caught and thrown into the same cell block as Barney Cleever. The reverberations from that gunfight over at Bessemer Bend were still a topic of conversation here in Casper. With Cleever's boss, Hap Fleming, going respectable, the safecracker figured he was a painful reminder of Fleming's crooked past. So if tonight's haul panned out, the next few days would see him hauling ass for Denver.

The lock fell away after another solid, soft-ringing blow from the safecracker's hammer. Carefully, he replaced his tools in the toolbox. From it he lifted out a folded leather pouch. An expectant grimace found him raising the lid on the strongbox.

"Glory be," he exulted, "greenbacks galore!"

He wasted little time in transferring the money to his leather pouch. Then with the pouch and his toolbox in hand, he blew out the lamp and let his eyes adjust to the darkness, while at the same time zeroing in on the sound of the wind. The banging noise had gone away, the wind picking up a lot, the rain still pounding away at the wooden roof. Now he scurried out of the office and frontward, squinting outside through the curtain lowered over the window in the door.

"Come on, old man," he scolded himself, "on a night like this, even the alley cats are holed up."

He eased outside, just as quickly wishing he hadn't when he found himself suddenly accosted by a pair of rain-slickered gunpackers.

"Well, Dandridge," muttered Sheriff Lon Echohawk, "I do hope you like the way we baited the trap." He held back as Hack LaVoy moved in and relieved the safecracker of his toolbox.

"The way it goes," John Dandridge said resignedly. "I ain't packin' any iron."

"I've heard that song before," said LaVoy. "Spread out and brace agin' that wall . . . stretch those arms out . . ." He brought his handcuffs shackling around the safecracker's wrists. Holstering his six-gun, he began checking the pockets for a weapon, finally declaring, "He's clean."

"You get lucky or what, Sheriff?"

"It was *or what,* Dandridge. We were tipped off to you by Barney Cleever. Just wonder how you'll like sharing the same cell." He motioned his prisoner out into the street, and after LaVoy picked up the toolbox, the three of them trudged eastward.

The safecracker had been a handful of names that Barney Cleever had grudgingly disclosed. Lon Echohawk knew the bunco-artist-turned-murderer was just buying himself a little time. As so far, Cleever had refused to discuss his relationship with Hap Fleming. It could be that Cleever expected to be busted out of jail by some of Fleming's hired guns. What Lon suspected strongly was that an attempt would be made to kill Cleever. Something that he'd come flat out and told the man, who'd scoffed in response. But he knew the seeds of doubt were eating a hole in Cleever's mind.

In the last week two events had taken place, the first when Lon was told of a tragedy that had occurred at a ranch north of Casper. One of the cowhands working for a rancher named Sinclair had ridden in to state that the man and his wife were drowning victims, with strong suspicions they had been murdered. A quick trip up to the Double S spread had revealed to Lon the evidence, in hoofprints spearing around the pond, that at least five horsemen had been there. He was told, too, that the week before Toby Sinclair had driven some land agents away at the point of a gun.

The other startling discovery had been revealed to him by a young woman he'd come to admire. Even before this, Lon had puzzled over Sylvia Valcourt's reason for hiring on at the Golden West Land Company. It just didn't fit her style to work as a clerk. Could be Sylvia was one of those eastern debutantes out here on a lark, he mused.

Reports had come his way of the heavy-handed methods employed by agents working for the land company. A lot of these accusations had come from Crown Oil's Nathan Fry. Lon just couldn't dismiss them, not when he knew Hap Fleming was involved. They were a team, he'd learned recently, Fleming and land company owner Ole Lundahl. So what Lon Echohawk had to do was to get at Lundahl's records in the hopes he'd turn up something. This was the reason he'd asked Sylvia Valcourt out to dinner.

"We came here that first time," murmured Sylvia as she gazed around the dining room in the Plainsmen's Club. She wore a western-cut jacket and a pensive smile.

"A lot has happened since then," remarked Lon as he lifted the spoon out of his cup. "One thing is that I won't be around here too much longer."

"Until you told me, I hadn't realized just how much territory lay under your jurisdiction."

"That's a lawyer's word."

"Yes . . . well, Lon, I believe a confession is in order. I am a lawyer; at least I was back east. Though I've yet to open an office."

His smile widening, Lon said, "You could put up your shingle and give Sean Fitzpatrick some competition. Casper, the way its growin', it'll need women of your caliber."

"Why, thank you, Sheriff Echohawk." Her eyelids fluttered down, and when her eyes centered across the table on Lon again, sadness radiated out of them. "Speaking of Sean, I feel he's been taken advantage of. By Megan Randsley. She's . . . capable of anything."

"I knew they'd split up," Lon commented.

"Did you also know that Megan and your brother are seeing one another?"

Lon absorbed this through a frown. "Though he's my brother, I can't excuse Tyler for what he's done."

"Don't blame him for this," she said. "Most of it is Megan's fault."

"That's what I've been told." He saw the questions dancing in Sylvia's eyes. How could he tell her that giving his brother a badge had been an error in judgment? Time and again he'd gone over the events of the past few weeks, back to when they'd been ambushed and Martin Colhour had been killed. It seemed that ever since then bad luck had been dodging their heels, as whoever was behind these killings seemed to anticipate Sheriff Lon Echohawk's every move. Only lately had he come up with enough evidence to convince him that his brother was a Judas starpacker.

He reached over and touched Sylvia's hand. When he spoke, it was with a soft urgency, "I have reason to believe the man you work for is involved in murder. To be honest, Sylvia, the reason I asked you to dinner is that I need your help. . . ."

Plainly, she said, "I expected this. Lon, please, you must understand. The reason I came out here was to find my father. Yes, I found him . . . and . . . and he gave me a job."

"Are you saying that Ole Lundahl is your father?"

"I've been deceitful about something else. Valcourt is my mother's maiden name . . . and that's another story. Yes, I found my father, he's Harold Fleming. And I know he's mixed up in all of this."

"He is deeply involved. Not only in murder, but in a lot of other criminal activities."

"Lundahl and Hap were partners in crime back

in New York. I have picked up on a few things at work, which I'll testify to in court. When I do, I'll also have to testify against your brother."

"I know that, Sylvia. Which means that both of us are going to get hurt. Would you know if Lundahl kept any records at the land company offices?"

"He keeps anything of importance in a safe in his office. Lundahl's a cautious sort. So it's highly likely he'll retain papers that could incriminate his associates."

"Just what role does Tyler play in this?"

"I'm not all that certain. But since Barney Cleever is out of it, I strongly suspect your brother is filling that role."

That night with Sylvia Valcourt faded away as Sheriff Lon Echohawk sidestepped the rainwater falling down a wooden spout into a barrel stacked in front of a building. But still remaining in his thoughts was that safe of Ole Lundahl's. Judge Childress had gone over to Cheyenne on territorial business, which ruled out his securing a search warrant. But he had the next best thing in safe-cracker John Dandridge.

"Hack?"

"Yeah, Lon?"

"Cell block's loaded with prisoners?"

"Yup, except for Barney Cleever having that cell to his lonesome."

"Guess that's it, Dandridge, you and Cleever being bunkmates." As they came onto Center Street and the dim confines of a streetlight, Lon took in the safecracker's face pinched with fear. "Unless—"

"Please, Sheriff, I'll tell you all I know about him . . . about Cleever and that Hap Fleming, but don't cast me in that cell."

"Here's the deal," snapped Lon Echohawk. "I reckon you're willin' to testify as to what you know about Fleming's operation. But that ain't enough, Dandridge."

"What else is there, Sheriff? I'll do anything . . . please."

"There's one more chore to tackle, Dandridge."

The sheriff of Carbon County never reckoned that as a lawman he'd have to break the law. Along with breaking and entering, Lon Echohawk could add aiding and abetting a crime to the list. Which were felonious charges he brushed aside when weighed against murder.

The rainstorm had long since chased away the heat of day, and it was cold in Ole Lundahl's office in the Golden West Land Company. They'd drawn the shades and lit a pair of coal oil lamps, with both lawmen soberly taking in the safecracker going about his business.

"Generally, I like to use nitro."

He stared at Dandridge's face covered with sweat and a lurking smile, and at the stick of dynamite the man held. "I reckon two things can happen: You'll either crack that safe open or blow us sky-high."

"Don't worry, Sheriff. I'll just wedge this stick

in that hole I bored. Used it dozens of times, so—"

"You confessing this to me?" chided Lon.

"Just sayin' I'm about the best around at this business of crackin' steel boxes. Just what do you expect to find in here, Sheriff?"

"Incriminating evidence, I hope."

"One thing is, that being Lundahl hired me to crack open a safe owned by Bascome . . . yeah, Bascome the city councilman."

"You're saying that Bascome could be mixed up in this?"

"Could be. You know, when you crack open a safe, sometimes it's the same as openin' a man's chest to get a peek at his heart, or gettin' a gander at some diary or private ledger. Yup, Sheriff, I've peered at the secret shames of a lot of so-called respectful folks. Or it could be like catchin' a man with his skivvies down." The safecracker cackled to show stumpy yellow teeth. "There, now, if one of you gents have a match . . ."

With the fuse sizzling behind him, the safe-cracker, Echohawk, and Hack LaVoy hurried out into the hallway to crowd along the wall. When it came the explosion was brief and violent, the earsplitting sound quickly dying away. Back in the office, Lon saw, to his relief, that though the safe door sagged open, the contents of the safe seemed to be untouched by the exploding dynamite. He turned slightly to look at LaVoy and the safe-cracker. "Hear anything?"

"Just the rainstorm," said LaVoy.

"Maybe our luck's holding." Lon turned back

and reached into the safe, to pass out piles of greenbacks tied together and some thick manila folders. Another item was a thick green ledger, which he lifted out and brought over to the desk. Easing down on the edge of the desk, with LaVoy opening a manila folder, the safecracker drawn closer by curiosity, Lon Echohawk began thumbing through the ledger. He realized that what he had was a daily record of activities penned down by Ole Lundahl.

"Hack, take a gander at this."

"T. Echohawk . . . five thousand dollars."

"The entries on this page are for the last Monday in July, as I recall, the day before we were ambushed on our way back from the railhead." Farther along Lon Echohawk came across his brother's name followed by a dollar amount. Angrily, he closed the ledger. He knew there'd be more entries involving his brother, and it was as though a heavy weight had descended on his shoulders. He let the names of those who'd been murdered chase away any loyalty he felt toward Tyler.

Heavily, he remarked, "How blind I was, Hack."

"We all were. Way I figure it is that Tyler is ramrodding this pack of hired guns. You know they'll come for Cleever, as sooner or later he'll realize tellin' what he knows just might keep him from the gallows."

"He's my only brother."

"Don't blame yourself, Lon."

"They say everyone's entitled to one mistake.

I've made mine. Tyler's was in coming here. If I have to remove that badge from a dead man, so be it, I reckon."

Seventeen

Deputy Sheriff Sy Hagen came awake when he realized somebody was rapping at the door. He threw the woolen blanket aside, rose from the cot, and picked up his six-gun from the desk. Bootless, he eased over to the front door, with a cautious look outside revealing the nighttime intruders were his fellow lawmen. He threw the bolt and swung the door open, declaring, "Must be three, four in the morning . . ."

"About that," said Lon. He set the ledger alongside the lamp on the desk. He lit the lamp but turned the flame down low, and then he shrugged out of his rain slicker. "Sy, I anticipate they'll make a try for Cleever just before sunup."

"You know something I don't?"

"Sorry to say it involves my brother. Seems Tyler is part of these killings."

From the land company building, Lon and Hack LaVoy had beelined over to their boarding house, where they'd roused Raleigh Carr. They'd left the safecracker shackled to the bed in Lon's room. Now Lon stepped past the desk and peered back through the window in the door at the cell block. There were four cells on either side of a narrow corridor, along with the barred back door. His prisoners consisted of Barney Cleever and two others, one arrested for fighting and the other a petty thief.

"Hack, release those other prisoners. And Sy, I want you to get dressed. I want one of you up on that building across the street."

"I'll tackle that chore," said Carr.

"Hack, you can hang out back someplace. I figure there'll be at least a half dozen with Tyler."

"I'll hang on in here, Lon."

"No, Sy, I was the one responsible for giving my brother a badge . . . you might say a license to kill." He glanced at Raleigh Carr lifting a Winchester out of the gun rack. Then Sy Hagen pointed to some paperwork on the desk.

"Picked up the mail late this afternoon. This letter's for you," Hagen told him.

Once his deputies had filed out, Lon Echohawk locked the front door and settled down tiredly behind the desk, where he opened the letter that had come from Oregon. He wore a tender smile as he gazed at his mother's familiar handwriting. The first few sentences went on to say his parents were in good health and enjoying the balmy Oregon weather. Following that came his mother's hesitant way of saying that Tyler had gotten into serious trouble back there—bank robbery among other things.

He lifted his eyes away from the letter in silent recrimination. Had he done his job properly by checking up on Tyler, some of these murders could have been prevented. His mother had left out the cold-blooded details of what Tyler had done back in Oregon. Maybe backshooting or worse, Lon mused. Dousing the flame in the lamp, he propped his feet on the desk and settled back in the chair in an attempt to get some sleep.

"If they do show up, am I up to gunning down my own brother?" he questioned himself.

There'd been an eerie silence after that last thunderclap, the horsemen hunched in their saddles as they came onto the bridge spanning the North Platte. Here shod hooves drummed a loping canto of urgency on the planking.

Tyler Echohawk was the first to clear the bridge. Although it was almost sunup, the rainstorm made it appear as if there were still a lot of night left. If anything, the rain was coming down harder through the mist that spilled away from the riverbank and obscured the riders. Despite the fact he hadn't been to bed, Tyler was in high spirits. For Barney Cleever was the last obstacle that would keep him from the riches he expected to acquire.

"Thick as I've seen it, Cap."

"To keep from being discovered, you know we'll have to kill any lawman keeping watch over the jail."

Tyler just grinned from where he was tucked into his rain slicker, his hat pulled low over his forehead and dripping water. "If it'll pain you all

266

that much, Cap, I'll do the killing, while you punch out Cleever's lights."

"That I can handle. You were right about this bein' better than robbing banks. I always hated those long rides afterwards, 'cause my lumbago sure gave me fits for days on end. You think Oregon'll double up on sendin' out wanteds on us?"

"Paper's cheap, Cap. But, no, there's a heap more out there than us breakin' the law. A few more months, I figure, and they'll forget about us."

"Mist ain't so thick amongst these buildings," Cap Bentley remarked. "Town's awful quiet, too."

"Graveyard-quiet is the way I like it," said Tyler, bringing his bronc to a halt opposite a mercantile store. Within the hour, he realized, some sunlight would come poking in to drive back the shadows. But that didn't ruffle him any as he spoke to everyone closing in. "From here we cut up Center Street. Me and Cap'll hold back a little to let you boys get in behind the jail. If anybody comes out the back door, drill 'em."

"By my watch it's about five-thirty."

"Too early for the drunks or early guzzlers or any lawmen to be up."

"What if the sheriff's keeping watch in there?" Emmet Haskell asked.

Every eye slid to Tyler Echohawk. "Any lawman is expendable, even my brother. Way I see it, he'd see me hang same's any other outlaw. Peel out now, but keep it nice and easy."

As the three with Emmet Haskell rode away, Tyler Echohawk began to calmly roll a cigarette

267

into shape. From a shirt pocket he came up with a dry match, which he used to light the tailor-made. Flicking the match away, he gazed at Bentley staring back at him. Amusement danced in Bentley's eyes at the way the slanting rain was hitting and soaking the cigarette. But he knew bravado was Tyler's way. Cap Bentley began to ride on now, trying not to think about what could go wrong.

They found Center Street as quiet as the Sandbar District had been, the mud muffling the sound of their passing horses. Alongside one another, they pulled in toward the jail battened down for the night. Force of habit brought their watchful eyes farther along the street, to the tops of nearby buildings and the gaps in between. Easing out of their saddles, they tied up their reins, and it was here that Tyler Echohawk ghosted ahead of Bentley onto the boardwalk, to stop under the overhanging porch. From the folds of his rain slicker he lifted out his six-gun and walked up to the closed door, with Cap Bentley slipping against the wall.

Tyler's heavy rap hit the door just below the barred window. "Hey, it's me, Tyler. Morning's just around the bend." He pulled his hand away at the faint response pouring through the door, thumbing the hammer back, teeth barred in killing anticipation.

Inside the jail, Lon Echohawk had dreaded the arrival of this moment. Strange, what cropped to mind was that long-ago time when he'd taken his departure from the wagon train. He blamed himself for what Tyler had become, believing if he'd gone on to Oregon, he could have been a stabilizing force in his brother's life.

Lon had found that he hadn't been able to sleep. It was while pacing to check out the street that he'd come up with the idea of unbolting the door, as he knew Tyler would be ahead of his men. Perhaps if he could get Tyler inside the jail, he could disarm him, since Lon really couldn't determine if he had the willpower to kill his own flesh and blood. The only trouble was it was as dark inside the jail office as it was out in the street, so even if he tried winging Tyler, it could prove to be a killing shot. Now he held back behind the desk, one hand wrapped around his Colt as he called out, "That you, Tyler? The door's unlocked."

He saw the door opening slowly, a vague shadow outlined in the doorway, then flame lancing from Tyler Echohawk's gun. And with bullets flying around him, the sheriff of Carbon County barely had time to duck behind the desk even as he opened fire. From outside came the heavier pounding of rifles answered by six-gun fire.

"A trap!" Cap Bentley had yelled as he reeled under the impact of a slug punching through his shoulder. He managed to get the reins untied and was swinging into the saddle, when Tyler Echohawk was there to climb aboard his bronc. Together they ran south along the street, Bentley just clinging to his horse, with Tyler firing back blindly.

Sheriff Echohawk bolted out the front door and

hammered out several shots at the pair of outlaws running down Center Street. Then something happened that chilled his blood: Tyler Echohawk turned his six-gun on the man riding alongside him. The outlaw tumbled out of the saddle, and then Tyler was grabbing the discarded reins and wheeling both horses down a side street.

It took a moment for Lon Echohawk to realize the firing had ceased. Cautiously, he went over and peered around the side wall, noting that the heavier darkness of night had cut away. "We've got three down back here and one giving up," Raleigh Carr called out.

"All clear up here," Lon yelled as he hurried back along the side wall. Two of the outlaws' horses had broken away. In the empty lot in back of the jail, he glanced at one outlaw sitting hunched over, another standing with his arms stretched over his head, and the motionless forms of two others, with Hagen and Carr emerging from concealment.

"You boys get nicked?"

"Nope," Raleigh Carr replied.

"My luck held, too," observed Lon. "Only thing is, my brother got away. "Sy, you see to saddling our horses. Me an' Carr'll take care of these hombres."

As Hagen hurried away, Carr said, "I'll get these two into a cell, then go get a sawbones. Where'd'ya figure Tyler is heading?"

"Breaking for the mountain, is my guess."

* * *

In a crazed moment during the gun battle all Tyler Echohawk could think about was that he'd survived. Strangely enough, it had been Slater Moore's face he'd seen instead of Bentley's. The same surprised look, the quick gaping of the eyes just before Tyler's gun had barked.

He was riding slower now on sloping ground, which took him to the higher reaches of Casper Mountain. Closer to the mountain, the wind was ripping the rainstorm to fleeing shreds. Patches of blue sky showed overhead, while away to the northwest it had cleared. He didn't have any co-herant plan of escape, just the wild idea of getting over the mountain and down into the timbered breaks.

"Waited too long in going after Cleever," he muttered harshly. "They know about me, they sure as hell know about Hap Fleming."

Farther up he let the horses labor along the narrow switchback road to the east. Below the breaking clouds sunlight struck down on Casper, Tyler's eyes anxiously scanning the beginnings of the road as yet unoccupied by any horseman or vehicle. But he knew the bulldog tenacity of his brother would make it difficult for him to get away. How could he have missed hitting Lon back there? "Too damned dark, it was," he muttered. "Next time I won't miss."

About a half hour later, Tyler Echohawk was on a section of road close to the mountain summit, a higher hunk of mountain cutting off his view of the plains below. The climb had taken its toll on the horse he was riding, but Tyler held to the saddle, knowing that the mining camp was around the next sharp bend in the rising road. Pine trees hemmed in the road, and they were glistening wet from the rain but not stirring their branches. The one time he'd been up here he'd learned that the road continued on past the mining camp, where it then dropped down and meandered toward the southern reaches of the North Platte River.

He passed a cabin set back in the timber. Farther along he saw several men in rough garb, and then he was in Eadsville. He rode toward a tank used to stock water, beyond which there was a tent store. A man with suspenders looped over his shoulders came out and eyed Tyler swinging down from his horse.

"A dollar apiece to water your horses, mister."

Tyler turned around to draw attention to the badge still pinned to his shirt. "Charge it to the county. And I'll need a sack of grub."

"This ain't no Salvation Army way station, damnit all. I want cash on the barrel head."

His eyes filling with a deadly glitter, Tyler Echohawk let the horses have their full as he swung away from the water tank to confront the storekeeper. He came in on the man, grabbing a handful of unkempt hair with his gloved hand, Tyler forcing him back into his place of business, where he unleathered his six-gun. He shoved the storekeeper toward the small table he used as a counter.

"You've got two minutes to fill one of those

gunnysacks with grub, or so help me, you're a goner."

"No . . . I'll do it, Sheriff . . . easy with that gun now."

While the storekeeper was stuffing food into the sack, Tyler picked out a few items. He set them on the table, then reached behind to lift out several boxes of shells from a wooden crate.

"About all it can hold," the storekeeper said.

"If anybody else shows up, you tell them Tyler Echohawk was here." Hefting the sack, he spun away and trudged out of the tent, tying the gunnysack to the saddle of the horse he'd ridden up the mountainside. From here on, he knew it would be a long, hard haul getting away from his pursuers. One thing he didn't like was his not knowing the country to the south. Coming up from Rawlins, he'd taken note of all the mountain ranges, and Tyler knew if he could get up into one of them, he'd have a better than average chance of escaping. Swinging aboard Cap Bentley's horse, he reined away from the water tank, the other horse whickering its displeasure at having to move out so soon.

Shortly, he was beyond Eadsville, loping along the narrow confines of a road that was becoming more of a trail cutting through the pine forest of the mountain. At the moment, he saw no sense in setting a faster pace, as Lon and the others would have to take a breather as he'd done back at that mining camp.

Resentment burned in Tyler Echohawk. It was all Fleming's fault for not taking out Barney

273

Cleever before this. What a sweet setup they'd had going, with the promise of gaining millions. "Fleming, now he'll get it all," came Tyler's bitter-rasping voice. "Should turn around and head back. But damnit, with my luck, I'll run into them damned lawmen."

Got to think, damnit, he mused. How many'll be after me? Just the four of them. No, for sure Lon'll leave one of his deputies behind to watch the jail. From here on, Tyler Echohawk's rambling thoughts included finding a good spot to lay an ambush. Then once he got rid of the lawmen, it was back to Casper to blow a hole in Cleever.

Through gritted teeth, he proclaimed, "Then I've got clear sailing to all that money."

It wasn't all that far out of Casper that they'd picked up on tracks left by two horses. The cloud cover had lifted away, leaving in its path rain-freshened air and a clear view all the way up the mountain. As they moved in, the lawmen kept scanning the lay of the road curling upward. Around them the land was wide open with no place to hide, which told Lon Echohawk that Tyler could be as far as Eadsville.

"I could say I know my brother," declared Lon. "Which I don't. Like I just told you, he's wanted back in Oregon. But I saw enough of Tyler to know he wants the edge."

Under his shading hat brim, Raleigh Carr studied high outcroppings for signs of movement. A little farther on were the beginnings of the tree line. He'd nicked himself while shaving yesterday morning, the small bit of dried blood surrounded by growing black stubble. He rode last in line, back at least ten yards just in case Tyler opened up on them. When he spoke, it was not all that loud, as even a whisper carried up here. "I figure what he'll do is put space between us and him. Eadsville; he'll pull in there to water up and grab some grub."

"Timber's thicker up there," said LaVoy.

"Timber means we'll have cover, too," Lon threw in. "The other side of the mountain isn't as steep as here and rolls down into a valley. Mostly open country from there onto the North Platte, where here we don't have any place to hide."

Over two hours of steady riding brought them ghosting into the mining camp, but they came in cautiously, keeping to the fringes of the narrow road and under the trees. Sheriff Echohawk eyed the new roadhouse. There were no horses tied out front or at hitching posts strung along the side wall, and as he swung his glance back to the street, Hack LaVoy spoke. "There's a stock tank over by that tent. Tyler'll expect us to stop there. So?"

"He's gone," Lon said flatly. He pulled out from under the trees and brought his bronc walking away from the road toward the tent store. Immediately, he picked up on the tracks left by a couple of horses pulling away from the stock tank and striking eastward on the road, and then he was confronted by the storekeeper.

"Badge says you're the sheriff. You owe me for a sack of vittles."

"So he was here," Lon said calmly as he dismounted.

"Left about an hour ago. Held a gun on me, Sheriff. Can't believe he was a lawman."

What had happened to Cap Bentley prompted Lon to tell him, "You're lucky you're still alive." Dropping the reins, he let his horse drink, as he added, "Tally up what he took. We'll need some more grub; enough for two, three days."

"Sheriff, is this another case of give now, pay later?"

"Cash on the barrel head, mister."

They ventured, as Tyler Echohawk had done before them, across a wide, open meadow making up part of the lowering mountaintop. Here the trail was wide, and wherever a man rode, it spilled to the southwest. Each of them carried a field glass as part of his gear. But they didn't need any field glass to sight in on elk and some deer grazing way down in a valley, the other wall of the valley slightly lower in elevation and tapering off from there toward the Shirley Basin. Way off to the south and west rose jagged peaks marking varying ranges—the Ferris, the Seminoles, and the Shirleys.

Lon Echohawk felt he'd ridden over every mile of what he could view, and even so, it was a country that could surprise a man. He got to thinking about what he called restless spirits holding sway out here. The wind was yowling some, or was it really a gathering of these spirits in the hopes of claiming some more victims?

Another half hour passed before Lon called a halt. They were almost off the mountain, as going downhill had been easier riding. Lon pointed with his canteen at a distant draw, noting, "A lot of them knifing toward the North Platte. He could hold in one of them. But"—he shook his head—"even if he gets one of us, there's a lot of open country he'll have to cover to get to the Shirleys."

"Maybe so, Lon, but if he don't, he'll have to cross the North Platte. Which is some chore even at this time of year."

"He won't head east, as that's tenderfoot country," Hack LaVoy said quietly. "I figure west, maybe to get into the Seminoles. Tyler hails from Oregon, so I reckon it'll be kind of like a homing pigeon him keeping headin' west."

"He could have been some lawman."

Lon took in what Raleigh Carr had just said, knowing it was the deputy's way of putting in a good word for his brother. Inwardly, Lon felt he'd let his men down by not really checking up on Tyler a lot sooner. It was a mistake he'd never make again. "Much as it hurts, Tyler's no longer my brother," he told them. "When he opened up on me back at the jail, it was with the intention of leaving no witnesses. Could have been you, Raleigh, or Hack. He's armed and dangerous and doesn't intend to give up. Like a rabid dog, you've got to beware of his fangs."

Beyond the reaches of Casper Mountain, the

prairie was a series of deep-gorging draws lined with wide scatterings of scrub brush and sagebrush. All of them realized they were within three or four miles of the North Platte, the Shirleys humping a lot closer off to the southeast. It hadn't rained all that much down here, and for Carr, who was out front, it was a difficult task to pick up on Tyler Echohawk's trail. As Carr rode over a hump, he drew up briefly to gaze on ahead. Suddenly he felt a twinge of pain. Carr twisted in the saddle and began to pitch forward. The ugly rippling of a Winchester leaped past him as he tumbled to the ground.

Spurring ahead, they came in on Carr, with Lon riding up a little and Hack LaVoy jumping down. Lon had pulled out his rifle and levered a shell into the breech, all the while searching for a place where Tyler could be holed up. Then distantly he discerned movement, and he fumbled for his field glass, discovering it was Tyler's spare horse breaking to the east. Angrily, he spat out, "You damned killer! What made you like this, Tyler? Why?"

He wheeled the bronc around as he shoved his rifle back into the saddle boot, spurred back to swing down. Kneeling, he gazed anxiously into Raleigh Carr's ashen face, the deputy managing to say, "Ruined this new shirt of mine."

"A shade more to the left and—" LaVoy forced a smile. He had opened Carr's coat and shirt to reveal the wound still trickling out a little blood. "It ain't a killing wound, but—"

"No," muttered Carr. "Just plug it up and then get after Tyler."

"Over by those scrub trees. Gather some firewood while I take care of this." Carefully, Lon brought an arm under Carr's back to lift him up, then he carried the wounded man the short distance to a little recess away from the moaning wind. He managed to plug the wound with a torn piece of bandanna. Next he got both of their bedrolls and rain slickers, from which he created a shelter. He made Carr comfortable in one bedroll, using the other as an extra blanket.

"Raleigh, I wish I'd been out front."

"A man who'd take out his own brother ain't too much."

Glancing at the flames starting to eat at the small campfire, Lon said, "No matter what happens, we'll be back around nightfall. Goin' on noon. A lot of daylight left to ride him down. You sight anybody, pump away with your handgun."

"Quit fussin' over me, damnit, Lon. Why, my hoss is there . . ." He tried rising, only to fall back gasping in pain. "I'll . . . be awright. Both of you . . . take care . . . as good lawmen are hard to find . . ."

Tyler Echohawk found that he had stumbled into a series of sheer hills pitted with rocks. The flanks of the hills tapered to the west, and every time he crested one, another just as steep would loom before him. His horse was tiring, with Tyler cursing at how the spare horse had broken away.

He was hoping the lawman he'd gunned down had been his brother, and if so, he figured the

279

others would break off and head back to Casper. Lon wouldn't, he knew, jabbing his spurs at the bronc coming onto a hilly summit. He sought his canteen and, while drinking, surveyed the Shirleys still a long distance away. Lowering his glance just a shade, he suddenly realized that the sun was sparkling from the river water.

"From the size of it, gotta be the North Platte." Coming up from Rawlins, he'd kept to the other side on the main stagecoach road. He drank what little water remained in his canteen, knowing he couldn't push his horse much longer. It needed water and a breather, as did he. Tyler headed west with the flow of the hill, as yet unaware that he was nearing a section of river called the Fiery Narrows.

At the moment he was more tired than he cared to admit. Some of it was from not getting any sleep last night. The sun didn't help, either, striking at him from the west. Then he was aware of the horse cocking its ears and fighting the reins as it took to gazing to the north. He spotted them an instant later, two riders sweeping over a hill.

"Get!" he raged at his horse.

"Reckon he spotted us, too!" Hack LaVoy shouted over at Lon.

"Yup, but he made a mistake coming this way." Their quarry had disappeared below the prow of a hill. They could have moved out at a canter, but Lon knew the way Tyler was going would find him encountering a narrow passageway that opened onto the high cliffs guarding the narrows. Once Tyler got out by the river, he'd be trapped in a little parcel of level ground encircled by an unclimbable rock barrier and the high cliffs plummeting to the river.

Coming onto the hill where they'd spotted Tyler Echohawk, they cut sharply to the right and riverward. Here LaVoy jerked his head and shouted, "There he is, Lon, heading in to the narrows."

"Let's pick it up," urged Lon. "I want to get into that ravine before he realizes there's no other way out."

The distance between them narrowed. The mouth of the ravine was covered with a sprinkling of huge boulders thrown there eons ago by volcanic upheavals. The ravine was no more than a quarter of a mile long. Entering, they pulled out their six-guns and slowed the gait of their horses. The narrow walls of the ravine were a barrier the wind couldn't penetrate, the air still and heavy with suspense. Lon knew his brother could be in behind a boulder, with his finger tightening on the trigger of his rifle.

But Tyler Echohawk was out of the ravine and just becoming aware that he'd boxed himself in. A couple of times he tried riding his horse up through the webbing of high rocks, only to have it shy down again. He circled back over rocky ground, along the edge of the cliffs that plummeted to the river, in search of a way down. He found the cliffs were too sheer. Opposite him, the southern wall of the Fiery Narrows was no more than fifty yards away. He reined away and cut toward the only way out, just as his pursuers appeared.

"Give it up. Tyler!" Lon shouted.

"No, damn you!" He jerked out his six-gun and fired wildly while veering sharply to the south, enraged at how he'd let himself get trapped.

Once again he sought to find a way out to the south as the lawmen swung down while holding their fire. The front legs of his horse buckled. Tyler whipped the animal back up and brought it at a gallop straight toward the river cliffs. As he rode, he cut loose with his six-gun and shouted, "I'll see you in hell before I give up my guns!"

"No, Tyler!" Lon cried out in disbelief.

Tyler Echohawk's bronc had surged beyond the edge of the cliff as the hammer of his six-gun slammed onto an empty chamber, his eyes crazed as though he didn't seem to be aware of what was happening. That was the last view Lon had of his brother, until he reached the cliff and saw the pool of blood on the rocks below. For just a brief instant, he glimpsed the rapids clutching at the limp form of Tyler Echohawk. Lon dropped to one knee. He found the hand he brought to his face was trembling, and in him was a deep sense of agony.

"You all right, Lon?"

He groped for something to say as the wind

around them started to pick up, moaning down into the narrows.

"I guess . . . the maverick spirits have come to claim him. Maybe it was the way he wanted it."

Eighteen

Nobody had paid much attention to the man in the cattleman's coat taking his ease by Casper's new railroad depot. Most likely they would remember this Friday, September 13, as the day three men went to the gallows. Being overshadowed by the long trial and the hanging sat all right with Lon Echohawk.

After the tragic death of Tyler Echohawk, Lon and Hack LaVoy had gone back to find wounded Deputy Sheriff Carr. They returned to Casper, only to discover that Hap Fleming and his confederate, Lundahl, had taken flight. To no avail, as both men were arrested in St. Louis. From there, Fleming used every legal device he could to keep from being brought back to Wyoming to stand trial.

Then for Lon Echohawk came the day when he no longer had jurisdiction in Casper, which in a close election had been declared the new county seat. Accompanied by LaVoy and Carr, who'd recovered from his wound, it was to return to their duties in Rawlins, though Lon knew he would be called back to testify against Hap Fleming and his cohorts.

A distant, mournful wail reminded Sheriff Echohawk of the arrival of his train. He held to the bench under the shading depot porch, as did the pensive glint in his eyes. One aspect of the trial had been Sylvia Valcourt testifying against her father. Even with Judge Childress presiding, the trial had taken almost a month. Dozens of other witnesses had come forward with damning evidence. The real damage had been the ugly verbal assault by Barney Cleever against Fleming and Lundahl, along with Cleever confessing to the murder of cowhand Dan Easton.

The county had paid for Lon's room at the Wyoming Hotel. There'd been some evenings he'd dined with Sylvia Valcourt, either at the hotel or elsewhere. Somehow their conversation, at least Sylvia's, always got around to Sean Fitzpatrick. Lon liked Sylvia more than he cared to admit.

He rose when everyone began surging to the edge of the platform to watch the train arrive.

"Sheriff," came a voice he knew. Lon turned to see Sylvia Valcourt stepping down from a carriage. She came up the steps onto the platform. "I couldn't have you leave without saying good-bye."

"Awful nice of you," smiled Lon.

She gazed up at him through the black lacy veil covering her face. Lon could make out the vestiges of grief in those eyes. He knew Sylvia hadn't watched them hang her father, and right now he didn't know what to say to ease her inner pain. She touched his arm, and they drew away from the crowd. "Lon, thanks to you, I made it through the trial. I . . . my father will be buried tomorrow morning."

"Just remember, Sylvia, Hap Fleming knew the risks when he got into this. I reckon you might say he was too ambitious."

"Ambitiously greedy," she murmured. "Mother, I suppose, will be ungraciously relieved. As for you, Sheriff Echohawk, you never did make a pass at me." She smiled at the sudden blush on his face.

"It wasn't because I was that much of a gentleman. Been a lawman a long time. A lonely way to make a living; reckon it'd be lonelier for a man's wife."

"I suppose it would. I will see you again?"

"Rawlins isn't all that far. I have to say I spotted Megan Randsley leaving day before yesterday."

"Perhaps that's for the best, Lon."

"Now, you give my regards to Sean. I expect you'll be getting married soon."

"Why, he hasn't asked me yet. I don't even know if he loves me."

"Just got a hunch Sean'll find that out, along with how to cope as Casper's new mayor. The only way this place will grow proper is if people like you, Sylvia, and Sean Fitzpatrick take a hand in its destiny. So, that whistle means I've got to

286

board." She came closer and brought a wistful hand to his face.

"In losing a brother and a father, we seemed to have gained strength from one another. Good-bye, Sheriff."

After Sheriff Lon Echohawk boarded the train and found a seat in a passenger car, the conductor appeared to quietly pass over a brown envelope. Lon opened it to find a telegram, which he determined must have just arrived. "Bank robbery at Green River . . . believed to be the Curly Brocus gang . . ."

With a flicking of his eyes, he let all that had happened in Casper ebb away. Already, he was anticipating avenues of escape for the Brocus gang from Green River, along with what his role in apprehending them would be. He caught himself, and a kind of shrug lifted his shoulders.

"Guess it wouldn't have worked for Sylvia and me. As the truth is, Echohawk, the law and this badge is what you want."

He swung a glance toward Casper Mountain, going beyond that to sage country and the lonely grave of a Mex sheepherder. He knew that grave was a monument to how it was out here. "Just hope the epitaph 'he froze to death with a bullet in his head' doesn't mark my final resting place."

"What's that, mister?" a passenger across the aisle asked Lon.

Pushing up his from seat, Sheriff Echohawk said politely, "Just saying farewell to a man who didn't deserve to die." Then he was moving up the aisle to find the club car and a game of stud poker.